Marked

Marked

Ally Wagner

Cover art by Jaqueline Kropmanns
Edited by Christina Ramos
Formatting and interior design by Jennifer Roachford at Curly Tales Publishing

ISBN 978-1-7367220-2-2 (paperback)

First paperback edition July 2022

To those of us who have suffered the cruelty of being bullied, we are, and always were, perfectly fine as is.
To the bullies of the world who have irrevocably maimed the self-confidence and self-esteem of their victims...
Go fuck yourself.

Author's Note:

This book is a Dark Fantasy/Dark Romance. It may contain sensitive material that some readers may find triggering. These topics include: explicit consensual sex scenes, violent murder scenes with decapitation, gore/blood, vomit, alcoholism, bullying, and the fact that the word "fuck" is used exactly ~~140~~ 141 times.

One

*T*he high-pitched chime of a cell phone echoes in the room, and I glare at it from my reclined position against the headboard. I consider letting it go to voicemail, ignoring the duties that await me. I already worked my day job as a detective, and it had been a fucking shit show of a Thursday.

After a vampire was found guilty of abusing an adolescent boy, we had to stake him. It was a long, drawn-out chase that ended in a violent scuffle. While nursing a bite to my forearm, we had to go confront the Lord of Las Vegas, the ruler of all the vampires in the city, to inform her of her coven member. That also ended in a screaming match, but at least I didn't have to stake anyone else.

Now that I'm finally relaxing, why would I want to hunt down another lead? The answer is simple: I don't. I earned this night to myself. I deserve—I frown when I realize the ringing stopped. Oh, no, that had been too easy.

Before I can dwell on it, my mind goes blank, the suspicion vanishing as pleasure ripples through me at a particularly well-placed kiss. My eyes flutter shut, back arching against the black wood as a skillful tongue replaces those soft lips. Fingers dig into the flesh of my thighs, gripping them to keep them in place as I wiggle against his mouth.

Suddenly, a white-hot pain bursts at the base of my sternum. Fuck! I sneer down at the black pawprint seared into the skin right below my breasts then turn to glare at the phone when it begins ringing again. I reach for it at the same time my lover tosses the sheet over his head, peering up at me with irritation gleaming in his green eyes.

"Let it go to voicemail, Val." Seth demands.

I look down at him as I grab my phone. "As much as I'd like to, I can't. It's work; you know how it is," I say with a shrug. Seth knows I'm a detective, but he's oblivious to my second job. And quite honestly, I prefer it that way. I mean, how does one explain that they mark people for the underworld?

With a soft sigh, I answer the call. "This is Val."

"You have another one, Val," comes the deep voice from Cerberus. Well, from one of the triplets anyways. "Try not to let this one go."

I don't miss the warning in his voice. Really, it's not my fault my last mark slit his wrists in guilt before I could get to him. "I need fifteen minutes." I nearly snort when Seth looks up at me, affronted by the time limit. "Thirty would be ideal." He smirks in triumph before flipping the sheet back over his head to resume his task.

"You are one of our hellhounds. We don't work on your time; you work on ours," a second, but almost identical, voice says after taking over the phone. After over a decade of working for Hades' hound, also known as the Guardian of the Underworld, I can usually tell when a new triplet speaks. Usually.

"The Fates have decided the next soul for you to mark." The third chimes in. "And it needs to be done soon. Thanatos is standing by to guide them to Styx."

I roll my eyes. When is the grim reaper ever not standing by? My amber eyes slide back for an entirely different reason when Seth returns his tongue to my clit, a single finger tracing the opening between my thighs.

"I'm kind of busy—fuck!" I curse as he presses his finger into me and curls it toward him, making my body spasm with pleasure.

"Not our problem," one of them replies.

"Can't someone else do this?" I pull the phone away from my ear as a breathy moan escapes me when a second finger slides in to join the first. "I've had a long day."

"No, you are the closest. We're sending the information to you now. Do not fail." With that the line goes dead.

I toss the phone onto the pillow next to me and rub the bridge of my nose in annoyance. Well, at least I won't be the only one frustrated tonight. I pull the sheets away from us and put my hand on Seth's golden locks, pushing his head away. "I have to go."

His gaze fixes on me, studying me incredulously. "Are you serious?" When I just stare at him, he sighs and pulls his hand away. "You are."

"I told you, it's work," I reply, swinging my legs over the bed to stand. When I turn back to grab my phone, I catch him dipping a damp finger in his mouth. Heat creeps up my neck as I snatch my phone from the black pillowcase. "Tease."

"Oh, I'm the tease?" He shoots back as he rolls onto his side, looking at me with a cocked brow. "Who is leaving who during the throws of passion, Val?"

I shake my head and slip on my discarded nude panties. "Who even says that?" I question as I step into black slacks and button them.

"I do," he answers flippantly before grinning. "But I'll always lick you clean, you taste divine. Like a sinful wine made of the rarest berries."

No, but really, who talks like this? "Well, you would know about wine." I laugh, tugging on my white, V-neck shirt over a beige bra.

Sometimes I forget Seth is a warlock. He's not like others I've met. He makes his own wine and essential oils for all things. Whatever pain or ailment I might have, chances are Seth has a cure for it. The oil he makes for menstrual cramps is a damn godsend. I told him he could make a fortune from it, but he simply said that he enjoys it as a hobby and has no desire to get monetary gain from it.

"Speaking of such, I've been working on a new flavor and just finished bottling it. Be my test subject?" He asks with a pout.

After holstering my gun, I grab the pack of smokes from the nightstand and tuck them into my pocket along with my lighter. I turn to him with my hands on my hips and quirk a questioning brow at him. "You really need a girlfriend to do these things for you."

We met about two months ago when he first moved to Las Vegas. Or Hades' ass crack, as I so fondly call it. I had just finished marking a soul at the Luxor and needed a drink to calm down. I stopped at one of the bars on the casino floor and Seth happened to sit next to me a few minutes later. He introduced himself and one drink turned to five as we conversed. It wasn't long before we were upstairs in one of the hotel rooms.

The one-night stand turned into a fuck-buddy relation-ship. It works since neither one of us does commitment. My life is too complicated, and Seth enjoys his freedom too much. We make decent companions, each having our own twisted sense of humor that makes the other laugh. Every couple of nights, we'll meet up for drinks and sex. We don't talk about our day, don't discuss our woes and stresses. It's perfect.

He shrugs. "You're a friend who happens to be a girl, so why not ask you?"

Fair enough. "I'll let you know when I'm free and you

can bring it over," I say in way of agreement. Leaving him in his bedroom, I go to his kitchen and pluck my keys off the counter. "Later!" I say it loud enough so he can hear me across the apartment.

"What? No kiss goodbye?" He calls right as I shut the front door behind me. I roll my eyes because he knows damn well, I don't do kisses.

Once in his apartment hallway, I bring out my smokes and grab one with my lips. Tucking the pack away, I withdraw my lighter and ignite the end of it. After taking a drag, I put the lighter away again and pull out my phone. I open the text from the 666 area code, yeah real original, and memorize the picture and details of my target. I frown when I see the last known location and wince. I'm not a huge fan of going to strip clubs, but at least this club has a more open floor plan. The smells hopefully won't be too bad.

With an exhale of smoke, I make my way to my red F150 and slide into the driver's seat. I hate the leather seats when it's sunny, but at night they're cool and welcoming. It's mid-September now, and Vegas is in that awkward stage where it's hot during the day, but chilly at night. In the next couple of months, I'll have to start bringing a blanket or jacket for the cold. Unfortunately, I'm sensitive to the cold, something Cerberus says is normal after my transformation.

And honestly, transformation is a bit of a stretch. Apart from my pawprint, nothing physically changed about me. I have heightened senses for hearing, smell, and sight, and can heal faster than a human, but that's about it. I don't have the speed or strength of a wereanimal, at least not in this form. I've only shifted once, and it was terrifying.

I take another long drag of my cigarette before snubbing it out in an old fast-food cup. I once got a ticket for littering when I flicked a butt out the window on a trip to California, and paying that hefty fine once was enough. Pulling down the visor, I check my appearance in the small mirror and wince. With a tsk, I run my fingers through my black hair, fixing the A-line so the longer ends fall neatly against my collarbones again. After flipping the visor back up, I put my truck in gear and head towards the I-15.

Pulling into Hustler's parking lot fifteen minutes later, I find a spot far enough away to avoid possible door dings and cut the engine. Since I'm off duty, I reluctantly take off my holster and put it in the center console. Not the safest place for it, but I dare someone to break into my truck.

I make my way to the expansive drop-off zone in front of the building, weaving through the lines of cars and limos waiting in the valet line. My heeled boots click against the polished black surface until they step onto the red carpet leading to the main entrance. The hair on the back of my neck bristles when the bouncer's eyes greedily rake over my body.

Clearing my throat, I hand him the thirty-dollar cover charge. "Here you go."

"Oh, babe. You sure you don't wanna dance instead? I

can get you an audition. I think you'll do just fine," he purrs, sizing me up once again as his fingers brush against mine when he takes the money.

Gross. "I'm good," I reply briskly, quickly wiping my hand on my pants.

He smirks and crosses his arms over his chest. "You sure, sweet cheeks?"

I shoot him a lethal glare that makes him step back. "Call me that again, and I'll shatter every bone in your fucking nose," I promise, hand clenching into a fist. He has three inches on my 5'10 height, but I can drop him to his knees if I have to.

"Bitch." He hisses but steps aside to let me through as a group of guys come up behind me.

I simply give him the finger over my shoulder and keep walking. Passing by the security check, I glance at a glass door on the right that leads to a sex store. Interesting. Venturing left instead, I enter the main club area. Almost immediately, there's an overbearing scent of sweat, sex, and alcohol. The loud music, mixed with the chatter of all the people, makes my ears hurt. This is why I hate strip clubs. It's nothing against dancers or the patrons that dabble in the pleasure they offer, but the smells and sounds make it hard to concentrate.

I maneuver through the crowd, avoiding the staggering drunks and the girls in towering heels that tug them along. Many tables are scattered around the main floor, and it takes a second to find one that's vacant. It's towards the middle of the room, giving me a view of both stages. I quickly claim the table and recline against the plush white chair, not at all surprised by the fact that it has wheels under it. Easier to drag a customer along, I'm sure.

A waitress dressed in a sparkly silver and black sequined corset comes over with a tray and a tight smile on her face. "What can I get you?" She asks, the pleasant demeanor so forced it's sad.

"Just a Jack and coke, please." I hand her a twenty. "Keep the change."

She immediately perks up. "Of course! Thank you so much!"

I wait until she's gone before beginning my hunt. I scan the stages then the floor, looking for the tall woman with the bottle-dyed red hair. The information said the woman is naturally 5'8, so I assume with the stilettos she's around 6'2, give or take an inch or two. Add in the flaming red hair and she should be easy to spot, crowded room and dim lighting be damned.

Halfway through my drink, I finally spot Ruby, also known as Stephanie Browne. She's wearing a red bikini top, her bottoms nothing more than a triangle of red cloth that covers her vagina. Her arm is linked through a customer's, a man who's grinning while staring appreciatively at her ample chest.

I watch them disappear into the VIP area and quickly

down the rest of my drink. Making sure not to look too eager or suspicious, I calmly stand from the chair and smooth down my white shirt. I head in the direction of the VIP room and am thankful to see that the women's restroom is right next to it. Turning into the hall for the bathroom, I stop and lean against the wall so I can keep my eyes on the VIP room. I'm going to wait for Ruby to come out, ask her for a dance, and then mark her for Cerberus. It will be quick and easy.

Except nearly fifteen minutes pass and Ruby still hasn't emerged.

"What the fuck?" I hiss under my breath, my patience nearly at its end. I just want to go to bed.

"You okay, babe?" a well-endowed, shapely dancer asks as she exits the bathroom, drying her hands with a paper towel. She has so much perfume on her, I take a step back as my eyes water.

"Peachy," I grumble in response. I'm trying to breathe through my mouth to get rid of the floral scent stuck in my nose when an idea strikes me. Straightening, I look at the curvy Latina woman and give her a shy smile. "Actually, I was waiting to get a lap dance. Any chance you're available?"

She gives me a flirty smile and tosses her dark brown hair over her shoulder. "Of course. What kind would you like?"

I point to the area Ruby disappeared in to. "How about one of these?"

The smile widens. "Sure. I'm Synn."

Matching her smile, I say, "I'm Val. Shall we go then?"

She nods and I follow her to the little stall where customers pay and nearly cringe at the cost of a fifteen-minute private dance. Still, it's worth it if it means marking my target and getting off Cerberus' shit list.

"Pick any one you'd like!" Synn offers as we walk in, gesturing at the two rows of semi-circle couches. They're only big enough for one person to sit in but tall enough to where someone can't see the people inside even if they're standing.

"Umm, let's see…" I trail off innocently before looking in each booth. I have to apologize more than once for interrupting some intense bumping and grinding. My snooping is making Synn uncomfortable; I can tell by how she keeps recommending a booth, but I have a job to do.

I'm starting to think I somehow missed Ruby leaving, but then I smell the familiar coppery scent of blood. Despite the flowers and arousal overwhelming my nose, I follow the faint trace of it to the final booth on the left.

I stare at the scene before me, my mind trying to catch up to what my eyes are seeing. Ruby's body is slumped in the chair with her chest torn open. Skin hangs in tatters around the opening of the hole, blood spilling from it like a crimson waterfall. Her sternum has been snapped in half, the attached ribs on either side ripped away to expose the chest cavity.

However gruesome the hole is, that isn't the most shocking part for me. It's the fact that her head is completely missing.

"Did you decide on a—" Synn cuts herself off by releasing a high-pitched, blood curdling scream right into my ear.

It makes my ears ring and head swim, causing my equilibrium to shift. I manage to stay upright until Synn's full body weight suddenly crashes into me as she faints. I'm knocked forward, making me thrust my arms out to brace myself. I end up landing on my knees between Ruby's, my chest pressed against the dead woman's torso.

My face is inches from the mutilated torso. At the close proximity, I can see that Ruby's heart is also missing. Someone took both her heart and her head. What sick bastard does that? Then my detective brain kicks in. Did they take the body parts before she died, or after?

I blink out of my thought as I finally grasp what they mean. Ruby is dead. Which means she died before I could mark her. For Cerberus. Dread and anger fill my veins when I realize I missed my mark again. "Fuck!"

Two

I'm absentmindedly washing my hands in the women's restroom, watching the pink-tinged water swirl down the silver drain. My gut feels hollow. This is the second person in a week that died before I could mark them. Cerberus won't be pleased by my failure.

Just like the stories say, Cerberus guards the gates of the underworld. Souls that pass over are not allowed to leave, and living beings aren't permitted to enter. When I was fourteen, I had a near death experience that led me to meet the guardian. I remember standing on the banks of Styx, the river of souls that flows between the land of the living and that of the dead. Even now, I can vividly see the transparent bodies floating in the murky water, their wails echoing in the darkness around me.

"You are not dead yet, girl."

I turn at the voice and stumble back at the sight of the massive three-headed dog that stands before me. A terrified scream catches in my throat when he suddenly shifts and splits into three identical men. They're wearing black suits that match their hair; the only contrasting color on them is the crimson of their eyes.

"We can send you back to the land of the living with a condition, or you can step into the river. Which choice do you prefer?"

It was such an obvious answer, I didn't think twice before answering. "I-I want to go back!"

Knowing now what I didn't then, I'm not sure I made the right decision. Marking souls as unredeemable is far from an easy thing. The actual task of marking is easy, but the emotional and mental toll isn't. Every time I brand someone, and they committed any sort of horrible sin, I see it as clearly as if I had committed it myself. Each soul I mark, good or bad, colors my own a little darker, makes me that much more cynical.

"Dalton!"

I startle when someone shouts my name. "Give me a second!" I snap back and splash some water on my face before turning off the faucet. I dry my hands and face before examining my appearance in the mirror. Grimacing, I try to fix the smudged eyeliner, but the blood-stained shirt is a lost cause. I won't be surprised if the techs have to take it.

Stepping out of the bathroom, I notice all the lights in the club are on. The place is mostly empty save for a few employees and dancers being questioned by various police officers of the preternatural branch. Spotting the new yellow caution tape warding off the dance area, I head toward my *favorite* lieutenant as he writes something on his notepad.

"They have anything yet?" I ask, sneaking up behind him.

Scott jumps, the notepad in his hand almost falling. He catches it and whirls towards me with a sneer twisting up his full lip. "Godsdammit, Dalton!" He curses. "How many times do I have to tell you not to sneak up on me?!"

I resist the urge to grin. "Sorry." But I'm not in the slightest bit and he knows that. I enjoy getting him worked up. We're natural enemies, but I couldn't imagine working for anyone else. "So, what do we have here?"

His brown eyes narrow suspiciously as they slide down my body and then back up, stopping to stare at my shirt. "You don't know?"

"Would I be asking you if I did?" I counter, crossing my arms over my chest.

Flipping his notepad open, his gaze hardens. "Tell me, Detective Dalton, what were you doing here tonight?"

My spine straightens at his accusing tone. "What are you implying, Scott?"

"Don't avoid my question, dog," he sneers.

"I prefer *hound*, kitten."

His dark skin flushes darker, the color spilling down his neck and disappearing under the collar of his dress shirt. I never thought cats and dogs were destined to fight until I met my boss, the werecat. Technically, he's a were*tiger*-I swear there's a were*everything*, but it's hard to call him that when all I see is a puffed-up kitten that had his tail stepped on.

Scott Carter tried to hide his identity when the preternatural creatures came out to the public twenty-six years ago. *Monster Movement* is the genius name the higher-ups called the equality law, ensuring the creatures that go bump in the night have the same rights and protection as humans. Many of the preternatural thought it was a ruse, a trap for the humans to finish off the so-called monsters once and for all. But, fortunately for us monsters, the law is real.

I was an infant when the law went into effect, so I don't know how the world was without monsters. But I doubt it was any better than what it is currently. A lot of humans hate us, and a lot of us still view humans as inferior.

Scott was forty when the bill passed, and he rants about *before* all the time. He once told me that before monsters came out of hiding, all he had to worry about was people hating him for being a cop. Now, they hated him for being a cop *and* a "monster". He used to be the most highly decorated officer in Las Vegas before the movement, but he got reassigned as the lieutenant for the Las Vegas Preternatural Crime Unit, also known as the LVPCU.

With the preternatural creatures out in the open, a lot of police forces created a subdivision of officers and detectives to handle related crime. It's been so successful that more and more cities are following suit. Let's be real, humans don't want to deal with monster messes. After all, it usually takes a monster to catch one.

So, when the higher-ups found out Scott was a wereanimal, they couldn't discriminate and fire him; so they relocated him instead. After all, who better to lead the new branch than a highly praised officer who they *thought* was human?

"This looks like something a dog would do," Scott hisses.

I roll my eyes. "Why would I attack her and then stay around to coat myself in her blood?" I gesture at my shirt. "Seems like a stupid thing to do if I wanted to get away with it."

"I'd be more than happy to arrest you if you're feeling guilty, Dalton."

"How much catnip have you had tonight? You still doing rehab for that?" I tilt my head at him innocently. I swear I can practically see his blood pressure skyrocket, but before he can shout, my best friend interrupts.

"Sir, I finished collecting evidence," the small blonde woman says as she ducks under the caution tape. She positively beams when she sees me. "Val! I knew that was your scent in there!"

I can't help but smile at the twenty-four-year-old bubbly technician. She's a werewolf, but she reminds me more of a golden retriever. Not just because of her friendly attitude and golden blonde hair, but because she always seems to be bursting with energy. She's also loyal. Somehow, she knows I'm not any kind of wereanimal, but I know she would never rat me out.

"Hey, Tay. Yeah, I was the one who had the joy of finding her." I explain with a sigh.

Taylor wrinkles her nose. "I'd hug you, but red's not my color." She laughs at her own joke and looks at Scott when he clears his throat in irritation. "Sorry, boss man, I collected what I could. The other detective says he's almost done examining it."

I blink at her words, brow furrowing as I glance from Taylor to Scott. "Other detective? Who does she mean?"

Pushing down his ire by taking a few calming breaths, he looks at me again. "We have a new detective that joined our branch. He was supposed to start tomorrow, but then we got this call, so I had him come with me to get seasoned with how things are done."

"Why didn't you tell me?" I ask with a frown.

"It must have slipped my mind," Scott brushes me off with a wave of his hand. "Now, are you going to answer my questions?"

"You know I didn't do this shit, Scott. You may not always admire my oh-so charming personality, but you know I wouldn't do this." I raise a brow, daring him to counter me.

"He might, but I do not," a deep baritone voice says from behind Scott.

I turn to the source and watch a tall man with tanned skin elegantly duck under the yellow tape. His hair is like black silk, the ends just barely touching his brow. When he looks at me with dark grey eyes, goosebumps pebble on my flesh.

Why does the color remind me of Styx's water?

"You must be Detective Dalton," he begins with a cool, albeit calculating expression. His gaze dips down to my shirt, no doubt looking at the blood smeared there, I hope. "I'd like to ask you some questions."

His voice holds an edge of power that trickles down my spine like warm honey. I glance at Scott and Taylor, but neither seem to sense it. Is it my imagination?

"About what? If it has anything to do with my alibi, then don't bother. I didn't kill her." Something about him makes me want to take a step back when he takes one forward, but I refrain. I won't be intimidated by this newbie.

"Your evasion of questions makes me think you have something to hide." He states, eyes locked on mine.

"Well, your opinion doesn't really matter to me." I manage to keep my cool. Even throw in a shrug for good measure. His aura just barely touches mine, but it makes the hair on the back of my neck prickle with warning. Whatever he is, he's strong. Maybe he's an alpha? But I've met alphas before and haven't been affected like this.

"It should, Dalton, because *if* you're cleared, Detective Khoury will be your partner on this case. But until then, you're off work." Scott interjects before looking between Khoury and I. "It's appropriate, two werewolves working to catch whatever did this."

"Hound," I correct automatically without hesitation.

The new detective narrows his eyes in question but

doesn't comment. He doesn't have to. I can tell by his stare that he knows I'm not a wolf. But then again, I have a sneaking suspicion he's not either.

"Detective Dalton, I would like to at least ask you a few questions regarding your time here at the club. That way I am on the same page as you since we might be working this case together." He holds out his arm, gesturing for me to step aside from the others.

I suppose it's a fair enough request when he puts it that way. See? Who says I'm unreasonable? With a huff, I turn to Taylor. "Can we postpone our coffee date until I'm free of suspicion?"

"Sure, just let me know when!" She beams. "Ah, and don't forget I'll need your shirt for testing."

Totally forgot already. "Fuck, alright. I'll give it to a tech before I leave," I reply then turn to Detective Khoury. "Lead the way, Detective." I wait until he starts walking to glance back at Taylor.

He's so hot, Taylor mouths and gives me a double thumbs up. Scott snorts in exasperation before ducking under the tape and disappearing into the crime scene once again.

I shake my head and turn back to follow my potential new partner. He leads us towards the deserted bar, out of earshot from the others. I plop down on one of the barstools and longingly eye the alcohol bottles. "How mad do you think they would be if I helped myself to a glass?"

He leans against the countertop and briefly flicks his gaze towards the bottles before looking at me again. "Considering you're being questioned for murder, I think it would be frowned down upon, even if someone was here to serve you."

Oh, he's a good cop then. Boo. "You're kind of a tight ass, aren't you?"

He doesn't flinch. "And you're kind of a bitch, aren't you?"

I blink at him for a moment, surprised by the mirrored blunt response. Then I laugh, unable to help myself. I'm not sure why I'm laughing, maybe the day is finally catching up to me.

Some of the tension in Detective Khoury's shoulders relax. "Perhaps we should start over," he offers and sticks out his hand. "Jack Khoury."

Oh, he wants a peace treaty. How disappointing. "Valkyrie Dalton, but I go by Val." I clasp his hand with mine and give it a firm squeeze. My dad always told me that handshakes should be firm, like a show of confidence.

Fuck, I really should call my family at some point. How long has it been now?

Jack doesn't release my hand immediately after the shake. Instead, he dips his head down, eyes never leaving mine. "You aren't a werewolf." My spine goes rigid as his powerful aura brushes mine again. "What are you?"

My heart stammers in my chest, but I refuse to let my nerves show. "Is that your first official question?"

He pulls back and studies me for a second. "Yes."

I scoff and rip my hand free. So much for a peace treaty.

"As you said, I'm a bitch. Ask your questions so we can get a start on this case, Detective Khoury."

His jaw clenches, but he goes back to leaning against the bar. "What brought you to the club tonight?"

"I wanted a drink." I casually reply, studying the chipped black polish on my nails. It isn't technically a lie; I *did* have a drink after all.

"Why come to a strip club and not a regular bar?" Jack presses.

"I like a show." I meet his disbelieving expression. "I think the female form is beautiful. Don't you, Detective? Or do you prefer something a little meatier? Maybe some sausage?"

He hums but doesn't rise to my bait. "Tell me how you came to discover the victim."

I glance down at my blood-stained shirt. "I asked Synn for a dance. I've never had one before; I thought I might as well try it since I'm here," I shrug and meet his eyes again. "She told me to pick a booth and as I was picking one out, I happened to smell the blood and found the victim."

"If you're a werewolf, wouldn't you have smelled all the blood beforehand?" He asks, staring at me knowingly.

I smirk. "Didn't you say I'm not a werewolf?"

He deadpans. "Touché." He pushes away from the bar and stands to his full height. "I'll question Synn once the paramedics finish checking her out and then review the security footage when the manager sends it to us. When everything corroborates with your story, I'll let you know, and we can get started with solving this."

I swivel in my chair but keep my eyes on him. "*When*, hm? So, you believe I'm innocent after all?"

He gives me a cool look, eyes unreadable. "I believe you didn't kill her, but I think you are far from innocent."

My smirk widens. "Smart man."

He surprises me by giving a small smirk of his own. "I wonder what your heart would weigh?"

What the hell kind of question was that? "Hearts usually weigh around a pound."

"That's *physically*," he explains before beginning to walk away. "I'll talk to you soon, Detective Dalton."

I watch him go, the tension in my muscles slowly ebbing once he's out of sight. "Fucking weirdo," I mutter under my breath as I spin my chair to face the bar again. In a scurry to evacuate the club, the bartenders left several of their bottles out. I grab the closest one and grimace when I see my prize is gin. Still, I proceed to pour myself a shot.

Holding the glass up, I nod to the floor. "Cheers, dog men. Here's to my punishment." I throw back the bitter, clear liquid and wince as it burns going down.

Three

*S*tumbling into my apartment, I throw my belongings on the kitchen counter, not caring if they spill off the other side of it. Today sucked, and I'm over giving a shit about anything. I promptly remove the loaner shirt a crime scene tech gave me and shove it into the trashcan under the sink. I scowl down at my bra crusted in Ruby's blood and quickly remove it as well. After shoving it in the trash next to the shirt, I make my way down the hall to the bathroom attached to my bedroom.

"For fucks sake!" I curse as I get a look at my reflection. I didn't see it at the club, but now I can see that blood had seeped into the waistband of my slacks. The pair I bought just a few days ago.

Undoing the button, I slide them down my legs before kicking them at the wall. I tug off my panties and throw them at the pile. "Throw the whole damn outfit away at this point," I mutter under my breath as I turn to the shower and crank it to nearly scalding.

I wait until steam starts to fill the small room before stepping under the water. A groan of delight escapes my lips as the water beats down on me. After scrubbing my body three times with extra soap to make sure all the blood is gone, I wash my hair and lean back against the cold tile.

Closing my eyes, I go through the night's events. Putting aside the disdain for failing to mark my target, I focus on the victim. What killed her? Who? And why? Was it the man who got a dance from her? Somehow, I don't think so.

Of course, it's going to be my job to figure it out once the video footage proves my innocence, but where do I even begin? I'll have to review the security feed after Jack does, but I have a feeling we won't get much. I doubt it'll be that easy. It never is.

Turning off the shower, I ring out my short hair and step onto the plush grey rug. After drying off, I wrap the matching towel snuggly around me and go to the kitchen to find my phone. I walk back down the hallway to the bedroom and plug my phone in, setting it down on the nightstand to charge. After pulling on a pair of hot pink, lacy boy shorts and an oversized t-shirt I stole from Seth, I flop down on the bed with a heavy sigh of exhaustion.

The pawprint burning on my skin is the only warning I get before falling through my mattress. Well, no, that isn't right. I don't physically fall; my soul is yanked down out of my body and thrust into a different realm. The only thing I can possibly compare it to is the free fall drop on a rollercoaster.

When the world stops spinning and the weightless feeling around me evaporates, I see three sets of shining black shoes before me. Aware I'm on my knees, I tilt my head back and look up at the triplets. Once again, they are dressed in black dress shirts, jackets, pants, and ties. Their red eyes fixed on me with matching disapproval.

"Valkyrie," they say as one, making me flinch ever so slightly.

I climb to my feet and brush off the pale green sand from my knees. "Look, it wasn't my fault."

Each head tilts the same way. "Oh?"

I pull on the hem of Seth's shirt, very aware that I'm in my underwear while facing the guardian of the underworld. "I missed her by fifteen minutes, if that. Someone murdered her before I got to her."

"We are aware." They comment.

I scowl at them. "You knew she was going to die?"

"Of course," one says with a lifted brow.

"You were told to hurry, no?" Another adds with the same eyebrow cocked.

My hands ball into fists. "Yeah, but you didn't say she was going to die that fast."

"We cannot tell you when someone is to die. That would be breaking the rules," the last informs me in a stern tone.

My eyes narrow. "Can you tell me who killed her?"

They pause for a second, their crimson eyes sliding over to the Styx then at each other. "The rules say we cannot."

"Fuck the rules!" I snarl. "Whatever killed her is brutal; it tore off her head and ripped out her heart. It's going to be my case and I need to stop it from happening again."

They shrug in unison. "Even if we knew, we could not tell you."

Useless threats fizzle on my tongue when the meaning of their statement becomes clear. "Wait, you don't know? How is that possible?" When they remain silent, I rub my face in exasperation. "Alright, where'd her soul end up? I'll ask her myself."

Their gaze returns to mine. "It is not here."

My lips part in surprise a moment before my brow furrows. "How is it not here?"

They give me a look that manages to insult my intelligence. "Because you did not mark her."

Oh, right. Still, I scoff. "So, what, it's just gone?"

"Yes." They sigh and steeple their fingers. "Normally if you fail to mark a soul it would mean that the soul just isn't *here*. The underworld is all forms of the afterlife. It is so expansive that there are different realms of it while still existing within one."

I blink. "What the fuck are you going on about?"

"Why do you think hell is depicted in several different ways in your literature? Think of all the mythologies and folktales within the land of the living. They are all correct. Different afterlives exist, but all within one underworld," they explain.

My lips purse together. "So, one person comes to our realm while someone else goes another, but they'll all be in the same underworld?" I rub my chin, thinking about all the possible different hells. "Is it similar to the different continents in the land of the living?"

"In a way, yes."

"That complicates the shit out of things. And here I thought just the Greeks got it right," I mumble.

"Every culture has it correct," they reiterate. "There is no one correct afterlife."

"I get it," I sigh and pull at the hem of the t-shirt once again. My modesty doesn't normally bother me, but Cerberus has a way of making me feel vulnerable. I don't quite like being half-naked in front of the guardian. My brow furrows again, and I meet their crimson stare. "Does that mean there are other guardians of the underworld?"

"Yes," Cerberus answers. "Each realm has their own being who judges the dead."

I glance down at the cool sand between my toes. If I had landed somewhere else during my near-death experience, would I still be alive? Would they have given me the same choice Cerberus did? Or, what if they had just let me go? If they didn't make me mark souls for them?

"What are you pondering?" A triplet asks curiously.

"My life choices," I mumble, looking at the vast dark grey around me. At the void of nothing that surrounds the Styx. Cerberus once told me there's a whole city on the other side of the river and that this is only the entrance to it. Part of me wants to see it, but the majority hopes I never do.

"We must discuss your failure."

I run my hand through my damp hair, knowing it will stay wet until I'm back in my physical body. "Like I said, it wasn't my fault. It's not fair to punish me for something I couldn't control."

They cross their arms, but only one says, "We have taken this into consideration, especially since the soul in question has ceased to exist."

"So, you are not here to be punished," another explains.

"We are warning you and giving you another mark," the third adds.

I bristle at their tone. "I'm not going to like this."

"Perhaps not. The being that killed your mark does not show up on our radar. The only reason for this would be due to the fact that they are from a different realm."

I blink at them and try to make sense of their statement. "You mean, they're also from the underworld?"

"We assume so."

I mimic their action, crossing my arms over my chest. "Let me guess, you want me to mark the killer?"

"Yes."

"You're going to drag someone from one hell to another? Is that going to be an issue?" Is that even possible? "And how the fuck am I supposed to take on someone like you?"

They preen, each one standing a little taller. "There is no one like us."

I wave my hand at them. "You know what I mean."

"You will accomplish your task by being smarter and swifter. People do not know what you are, Valkyrie. It's highly likely that this entity does not either, especially since they are from a different realm," they explain. "Find who stole our mark from us and mark them in return."

"You seem to have more confidence in me than I do."

Damn, I want a smoke. And maybe a shot of tequila. "What happens if I don't mark this...*person*? Is that even the right word?"

They ignore my last question. "Then they will continue killing."

I frown. "Won't they keep killing even if I do mark them? You won't get them until they die."

"If they are an underworld creature then they won't die regardless," they point out. "But if they are marked for our territory, we can at least do something about it. We can force them here if we must."

"How do I kiss a killer and not die?" I mutter more to myself than anything, but they still answer me.

"By being clever." They each hold up a hand at my snort to stop my rebuttal. "Mark them and we will do the rest. That's all, Valkyrie. You are free to return."

Before I can snap at them, they wave their hands and I'm slammed back into my physical body. I inhale sharply, eyes flying open as my body jerks with life once again. I shoot up into a sitting position, pressing a hand hard against the throbbing pawprint. Eyes stinging and watering, I continue to gasp in air and mentally curse Cerberus over and over again.

Once my racing heart calms and I no longer feel like I'm choking, I snatch my phone from the charger to check how long I had been away. An hour. That isn't too bad, but damn am I more exhausted than I was when I laid down.

Noticing a text notification, I click on my messages. I tap on Seth's conversation and roll my eyes at the eggplant emoji he sent. Still, I laugh and simply send him back a shrugging emoji.

Rude. Comes the immediate response. Why is he still up at midnight?

Oh, please. There are so many girls who will throw themselves at your feet, Warlock. I type back.

You're not wrong. But I was referring to you and me this weekend.

We'll see. I'm going to have a new case, but I'm not sure when I'm starting. Hopefully Monday. You know, unless more bodies drop before then.

Ouch. Potential serial killer?

My lips press into a hard, thin line. I don't like talking about work with Seth, or anything that's personal. It makes our situation seem deeper than it is. He's just a bed companion and someone I blow off steam with. I don't need, or want, any deep bonds with anyone. Taylor is the only exception.

Dodging the question, I send the sleeping emoji to him and mute my phone. Sliding open my bedside drawer, I take out the small bottle of tequila and swallow two gulps. I wipe my mouth, twist the cap back on, and put it away again. Snuggling under my blankets, I roll onto my side and pass out minutes later.

Four

"Y ou look like shit." Taylor comments.

I push my sunglasses further up my nose as the bright Monday morning sun beats down on me. "You know, you're probably the only person who could say that and make it sound cute," I say before taking a long sip of my latte.

Taylor laughs as she cradles a coffee cup in her hands. "Sorry, sometimes I don't have a filter."

I shake my head at her. "No, it's what I like about you."

The blonde grins. "That means a lot, Val. Thank you."

I hate when people thank me. It makes me uncomfortable. "Don't thank me. It's weird."

Her grin widens. "You're weird, but I love you."

I snort and set my cup down on the table, glancing away. Taylor is my complete opposite, and to this day I still have a hard time understanding how we became friends. Like Seth,

I tried to keep the crime scene technician an arm's length away, but the wolf had other ideas.

Despite me not responding to her persistent babbling when I first started at the LVPCU, Taylor wouldn't be deterred. She brought me lunch and baked goods but finally won me over by showing up at a stupidly early crime scene with an extra coffee for me. From there, I found myself slipping and contributing to the conversations she would begin. I never wanted to, but damn did the werewolf have something about her. And now here we are, two years later.

"Sooo," Taylor drawls out. "How was your one-on-one time with Mister Alpha?"

I quirk a brow at her. "Mister Alpha?"

She lowers her tone almost conspiringly. "Jack Khoury. You know, when he was interviewing you at the crime scene a few days ago?"

My eyes roll behind the glasses. "You mean when he was interrogating me? Just peachy."

Looking down at the lid of her Starbucks cup, she purses her lips. "He's like you."

Surprise makes me sputter on the coffee. I immediately cover my mouth to prevent the liquid from spewing out. After some difficulty, I swallow and clear my throat. "Come again?"

"Not a werewolf," she whispers in a serious tone.

I lean back in my chair, taking the cup with me. I never told Taylor what I am because I didn't want her to be burdened by the knowledge of it. Or maybe I just didn't want her to look at me differently now that I finally had a friend. "Can you tell because you are one?" I ask after a moment.

She shrugs. "I guess. But wolf or not, he's definitely an alpha of some sort."

"I agree, but I don't know what he is either. He could be some type of wereanimal, I'm just not sure what kind." Even as I say it, part of me doubts it.

"That's true, I guess." She hums and then glances at her watch. "Ah, we should get going if we want to be on time."

"Are you ever late?" I question as we stand from the table.

The Starbucks is conveniently located just around the block from the main Las Vegas sheriff's office. To make sure there is no workplace hostility, the Preternatural Crime Unit had its own building away from the human one. There are talks of the two joining under one roof, but I doubt it will happen anytime soon. Many states still don't have their own preternatural division, let alone a merged one.

I can't help but cringe at the thought of humans handling monster cases. I'm sure it was done unknowingly before the movement, but it still makes me uncomfortable.

"Nope, I take pleasure in being on time!" Taylor says proudly as she slings her purse strap onto her shoulder.

I sigh and pick up my small purse. "You're better than me. I'm frequently late."

"You were just off for a couple days! You can't be late on your first day back!"

My brows lift in challenge. "Watch me."

She lets out a soft laugh. "And you wonder why the lieutenant is always angry with you."

"He's just angry in general. I think it's a cat's nature to always be pissy."

Taylor shakes her head, but a smile curves up her lips. She knows that despite my crass words, I actually like Scott a lot as a person. "Maybe you two would get along better if you didn't provoke him, Val. He may even be nice to you."

"Lies. Filthy, filthy lies," I accuse as we walk through the automatic doors of our building.

The wolf bursts out laughing, making me grin in return. We make our way through the lobby, which has a seating area to the right and a small beverage station to the left. Straight back is a tall reception desk with a wall of bulletproof glass protecting the person behind it. Directly adjacent to the desk is a security door that can be unlocked by the receptionist, or by our microchipped badges.

Still cackling, we wave at the receptionist in greeting before tapping our badges over the sensor. We wait for the buzzer signaling the unlocked door then walk down the hallway towards the elevator.

"Lunch?" Taylor asks as the doors slide open on the second floor.

"I'll text you and let you know," I answer as we step into the small lobby. There are a few desks lined on either side of the open area and closed offices down the hall along the right back wall. The hall down the left leads to the lab Taylor works in. "I have to go over the case with Mister Alpha."

Seeing my friend's eyes widen in horror at something

behind me, I whirl around and nearly bump into Jack. Startling at how close he is, I jerk back in reflex. Unfortunately, my coffee collides with my ample chest, the lid popping off and spilling the contents all down my navy-blue blouse.

"Fuck!" I immediately try to pull the fabric back from my skin, trying to save both my flesh and my brand-new bra from the hot liquid. Someone takes the coffee cup from me, and I use both hands to pull at the soaked fabric. Stupid form fitting shirt!

A third hand joins my efforts while a fourth dabs a piece of charcoal silk along the saturated coffee. I look on in mild horror as the very masculine hands continue to wipe at the coffee, each sweep brushing over my breasts. I have to be seeing things. I must be because there is absolutely no way that Jack Khoury is trying to clean off my chest. There's no way he's that oblivious as to what he's doing, right?

I force myself to look up at Jack's concentrating face. I'm 5'10 so it's not often I have to look up at anyone. Most of my coworkers are shorter than me, especially on the rare occasions I wear heels to work. I hear Taylor's mortified squeak behind me, and it makes me sweep my eyes around the room to see that most of said coworkers are staring openly at us.

Blinking out of my stupor, I quickly bat Jack's hands away, cheeks hot with embarrassment. "I think that's good enough, Detective Khoury."

His brow furrows until it finally seems to click as to what he has done. He quickly takes a step back and clears his throat twice before speaking. "My apologies, Detective Dalton," he murmurs. He looks down at the fabric in his hand and sheepishly hands it to me. "Here."

I snatch it out of his hand and turn slightly away from him so I can dab at the shirt. When I finish, I realize with disdain that it's his tie. Balling it into my fist, I thrust it back at him.

He takes it without a word and tosses it into the closest trash can. His eyes are cool when he looks at me again, but his lips are pressed in a tight line. He must have felt the occupants of the room staring at us because he turns his head sharply towards them with a cold glare. "What?" He snarls out.

Everyone quickly turns back to their work at the snarl, but a few snickers still echo in the room.

I pinch the bridge of my nose before turning back to a wide-eyed Taylor. "Rain check?" Which really sucks because I could have used a drink. Actually, I just happen to have a mini bottle of alcohol in my desk drawer.

"Uh, okay." She glances at Jack and then back at me. "Good luck," she murmurs before scurrying off to her lab.

I take a deep breath and face the tall detective once again. Ire prickles when he simply stares at me. "Did you need anything, Detective? I mean, besides to cop a feel? Or is this your way of greeting your new partner? I have to say, it's a bit tasteless."

His cheeks tinge pink before he runs a hand through his hair. "That wasn't my intention," he replies in a low tone.

"I'm sorry."

"It's fine," I snip though I don't mean it. Not yet.

He nods once before continuing. "I was wondering if perhaps you would like to get a start on the case?"

"I'm going to try to clean up a little and I'll meet you in my office in twenty." I turn and stalk towards the bathroom, not giving him a chance to answer.

Twenty-five minutes later, I stalk into my office with a slightly calmer demeanor despite needing a smoke. After making sure my nipple piercings were clear of coffee, I rinsed the shirt under the faucet and tried to dry it under the hand dryer. It's still fairly wet and smells like coffee, but I have a hoodie in my truck that I can change into at lunch.

Jack's sitting in the chair across from my dark brown desk, looking at the items that decorate my small workspace. There's not a lot, just a few knickknacks my parents and younger sibling decide to mail me every year on Christmas, despite my lack of acknowledgement. Keeping people at an arm's length is what I'm good at. Even if I feel guilty for doing so.

I shut the door behind me and head to my desk, slide off my holster as I do. After setting my service gun on the desk, I roll out my black leather chair and sink down into it. When I'm finally situated, I level my new partner with a blank expression. "So, where do we start?"

His eyes meet mine and my stomach somersaults at the look he gives me. How does he keep doing that? "I really am sorry, Detective Dalton. I reacted without thinking."

Shrugging, I look away from him and those intense eyes. "Let's just forget it happened. So, the case?"

He gives a terse nod and gestures at my computer. "I sent you the footage from the security cameras. I'd like for you to watch it and give me your opinion before I give you mine."

"Alright." I log onto my computer then my work email.

My phone pings, and I glance down to see a text from Taylor with about twenty exclamation points. Momentarily ignoring the message, I turn back to the computer and click on the email from Jack. A window pops up on my screen and begins to play the footage of the familiar dance area. The camera is at the back of the room, facing towards the entrance. It gives a clear view of the aisle and the people that come down it. It also happens to give an aerial view of the back booth Ruby was killed in.

I watch as Ruby pulls her customer to the last booth, takes off her heels, and proceeds to give him a lap dance. About fifteen minutes pass before Ruby steps away and speaks to her customer. He shakes his head and walks away. With a shrug, she sits down on the chair and begins to put her heels on before the screen then cuts to black. When it comes back on, I see myself walking towards the booth, Synn trailing behind me. After I watch Synn crash into me, I replay the video, paying attention to the background.

Nothing catches my eye outside of the cut on the footage.

I lean back in my chair and sigh. "Well, it could be a technical issue. Any other cameras cut out?"

"No." He responds, eyes staring intently into mine.

I resist the urge to look away. "Was it tampered with?"

"The manager on duty said that the footage could have only been tampered with through the office and he didn't touch it. There's a camera outside the office door, as well as one inside. I watched it to confirm. He was doing paperwork during the cut." He let out a soft sigh. "I suppose it's possible it's all some elaborate scheme, but I don't think so."

"I don't either. It's obviously preternatural interference, hence why we were called in after the initial responders got there."

"I agree," he replies, leaning forward to rest his forearms on my desk. "But, what?"

"Something capable of decapitating a human and tearing through their rib cage to rip out the heart." I muse.

"It's not a wereanimal," he states.

I lift a brow at him. "You seem so sure." I know it isn't due to my conversation with Cerberus, but how does he know?

He leans back in his chair and glances out the window to his right. "How transparent do you want to be with each other?"

The hairs on my neck bristle in warning. "We're partners, so the correct answer would be complete transparency."

"But," he prompts.

"But I don't trust you. We just met so I'm not about to

open my heart and spill all my secrets."

He gives a single nod and thrums his fingers on his knee. "Then perhaps we should get to know each other. We can start slow and go from there."

I cross my arms over my chest. "We don't know how long this case is going to take so what's the point? This is temporary, isn't it? You may be assigned a different partner later or something."

Jack lifts a brow. "Are you saying you'd feel more comfortable if I remained your partner?"

I shake my head, but I won't argue that a daily view of him would be nice. The man is gorgeous. "Not really. I keep my circle of friends small. The less personal connections, the better."

His black brow stays up, his expression turning almost sardonic. "Wouldn't you prefer to have one partner who you knew and trusted?"

"I don't really trust anyone."

"What about Meyers?" He asks with a smirk.

Defensiveness has me tilting my chin up defiantly. "Taylor doesn't count. She was unexpected."

"Not even your significant other?" He hedges.

It's my turn to lift a brow at him. "Is that your sly way of asking me if I have a boyfriend?"

Another smirk tilts up those fine lips of his. "Perhaps."

Again, his honesty surprises me. Besides Taylor, I'm not used to someone being so frank with me. "I'm not dating anyone. I have someone who I see on occasion, but I don't have a boyfriend." What was the point in even answering that? It's not like I'm looking to date.

"Interesting," he muses. Is it my imagination, or does he seem somewhat satisfied? "How about I match whatever secret you give me?"

I study him carefully through narrowed eyes. "How do I know you won't lie to me?"

"How do I know you won't do the same?"

"Touché," I say with a sigh. "Alright then, let's test it out. I'm not a werewolf." He's not either, so if he isn't honest with me, then I know this won't work.

"I'm not either," he replies before giving a small smile. "Although, I'm not sure that's actually a secret since I knew you weren't one from our meeting on Thursday."

"I never actually confirmed it until now." I lift the small Cerberus figurine from my desk and run a thumb over each of the heads.

After the guardian sent me back to my body the day I met him, I became fascinated with trying to find out more about him. Greek mythology became my obsession when it turned into my reality. Mom surprised me with the figure on my fifteenth birthday, and I simultaneously hate and love it. Sometimes I envision it being the actual guardian so that I have an outlet for my frustration. After marking someone, I'll sometimes squeeze it until my knuckles turn white. The plastic figure has proven to be damn near indestructible over the past decade.

Jack studies me quietly. "Are you going to tell me what you really are?"

My golden eyes meet his. "Are you?"

His teeth clench together. "It's not something easily explained."

"Same." I echo nonchalantly, thumb brushing over the figure once again.

"May I be honest?"

I don't look at him. "By all means."

"Your aura is different than anyone I've met before. It's touched with darkness, but not the kind that comes with evil. Does that have something to do with what you are?"

His words couldn't have hit me harder. I can't see my own aura, but I suppose it makes sense that it's tainted. Still, the words sting. I take a deep breath and try to get my sudden self-pity under control. "Your aura is extremely oppressing. It's powerful and dominant. Does that have something to do with what you are?" I echo his question while deflecting it.

"Yes." He doesn't hesitate. "I suppose that's why you called me Mister Alpha."

I run my hands through my short hair to try and hide my embarrassment. "Well, this has been lovely, Detective Khoury, but I think I'm going to go over the witness statements. Alone. You can email me should you need anything."

He seems confused by the sudden, professional brush off but stands. "Alright then. If you have any questions, feel free to ask, Valkyrie."

I curse the shiver that runs down my spine at the way my name sounds on his lips. "It's Val."

"Valkyrie suits you better." He comments before slipping out my office and closing the door behind him.

I slouch ungracefully in my chair and release a groan. Somehow, I have a sneaking suspicion that this case is going to be one of my harder ones and not because of the victim. Pulling open my bottom desk drawer, I rummage through the loose papers and half-empty water bottles until I find the tiny bottle I knew was there.

I grumble when I look at what kind it is. I don't mind whiskey, but somehow the tiny bottle of Jack seems too coincidental. Fate's funny like that sometimes.

With a silent curse to whatever god is mocking me, I down the mini bottle.

Five

I'm very aware of Taylor staring at me in mild concern as I down my third shot of tequila. Momentarily ignoring her, I lick the rest of the salt from the rim of my glass and bite into the lime. Swallowing the sour juice, I drop the fruit into the small glass and set it down with an audible *clank*.

"That bad, huh?" Taylor asks, her margarita still mostly full.

"He's not safe to be around," I mumble in reply and glare at the glass of water Taylor slides my way. "I'm fine."

"We've been here for half an hour, Val. You can't just drink away your problems."

If only she knew. "Watch me," I challenge, pushing up the sleeves of my black hoodie.

Taylor slides the glass closer, the two of us staring at each other without blinking. After a solid minute, I gave in and take a sip. Smiling in triumph, the wolf leans forward eagerly. "There you go. Now, tell me why Mister Alpha got you all hot and bothered. You know, besides fondling you in front of the whole department."

I groan and rub my face, not caring about my makeup anymore. "I still can't believe he did that." The server brings us our dinner, and I move my shot glasses out of the way so she can set down the plates.

"Hey, in his defense, he was trying to help," Taylor points out before lifting her silverware to cut a piece of her smothered carne asada burrito.

"Yeah, well, that doesn't make it any less embarrassing." I answer, dousing my cheese enchiladas with hot sauce. "He's constantly checking my work and asking questions. We finished interviewing more of the dancers, but he kept going over our notes as if we both hadn't been there. He will straight up tell me when he thinks I'm wrong or doesn't like something I'm doing! I feel like he's constantly challenging me!"

Taylor chews thoughtfully before pointing her fork at me. "He gets under your skin."

I blink at her, fork pausing on its journey to my mouth. "Yeah, you could say that. I'm not used to someone being so honest and blunt."

She laughs. "You mean like you are?"

"And *you*." I give a half-hearted scowl and take a bite of my enchilada.

"I'm only that way with you, Val. You're that way with

everyone," she teases. "But really, I think it says something that he gets under your skin."

I groan. "Don't start."

Taylor gives me an innocent shrug. "You can't just keep having this fling with Seth. You have zero intention of dating him, so maybe you need to start looking at some other candidates."

I go to order another shot when the server checks on us, but Taylor's warning glare makes me refrain. "I hate talking about this," I begrudgingly admit after the server leaves.

"It's not bad having a boyfriend." She points out.

"You're just saying that because you and Bryan are perfect," I say without venom.

I love that Taylor met a fellow werewolf that compliments her so well. They met a month before Taylor and I did and have been together for two years now. I have a sneaking suspicion that Bryan is going to pop the question soon, but I'm just not sure if it'll be the marriage or the mating one. Most shifters do both at some point.

Taylor's dramatic pout makes me laugh. "I miss him so much," she whines.

"He went with your guys' alpha to meet with the Los Angeles alpha, right?" I ask, glad the focus is temporarily off me and my nonexistent relationship. "Or is it the LA County Alpha?"

Besides the typical hierarchy that is briefly taught in schools now, I'm not super familiar with how pack politics work. How does it go again? Alpha of the city answers to the alpha of the county, and he answers to the alpha of the state?

For my werewolf cover, I did the basic research directly affecting me. So I know the Las Vegas alpha is Dominic, and the Nevada alpha is Luis, but all the other information I get is from what Taylor tells me.

"The Alpha of Los Angeles." She clarifies, still pouting. "They're meeting with Cain to talk about some fae black market that keeps popping up."

"When do they come back?"

She lets out a heavy sigh. "Hopefully they'll be home by tonight, but Bryan said he's not sure."

I pat the top of my friend's hand. "It's been two days; you can survive one more." I laugh again when Taylor's bottom lip sticks out even more.

When I pull my hand away, my phone starts to go off, the theme from an old Meow Mix commercial ringing loudly. Taylor stifles a laugh, and I ignore the questioning glances from the other diners as I answer the phone. "Yes, Kitten?"

"...Kitten?"

I drop my fork at the sound of Jack's voice. I have to clear my throat and force a swallow before talking. "Um, Detective Khoury, sorry, I wasn't expecting you." Taylor starts laughing, and I promptly kick her in the shin.

"Ow!" The wolf yelps, glaring at me.

"Was that the crime scene technician?" Jack's smooth voice asks.

"Taylor," I inform him, knowing damn well that he

knows her name. "And yes, it is. We're having dinner. Can I help you with something?" I feel a hard kick to my shin and shoot an accusing glare at Taylor.

Be nice. She mouths, pointing her fork at me in threatening manner.

I flip her off and turn away, keeping my shins a safe distance away from the ruthless wolf. "And why are you calling from the lieutenant's phone?"

"I left my phone at home, and we have another victim. He's helping secure the scene until you arrive."

I straighten and shoot Taylor a serious expression. Catching on, the blonde instantly waves her hand at their server for the check. "Where at?"

"The Crazy Horse." Before I can ask, he answers my next question. *"It's another dancer, and she was attacked in the same way."*

My eyebrows knit together. "That's less than a week between victims."

"Yes," his voice rumbles unhappily.

I rub the bridge of my nose. "Alright, we'll talk more when we get there." I hang up, not waiting for his reply. When I look at Taylor, she's already standing, the check paid.

"Ready!" Taylor announces, swinging her car keys on her finger. "I'm driving!"

I do a double take when I look at Taylor's empty plate. I know the full moon is tomorrow night and it causes wereanimals to have an increase in appetites, but damn. My friend is short and tiny, where did she put the giant burrito? I glance longingly down at my barely eaten cheese enchiladas then at Taylor's still full margarita.

As tempting as it is, I know Taylor won't hesitate to smack the drink out of my hands. With a sigh, I turn to my friend. "Let's go."

Taylor and I flash our badges to the police at the front door. To both our surprise, the two men stationed there are human.

"Monsters catching monsters? What a joke," one mutters under their breath when they think we are out of earshot.

Funny thing about monsters is that we have heightened senses. Such as hearing.

"They're probably all in on it together," the other replies.

I turn and glower at the two police officers. "At least we monsters know how to be professional at a crime scene. Maybe you should take some fucking notes."

They both bristle at being caught bad mouthing, but human, male pride is a fragile thing. "You dare call me unprofessional?"

Taylor tightens her hold on her crime scene kit as her lip curls up in a wordless snarl. "Better than calling you a dick." She growls, her tense back still angled towards them.

The second officer takes a step forward. "What did she

say? Turn around and say it to my face!"

I move and angle my body so I'm in front of Taylor. With the full moon coming, I know it won't take a lot to set Taylor off. The last thing the LVPCU needs is for her to shift at the crime scene. The human officers would have a field day with that.

"She told me to stop and let it go because you're not worth it. She's right, of course. No point dealing with disrespectful pricks." I step backwards, deliberately pressing my back against Taylor's to nudge the wolf forward and away from the confrontation.

Taylor remains rooted in place for a few more seconds until I press harder against her. She finally takes a stiff step forward then another until she's walking robotically towards the yellow crime scene tape.

"Your little friend left you," the first cop mocks with a smirk. "I guess monsters don't understand loyalty. Always out for themselves."

"That's because we have an actual job to do." I wave my hand at them. "You should get back to doing yours."

"Don't give me orders, *Monster*!"

My retort abruptly dies on my tongue when I feel heat at my back and a strong hand clamping down on my shoulder, warm knuckles brushing against the skin of my neck. His aura pulses against me and the anger behind it almost makes my knees buckle. Damn it, how strong is he?

"Is there an issue here?" Jack's voice is calm but cold.

The two police officers stare over my head at the imposing figure that is Jack Khoury and shake their heads. I catch a glare and a sneer from the man I was arguing with before he turns with his partner to resume their post at the front door.

Jack's grip tightens, and I feel a wave of heat shoot down my arm and across my chest despite the hoodie I'm wearing. I quickly move away before turning towards him. "I don't need you to come to my rescue, Detective Khoury. I'm a big girl, believe it or not."

He holds up his hands in defense. "I wasn't insinuating otherwise, Valkyrie. Taylor was angry when she came to the scene, and when the lieutenant asked her what was wrong, she said the guys at the door picked a fight. I heard them yell at you as I approached and reacted."

"Well don't!" I snap, hating how his closeness makes me feel. When he was in my office, and even in the car on the way to Hustler for interviews, I was super aware of how his aura made me feel. It's not normal.

I try to brush past him, but his hand encloses over my bicep. I curse when I feel his heat through the thick sleeve of my hoodie and try to twist out of his grip, but it's like a steel band.

"You smell like vodka," he says quietly, but his eyes are narrowed in a glare. "Are you drunk?"

"It's tequila, actually," I growl angrily and try to break free of his hold again, but he doesn't budge. "And no, I'm not. I wouldn't put my job at risk like that." Not that the tiny alcohol bottles in my desk would prove otherwise. "Not that it's any of *your* business, but it takes a lot for me to get drunk."

He stares, studying me carefully. He then reaches into his suit pocket and pulls out a small, tin rectangle. He flicks open the lid with his thumb and holds it out. "You may want one before confronting our boss."

I glare at him then look at the mints in front of my face. With my free hand, I grab one and pop it into my mouth. I chomp on it and swallow before blowing a breath at him. "Better?" I hiss.

He meets my seething scowl, nods, and releases his hold. Almost immediately, I grab the lapels of his jacket and use it as leverage to throw my knee up towards his nether region. His breath hitches when my knee lands on his groin, just an inch above his crotch and its precious cargo. With the hold I have on his jacket and the pressure on his groin, he's forced to bend towards me, our faces close.

"Do *not* grab me," I growl low. "The next time you do, I'll shatter your balls and dislocate your dick. Do you understand?"

Jack holds my fiery stare for a moment, and I falter when I see the embers of desire in his eyes. I'm threatening his future children and he's turned on by it? Why is that kind of hot? His gaze falls to my lips and my stomach tightens.

No, no, no. *No.* No matter how much he presses my buttons, I would never do that to him. Even telling myself that, it takes me longer than I would have liked to release him.

I force my hands open to release his jacket and whirl away from him to head further into the club. As I make my way along the left walkway towards the commotion, I try to calm my racing heart. I need to focus on my job, not these wild hormones.

After passing all the plush leather chairs, and long rectangular stage, I approach the VIP entrance. The area is more lit up than the main floor, the gold embellishments giving off the feel that this was only for the wealthy. On the other side of the second bar is a taped off area near two doors.

When I get to Taylor, my friend hands me a pair of gloves with wide, questioning eyes. After tugging on the plastic gloves and snapping them into place, I hold up a finger to Taylor when she opens her mouth. "Don't."

She puffs out her cheeks with a huff. "Later?"

"Fine." I turn to the scene, putting all my anger and emotions away so I can properly focus on the victim. "So, what do you have for me?"

"Another female in her early twenties," Scott begins, squatting down next to the body.

I follow his lead, kneeling to get a better look at the victim. Once again, her head is missing. The spinal cord is visible through what is left of the neck, the skin and tissue in tatters as if the head was ripped off. Blood runs down the woman's dark skin from the stump of the neck, leading straight to the gaping hole that used to be her chest.

"Head was torn off," I comment, leaning over the body

to get a better look at the chest. At the first scene, I hadn't been able to examine the body since I was a suspect. Being shoved face first into the victim didn't allow me to professionally analyze it as I am now. However, it's identical to what I saw up close and personal. "Ribs and sternum have been broken; the heart is missing."

Jack squats down next to me, gesturing at the snapped bones with a ballpoint pen. "The bones have been broken away from the body. You can tell by the splinters along these edges."

I follow his line of sight and nod. "As if whoever did this pulled the bones away from the body to get to the heart."

"Why is that important?" Taylor asks.

Jack and I shrug at the same time, much to my annoyance. "It might not be," I explain. "But most of the time, if someone has the strength to do this, they'll just punch through the ribs, grab the heart, and yank it out. Why go through the trouble of breaking them apart first?"

"Does that mean they weren't strong enough to punch through?" Scott questions, standing up and stepping back from the gruesome scene.

"It takes more strength to do this," Jack turns to me with an expectant look. "What else do you see?"

His challenging tone has me gritting my teeth before turning back to the victim. I study her carefully, eyes slowly roaming over her body. There are deep scratches along her arms and shoulders, her lime green bikini and white stilettos stained with blood. Ah, the blood. I stand up to get a better view of the area around the body. "She wasn't killed here. There's not nearly enough blood for the trauma done to her body."

"Exactly." Jack's approving smile makes my stomach flutter. I hate it. I think. Or do I like the praise?

"Then where was she murdered? How long has she been dead?" I counter and look at Jack as he hovers his hand over her body, brow furrowing as he does. I scowl at him. "What are you doing?"

He hesitates briefly before answering. "Checking the body temperature."

Did he just lie to me? Or am I just on guard from our interaction a few minutes ago? Taking a deep breath, I let it go and ask my next question. "So how the fuck did her body get here?"

"*Dalton.*" Scott scolds my cursing, but I wave my hand at him.

"We don't know yet. The medical examiner will have to determine the time of death. We should get our definite results in a few days. As for the original murder scene, we have no idea. Not yet anyways." Jack straightens, tucking his pen into pocket.

"Who is she?" Taylor speaks up again, stepping aside so a different tech can snap pictures of the scene.

"We don't know." Scott sighs.

I turn on my lieutenant. "What do you mean? Didn't you ask the managers? The other entertainers?"

I can practically see the weretiger puff up. "*Of course,* we asked everyone. I don't need you telling me how to do my job, Dalton. No one here recognizes her body."

"I understand she's missing her head, but they should still be able to identify her body if they work together, shouldn't they? And, speaking of which, who found her body?"

"It was a bouncer and I already questioned him when you were on your way here. You can read the notes tomorrow," Jack answers. "But no one has recognized her yet so we will have to go off of her fingerprints."

I look down at the decapitated entertainer and then the area of the club we're in. There's an emergency exit a little too conveniently close by. "Do you think it's possible she didn't work here? That she was just dumped in this club?"

Again, my partner looks pleased. "I was thinking the same thing."

"What the actual fuck," I mutter under my breath, looking at the girl once again. "That's insane, right? Someone coming here just to throw a headless woman into the back of a club?"

Jack nods once. "It's definitely strange. I have a feeling this case isn't going to be easy."

Didn't I say the same thing to myself earlier? Damn it.

Six

I can't wait," Seth pants below me, sweat beading his fore-head.

"Seth, *no*," I groan in frustration as he removes his thumb from my clit, making me lose the orgasm that had finally been starting to crest.

He grabs my waist tightly as he thrusts his hips up, pounding his erection into me. "I can't—I'm going to come!"

I have to brace my hands on his smooth chest as he bucks into me, his thrusts becoming jerky and frantic with his impending release. He gives a final hard thrust, burying himself in deep before going rigid. A few long seconds later, he relaxes against the sheets, his head falling heavily on my pillow.

His hands lazily trail over my thighs as he tries to regain his breathing. "I'm sorry," he pants. "I tried to wait until you were there."

Frustrated, I climb off his lap and flop down next to him on the bed. "It's fine." I huff as I stare up at the ceiling.

He laughs and rolls onto his side to face me. "I can always finish the job in other ways," he offers, walking his fingers down my torso towards the part between my legs. "I'm always a hungry beast when it comes to you."

I shake my head, the mood lost. "Really, it's fine. I think I just have a lot on my mind."

"I want to hear about it after I take care of this," he gestures at the condom before standing from the bed. He presses a kiss to my cheek when I turn my face from him. Gods, I hate when he tries to sneak in kisses. "Be right back," he adds with a wink.

I sit up as he leaves and frown at the empty room. Is he asking me to share my day with him? That goes against our rules. We don't talk about our personal lives. It just wasn't something we did. Maybe I need to distance myself from the warlock.

Reaching for my phone on the nightstand, I see a missed text from Taylor. I click on the message and smile at the grinning selfie of Taylor and Bryan.

Happy he's finally home. Have lots of sex. I'll see you tomorrow. I type in response.

Oh, don't worry. We covered that. Details tomorrow!!! She sends back, making me laugh.

"What are you smiling about?" Seth asks as he walks back into the room, stark naked and holding two copper goblets and a dark-tinted wine bottle.

"Taylor's boyfriend came home and she sent me a self-ie," I answer as I place the phone down on the mattress.

"Cute," he comments before handing me a goblet. When I hesitantly take it, he laughs and uncorks the bottle. "Why do you look so skeptical?"

"I'm not." I lean back against my headboard and grab my pillow, placing it in my lap to cover my nudity. When he fills my glass halfway, I lift it to inhale the scent. My nose instantly scrunches at the stench of the metal. "You and these damn goblets."

He sits down in front of me and gives me that charming grin before putting on a horrible British accent. "My dear, everything tastes better in a chalice. I made a wine fit for royalty and so we shall drink as such." His accent goes away as he looks lovingly down at his goblet. "These are my favorite treasures, I think. I found them for sale during one of my trips to the Middle East. They're said to be meant for a god, so naturally I had to have them."

I roll my eyes at him and take a tentative sip of the wine. It's room temperature, as Seth likes his wines, but it makes the subtle undertones of fruit pop. "Cherry?" I guess, mulling around the flavors sitting on my tongue while trying to ignore the metallic scent.

He smiles behind the rim of his cup. "Yes, a bit of raspberry as well."

I swirl my glass and take another sip. "It's good," I

praise. "A little heavier than what I'm used to, but it's good."

He nods. "It's more like juice, isn't it?"

"Adult juice." I laugh.

"I'm glad you like it." He rests his goblet on his knee and looks at me seriously. "Why don't you tell me what's on your mind? Does it have something to do with pushing back our meeting time tonight?"

I can't help but bristle. "Seth, I thought we agreed not to mix personal life with this."

He lifts a blonde brow. "I asked about your day, not for your hand in marriage."

I put the cup down on my nightstand and hug the pillow to my chest. "Talking about our day and what upsets us is too much like a relationship."

Seth glances down at his wine for a moment. "Would that really be so bad, Val? What if I want you to be mine?"

I recoil back against the headboard. "I can't be yours." I wince at how cold that sounded. "Seth, you're great, but my life is too complicated. I can't have a normal relationship."

He narrows his eyes. "Don't sugarcoat it now. Your first sentence said everything."

"I didn't mean it like that."

"I think you did," he replies as he stands from the bed. He sets his glass down next to mine and proceeds to collect his clothes from the floor, slipping them on as he does.

"No, I'm sorry, that's not how I meant it. I mean that I *can't* be yours. I can't be *anyone's*. Plus, I come with too much baggage, Seth." I try once again to explain. "You deserve someone better."

"It's fine, Val," he says, his words clipped and angry.

I've never seen him mad before and it makes me uneasy, sending the hair on the back of my neck prickling. I don't know what to say so I just watch as he gets dressed and picks up his belongings. He downs the rest of the wine in his cup and shuffles towards the bedroom door with it in hand.

"You can keep the wine and cup. Consider it a parting gift." He throws over his shoulder in a bitter tone.

When I fail to reply, he scoffs and disappears from my sight. When I hear my front door slam shut, I sigh and squeeze my eyes closed. Standing from my bed, I grab my cigarettes and lighter and head to my balcony for a smoke.

Today fucking sucked.

Taylor winces when I finish telling her what happened last night with Seth. We're hiding in my office, eating lunch as we fill each other in on our nights. "Well, to be fair, you did try to explain it."

"Yeah, but the damage was already done." I pick at my salad. "I really thought we were on the same track when it came to what we wanted."

"Maybe you were at first," she starts. "But feelings change, Val. His clearly did."

"Mine didn't," I sigh, setting down my fork. "The worst

part is I think I meant what I said the first time. I can't be his because I don't want to be. He's too bubbly to my cynical."

Taylor shoots me a pitying look. "You know, I did say this would happen."

My glare is weak. "Why do I keep you around?"

"Because I'm the *real* bubbly to your cynical," she laughs. "But you can't get rid of me so don't even try."

Despite my best efforts, I laugh as well. "So, happy that lover boy is home?"

Her cheeks burn red even as a smile curls up her lips. "I missed him so much. I know he was only gone for a couple days, but when he's gone it feels like a piece of my soul is missing. I feel empty inside." I make a gagging noise, and she swats at my arm. "Val, I'm serious!"

I smile. "I know, I know, I'm just being a bitch. Bryan's perfect for you, and maybe I'm a little jealous that you seem to have found your soulmate."

Her blush deepens, and she looks down at her lunch. "Funny you should mention the word *mate*."

My eyes widen. "He finally asked you, didn't he?"

"Yes!" She squeaks before blinking owlishly at me. "Wait, you knew he would?"

"Duh, anyone can see he's crazy about you."

"Really?" She squirms in her seat when I nod. "I'm so happy I'm going to be his mate, Val."

I cup my ear, leaning towards her. "I'm sorry, I don't think I heard you. I know a newly intended mate would be much more enthusiastic about this!"

Tay grins and jumps from her chair, throwing her hands up with a fork still clenched in one of them. "I'm going to be his mate!" she all but screams.

"Fuck yeah you are!" I stand up as well and high-five her over the desk. "I'm so happy for you, Tay!"

We fall into a fit of giggles I'll deny I ever let out before heading back to our seats to finish lunch. I turn to the door when a knock echoes on it, telling them to come in. I sit a little straighter when I see that it's Jack. His tanned skin looks even darker against the cream button up that fits him perfectly, the black blazer he walked in with that morning nowhere to be seen. His hair is slightly disheveled, as if he ran his fingers through it a couple times.

I mentally curse myself when I picture it being my hands in his hair. Get a fucking grip, Val. You've known the guy for less than a week.

"Hey," he begins and looks at the meals on the desk. "Oh, I didn't realize you were on your lunch break."

I point an accusing finger at him. "You've now interrupted two of my meals and ruined a precious cup of coffee. Why do you hate—*ow!*" Did Taylor just fucking pinch me?

Taylor gives Jack a warm smile as she settles back against her chair, ignoring my cursing. "You aren't interrupting at all, Detective Khoury."

"Please, call me Jack," he says, giving her a smile in return.

"Jack," she repeats before her smile twists into a conspiratorial smirk I know all too well. "You know, Val's right, you *do* owe her." When his brow furrows in question, she continues and moves a safe distance away from me. "You ruined her coffee *and* her dinner yesterday. Do you know what my friend is like without caffeine and food? Let me tell you, she turns into a bitch." She cups the side of her mouth and loudly whispers, "Worse than usual. Like, a *mega* bitch."

"Taylor!" I snap, knowing exactly where the wolf is going.

She jerks her thumb at me. "See?"

Jack glances between us and lifts a brow at me, the corner of his mouth tilting. "I think I know exactly what you mean. She *did* threaten me yesterday. I suppose it makes more sense now."

Oh, I'm going to wipe that smirk off his face.

"Great! So, you agree you owe her!" Before he can reply, Taylor claps her hands together. "It's decided then, you can make it up to her on Friday after work! I happen to know that her booty call dumped her last night so she's free."

"*Taylor!*" I hiss again, shooting from my chair and reaching for the blonde across the desk.

Agile as ever, Taylor slides out of my reach and stands up to keep distance between us. "You should already have her number, but I'll email you her address in case she tries to leave work early. We almost had Mexican for dinner yesterday, so I suggest taking her to a place where she can get her enchilada fix." She quickly grabs her takeout box from the desk and blows me a kiss. "I'll send you the reports from the crime scene as soon as I can! Love you, bye!"

I stare dumbfoundedly at the door after Taylor leaves. Oh, I'm going to kill her. There is no way she's going to get away with trying to set me up on a date with Jack. Hell no.

I clear my throat and look at the man in question in my doorway. "Please ignore her, Detective Khoury. I'm convinced she's bat shit crazy. In fact, we're not really friends. I don't even know her. She's like a lost puppy I fed once."

He gives me a once over. Immediately, my sleeveless, dark green chiffon blouse feels suffocating. "I'll see you at seven on Friday," he states before setting a file down on my desk.

"W-what! No!" I protest, throwing up my hands. "Really, Khoury, you don't have to. Neither one of us agreed to this so let's just pretend it didn't happen."

Jack shoots me that sly smirk that makes my stomach flutter. "You have three days to come to terms with it."

When he too vanishes from my office, I sink down into my chair and stare at the file on my desk with wide, disbelieving eyes. What the hell just happened?

Seven

*F*riday came in a fucking blur, and I'm in all kinds of knots over it. My stomach is tight as I sit at my desk after lunch and a cigarette. My eyes keep darting to the clock on my computer screen, the minutes taunting me with the impending date that I keep telling myself I don't want. Because I don't. I do *not* want this date.

Then why did I choose my favorite dark grey pencil skirt and a black blouse that showed off just a tad too much cleavage? Why did I pair it with a pair of black heels that makes my ass look even better?

"I did this for me," I argue into the compact mirror in my hand. "I'm allowed to look nice for myself. I deserve to look hot and be confident. Maybe I'll buy myself some flowers, too. Yes, treat yourself, bitch."

"Am I interrupting something?"

I whirl my chair towards my door so fast I slam my

knee on my desk with a cry. I'm going to blame my inflamed cheeks on the embarrassment of being caught talking to myself. Because dear gods, Jack is standing in my doorway looking delectable. He's dressed in a silk, dark blue button up that clings to his physique, his black slacks clinging just enough to tell me that he has a nice, probably firm, ass.

"Something I can assist you with, Detective Khoury?" I ask, refusing to give him the satisfaction at seeing me flustered as I rub the sting out of my knee. "Please tell me you have something for the case."

Jack and I have gotten nowhere in our investigation. We have no suspects or leads. After talking to the friends and family of Ruby, also known as Stephanie Browne, the only possible motive we could come up with was a scorned customer. And even if that was the motive, we have no idea who the customer could be. The problem is that none of the staff or entertainers we interviewed could recall a single altercation between Ruby and a customer.

We went to her apartment, searched the unit from top to bottom, but the only thing we found was a phone tucked in a drawer next to a rather large dildo. The techs that investigated the phone, but determined it was most likely just an old phone she kept.

I had been tempted on more than one occasion to contact Cerberus and ask why exactly Ruby had been chosen to be marked, but I knew he wouldn't tell me. It went against the "rules". Either way, the fact that she was supposed to be marked so urgently meant something, didn't it?

Normally, when I mark souls chosen by the Fates, it's a

gamble for me. I see every sin that person has committed, no matter how big or small, but I'm not their judge. I don't know what happens after Thanatos takes them to the Styx or where their souls end up in the underworld. Do they go to Elysium, our version of heaven, or Asphodel, the city Hades created for the souls that are neither bad nor evil? *Or,* do they end up in the black empty pits of Tartarus?

And for all the options, what is the deciding factor? How much of a sin is *too* much?

This uncertainty is the main reason I've kept away from my family.

He stalks over to my desk and sets down a manilla folder from the lab. "The medical examiner's report on Jane Doe is in."

Perking up at the news, I lean over and snatch the report off the desk as he sits in the chair across from me. I skim through the report before finding the information I'm looking for. I read the line three times before I look at him. "This can't be right."

"I said the same thing," Jack says. "I asked her to check it again. That was a mistake I'll never repeat."

I wince in sympathy. "Latisha is meticulous in her work. She's never made a mistake and to insinuate one will immediately put you on her shit list."

"So I discovered. How do I get off it?" He asks as he rubs the stubble along his jaw. "She hit me with my own folder."

I laugh at the image of it before I can stop myself. "Tell her you're sorry and that Val is going to whip you into shape.

That should give you at least a chance to redeem yourself."

"Whip me into shape?" He repeats, his eyes darkening as a hint of a smirk tilts his lips.

I press my thighs together at the suggestion in his tone. This is how it has been between us all week. We can be completely professional and swamped with work, but occasionally, these moments happen. Banter with underlying flirtation. I know I'm drawn to him, his energy calling to mine, but damn does he get under my skin sometimes. It isn't that he's cocky or pompous, no. He's confident and sure, but also honest and straightforward. He says what's on his mind and doesn't hesitate to call me out on shit. Alternatively, he never hesitates to compliment or praise me. A small part of me, although I will never admit aloud, basks in his praise.

I don't understand it, and it scares me.

I'm well and truly fucked for tonight if I can't get my shit under control.

I clear my throat and look at the file once again. "Latisha is saying that the blood we can see isn't hers?" I lay the file down on my desk and turn back to my computer, bringing up the case file so I can view the photos taken at the crime scene and compare them to Latisha's.

Jack wheels his chair around my desk so he's sitting next to me. "That's what I didn't understand. I asked her if it could simply be her killer's blood and that's when she smacked me with the folder."

"She would have noted that in her file," I muse as I bring up the photos of Jane Doe. I zoom in on the jagged stump that's left of her neck and look at the blood. "She's saying all this wet blood is someone else's." I hum and scroll to the next picture of her mutilated sternum. "This as well."

He flips through the file on my desk and reads, "Upon further investigation and testing, the body is showing signs of vapor and blood cell rupture."

I glance at him. "What does she mean by blood cell rupture? I'll be honest, she usually dumbs this shit down for me."

He lets out a huff of a laugh. "It's a process that happens to blood cells when they're frozen and then thawed."

I whip my head towards him and almost smack our foreheads together when I realize how close he is. Rearing back, I take the file from him and read over Latisha's notes again. "She's saying the body was frozen at some point?"

He nods. "Yes. She's unsure how long the victim has been dead because of how well it's been preserved. However, she states that the body was almost completely thawed when we found it. She left a little note down here for you saying that bodies take up to a week to thaw if done correctly in a cool environment."

"Did she really? Or are you making fun of me now?" I ask with a lifted brow. When he hands me a skull-shaped sticky note, I can't help but smirk. "I love that woman. She really gets my level of laziness."

"As a detective, you really shouldn't be lazy," he points out.

"Seeing as you're not my mother, you really shouldn't be chiding me." I retort and childishly stick out my tongue. Something heats in his gaze, and I instantly draw it back into my mouth. "Anyways, so, we have no real TOD for Jane Doe's death."

"No," he responds and slides his chair back around to the other side of my desk.

I run my hand through my hair as the stress of the case doubles. "But the murders are identical. There's no way it was a different killer. The question is: why would the murderer freshly kill someone and then a week later dump another victim at a different club? What's the point of that?"

Jack shrugs, but I can see the tension in his shoulders. "I don't know, but you'll be interested to know that we finally got the camera footage from Crazy Horse."

At his tone, I can already see how this was going to go. "Let me guess, it cuts out once again?" When he gives me a single nod, I sigh. "Of course. It would be too easy if it didn't."

"Agreed." Jack says. "Latisha sent our vic's fingerprints into the Las Vegas Missing Persons Detail, but there hasn't been a hit yet." He reaches for the Cerberus figure on my desk, and my hackles rise. It takes every part of me to not snatch it back from him.

"I'm guessing she sent off a DNA sample to the Missing Persons DNA Program then? I wonder how quickly the FBI's database can match something." I muse, but my eyes are transfixed to the plastic three-headed dog in his hands.

"The FBI's Combined DNA Index System will compare samples across the nation but filling it out and getting the sample to them takes a bit of time." He looks up and tilts his head at my intense stare. He holds up Cerberus but doesn't offer him to me. "This is sentimental."

I blink at his statement. My lips purse together, a denial on my tongue, but something tells me he'd spot a lie. I go with a partial truth instead. "My mom got it for me when I was a teen."

"Kind of a random gift," he says as he looks at the figure again. "Why Cerberus?"

I shift in my seat and look at the miniature guardian. "I became obsessed with Greek mythology after—" I cut myself off, tearing my gaze away to glare down at my desk instead. "After I almost died. Well, I *did* die, technically."

Jack's head snaps up, and I can feel his sharp gaze on me. "You died?" Why does he sound angry?

I nod once. "I think it was karma." I blink at the admission. Never once have I spoken out loud about my speculation. With a dry swallow, I tuck my hair behind my ear and try to shake off the heavy feeling. "But it doesn't matter, does it? I'm still here blessing the world with my bitchy sarcasm and unparalleled wit."

Jack continues to frown at me. His lips twitch and then press together like he's trying to find the right words to say. His gaze drops back down to the Cerberus before he hands it to me. "What did you see when you died?"

Our fingers brush when I reach for the figure and heat flares across my hand and up my arm. I meet his probing stare and something in me turns spiteful. I don't miss the implication of his question. Who is he to assume that I saw anything?

A snarl twists my lip and I rip the figure from him before hurling it across my office. It knocks a frame from the wall, glass shattering as it hits the carpet.

I take a slow, deep breath and relax back into my chair, not bothering to explain my outburst. "Nothing." I respond calmly and turn back to my computer. "When did Latisha send out the DNA samples? Oh, I see her note saying she sent them yesterday."

His look almost becomes pitying. "Valkyrie…"

I'm saved from biting his head off when my office phone rings. Snatching it off the cradle, I sneer my name into the mouthpiece. "Dalton."

"*You better pump the brakes on that attitude, dog,*" Scott says.

"What do you want, kitten?"

He scoffs. "*We just got a call from Crazy Horse that our person of interest is there.*"

I glance at Jack. "Person of interest?"

Jack shrugs unapologetically. "I was about to tell you."

The glare I give him non-verbally tells him that he's an asshole. "He's there now, Scott?"

"*Yep, he's a regular who usually stays for a few drinks and dances. Still, I wouldn't chance missing him. Get there ASAP and find out what he knows.*"

I set the phone down when my boss hangs up but continue to stare down Jack. "Maybe instead of prying into my personal life, you can stick to information relevant to our case."

He stands from his chair, completely unphased by the venom in my tone. "I was getting to it. Our person of interest was caught on camera by the emergency door a few minutes before our vic was discovered. I figured since our possible motive was a scorned customer, this guy would be a good place to start."

I push down my ire as my professionalism finally kicks back in. Well, more like I remember that I have two headless girls with no killer yet. I stand and slide my holster vest back on before grabbing my coat from the back of the chair. "What was he doing at the door?"

Jack leads me from the office, heading down across the precinct towards the elevators. "Not sure," he begins as we step into the small space. "His back is turned to the camera. He could be a suspect or a witness."

"You think he saw or helped the person who dropped her off?"

Jack's lips twist a little. "I don't know about helped, but I think he may have seen something. If he doesn't have anything to hide, why not come forward when our people were interviewing possible witnesses?"

"I guess we're just going to have to find out, aren't we?" We step out of the elevator and wave at the receptionist before heading out of the building. When we get to the parking lot, we both stop and look at the other expectantly. "We can take my truck."

He looks at my red truck and has the audacity to laugh. "What are you, a fireman?"

"That's fire*woman*, you sexist pig," I cross my arms over my chest.

"For fucks sake, Valkyrie, it was a joke," he says, lifting his hands in defense, but an amused grin spreads across that

fine mouth of his again. "How many fires have you put out
lately?"

"A lot, you want to see my hose?" A reluctant smile curls
my lips when a full-on laugh escapes him. I pull my keys out
of my purse and unlock the doors. "Alright, now that you
have enough ammo to get me a write-up from HR, let's go."

"Yes, ma'am." He salutes me and heads to the passenger
door. He slips into the leather seat as I climb into mine. He
looks around and nods approvingly. "All jokes aside, this is
actually really nice."

"Why thank you." I beam and pet the dashboard. "I
treated myself to her a year ago and haven't regretted it
since." When I turn to look over my shoulder, I notice Jack's
smirk. I lift a brow at him before backing out of the spot.
"What's the smirk for?"

"Nothing," he hums. "I mean, treat yourself, right? Did
you buy yourself the flowers too?"

I slam on the breaks and Jack laughs even as he's jerked
forward against his seatbelt. "You better watch your knee-
caps, Khoury. They're officially my target," I warn. He lets
out another snicker, and I can't help the stupid smile on my
face as I head to Crazy Horse.

Yes, I'm well and truly fucked for tonight.

Eight

*J*ack's breath caresses the shell of my ear as he bends closer to me. "How do you want to play this?" He asks so I can hear him over the loud music.

I ignore the shiver that runs down my spine. "I think we should just approach him calmly. If we ask him to come with us, he may freak out and run if he is hiding something."

"So, you want to walk up to his table and say hi?" Jack asks with a raised brow. "Isn't that just as likely to make him bolt?"

I offer him a shrug. "I guess it depends on how we go about it." When I turn to head to the suspect's table near the wide, rectangular stage, Jack grabs my arm. Ignoring the fire racing up my arm at the contact, I whirl on him. "What did I say about grabbing me, Khoury?"

He immediately releases me. "Sorry." He runs a hand

through his black hair. "I just think we need to be more cautious. Rushing at him isn't the way to go about it. Let's observe him for a bit at the bar."

I perk up at the mention of alcohol. "Okay, let's have a drink."

He shoots me a suspicious look but nods. Score! "Alright. It'll look more authentic, I suppose," he begins. "We should act like a couple then."

Really? A couple at a titty bar? "How many couples do you think really go to a strip club? It's not very romantic."

"You don't strike me as the romantic type." Jack bends closer once again. "Besides, I happen to know that some couples like voyeurism." He presses his hand to the small of my back and leads my speechless ass to the bar.

I swallow my surprise and look at him over my shoulder. "Voyeurism or shopping for a third for the evening?"

He lifts a brow at me. "What, you don't like another woman in the bedroom?"

"Are you making assumptions about my sexuality, Detective Khoury?" I purr as we get to the bar and take a seat.

He doesn't need to know that I've tasted more than a few women before. None of them lasted longer than a night or two. In fact, Seth was the longest consistent bed partner I ever had. But again, Jack doesn't need to know that.

The fucker has the audacity to smirk at me as he slides into a barstool. "I think I would be in for a rude awakening if I assumed anything about you."

I give him my most innocent smile before turning to the

bartender and ordering a rum and coke.

"Two, please." Jack swivels in his seat so he's facing me, but I know he's keeping our suspect in his peripheral.

Copying him, I turn as well but have to place my knees between his so we don't knock them together. Plus, I'm wearing a skirt and the world doesn't need to see the scrap of lace I call underwear.

He tentatively puts his hands on my knees and gives me a small questioning glance. When I nod, he grabs them more firmly. I know he's doing it for our cover, but damn does heat flare up my thighs. He jerks his head towards our suspect. "There's a girl with him now."

I lean towards him with a flirty smile. "If he is the murderer, do you think she's potentially the next victim?"

"Could be," he agrees. He leans slightly away when the bartender drops our drinks off. He reaches into his inner jacket pocket and pulls out a twenty for our drinks.

I pick mine up and discreetly watch Josh as I swallow down a healthy gulp. Josh Hastings is a thin man with too-pale skin covered in pock marks. His brown hair falls into his eyes, and even from here, I can see the light reflecting off the grease in it. He's leaning towards the dancer, the girl laughing a little too loudly at whatever he was saying. How much time do these dancers waste listening to their client's bullshit? I don't have enough patience for that shit. I would have punched someone by now.

Feeling Jack's stare, I turn my attention back to him.

"What?"

He looks at my glass. "Do you drink a lot?"

"What business is that of yours?" Even as the words come out, I know they sound defensive.

"Considering you're my partner, it's my business. Don't think I forgot how you reeked of alcohol at the last crime scene." His dark grey eyes take on a gleam of concern. "I saw the empty bottles in your trash."

I bristle at the mention of the miniature bottles. "Snooping through my work trash now?"

"They weren't exactly hidden." He points out. "Do you need help?"

More than he'll ever know. Instead of saying that, I down the rest of my drink and swivel away from him. "They're getting up. Let's go."

"Looks like they're heading towards the VIP area where the body was found." Jack murmurs, keeping close behind me.

He's right. The back of the club where the body was discovered is dark without all the bright lights on. The only real light coming from the empty bar. We cautiously approach and see the two of them huddled together by the doors, whispering in low voices. Everything seems fine until Josh slowly begins reaching for something in his back pocket.

"Stop!" Jack hollers.

Josh whirls towards us, bloodshot eyes wide with fear. He looks at me then at Jack, and his eyes damn near bug out of his head. He shoves the entertainer at Jack, forcing him to catch her as she stumbles in her tall stilettos, and bolts out the exit. Cursing, I kick off my heels, pick them up, and chase after him.

"Val, wait!"

I hear Jack's voice before the door slams shut behind me. It takes me a split second to see Josh running across the secluded parking lot at the back of the club before I chase after him. "Police, stop!" I'm not sure why I bother shouting it. They never stop. Not ever.

Josh turns towards me, and for a split second I think he might actually stop, but no. Instead, he chucks his beer bottle at my bare feet, and I curse as shards nick my shins. The real pain comes when I step onto most of the broken glass; it all happened too quickly for me to dodge it.

"Bastard, two can play at that game." I sneer and chuck one of my heels at him. It hits a car when he suddenly veers to the right, the car blaring its offense as the alarm goes off. I follow him down the alley alongside the club, chasing him into the main parking lot in front of the club. He leaps over one of the planters and I follow, cursing as I feel glass sink further into the tender flesh in the arches of my feet. When I see him head towards the sidewalk, I aim my remaining heel and throw it as hard as I can at him.

Fuck yes! I mentally cheer as it hits him square in the back of the head, making him tumble forward. I'm on him a few seconds later, trying to pin his lithe body to the concrete. He's stronger than he looks, but that could be a combination of the adrenaline and whatever drug he's on. And looking at those crazed, dilated red eyes, there's zero doubt that he is definitely on one of the many drugs that roam Vegas' streets.

With a thrashing wiggle and pivot of his hips, Josh knocks me off him enough to reach for his pocket. As I reach to restrain his arm once again, he slashes blindly at me with a pocketknife and gouges my forearm.

"You dick," I hiss before grabbing his wrist and slamming it into the ground, forcing him to release the blade. "It's not nice to stab people!"

"It's not nice to throw fucking shoes at people, bitch!" Josh shouts.

"You threw a bottle at me first!" I snarl, digging my knee harder into his back. Sweet relief fills me when I hear Jack's voice calling my name from behind me. I'm not sure how long I would have been able to hold him here without cuffs.

Jack rushes towards us with his gun in his hands. When he sees I've restrained him, he tucks it away and quickly cuffs Josh's hands behind his back. Once he's secured, I sit down next to him on the asphalt, the pain in my feet and arm throbbing. Jack is at my side in an instant, taking off his jacket and wrapping my arm in it.

"What were you thinking? And going out there without your gun drawn?" He growls, but his brow is furrowed as he puts pressure to the cut on my arm. "You should have waited for me."

"I didn't want him to get away." I wince a little at the tightness of his hold. "And I had my shoes in my hands."

"Sorry," he mumbles, loosening his hold. "I just—" He

takes a deep breath and meets my gaze with a serious expression. "I saw the glass and the blood, and I panicked. I thought maybe he had taken you instead."

Had he been worried for me? A small flutter warms my stomach. "I'm sorry," I relent with a small sigh. "I didn't want our one lead to the murders to get away. I should have known better."

"Murders?!" Josh squawked. "No, no, no! I don't know anything about no murders!"

Jack releases my arm, leaving me to keep pressure on it. "Then why flee?" he asks, staring down at the worm of a man.

"Because I thought you were going to bust me!" he cries, eyes wide.

"Bust you for what, exactly?" I press. When he presses his lips together, I shrug. "Alright then, have it your way. You'll be brought down to the station for questioning regarding the body that was dumped here earlier this week."

Josh frantically shakes his head. "No way! I don't know anything about that! Look, I just come here to do my business! These girls are some of my best clients!"

"Clients?" Jack asks, now writing down everything on a small notepad he pulled from his pocket. "What kind of clients?"

Josh bangs his head on the ground in defeat. "Drugs, man. Mostly weed and pills, but sometimes a bit of cocaine."

"You were here Monday night at 6:12pm." I phrase it as a statement rather than a question since we have him on camera. "When you were dealing in your little back corner, or at the door, did you see anyone suspicious? Anyone carrying large items? A car parked along the curb?"

He shook his head. "Nah, man. I was focused entirely on my deal."

"Think really hard." Jack squats down in front of him, his face a mask of cool indifference. "It would be a shame to have to take you down to the station after all."

Josh grunts, his face scrunching up in fear. "Well, I mean, there was one guy, I guess. He wasn't carrying anything, but he was just leaning outside the door. I thought maybe he was waiting for a girl or something, I don't know."

"Description?" Granted, as Josh said, it could have been just a person outside, but maybe they had seen something this guy didn't.

"Man, I don't know. It was dark!" he wails.

"Taller than him?" I ask, pointing to Jack's 6'3 frame. When he shakes his head, I point to myself. "What about me?" I force myself to my feet and wince at the instant pain it brings me.

Josh's eyes slither up and down my body, making me sneer at him in disgust. "Eh, I'd say around your height, I guess. I think his hair was light, but it's hard to tell with the lights."

I perk up at the sound of a car pulling into the lot and grin at the cruiser. "The cavalry is here to take you to the station." I tell Josh, who pales and starts thrashing again.

"What the fuck? I answered your questions!" He protests as two uniformed officers pick him up off the ground.

"You ran from law enforcement, harmed an officer, and admitted to dealing drugs," Jack tells him with a lifted brow. "What did you think was going to happen?"

"This is bullshit." Josh pouts as he's taken away to the squad car after being read his Miranda Rights.

"What do you think about the guy he mentioned?" I turn to Jack, but he's staring down at my bare feet with a glare. "Jack?"

He snaps his head up at my use of his name, surprise on his face before it morphs to anger again. "Your feet."

I look down at them and grimace at all the blood and dirt. "Did I mention I ran through glass?"

"Unbelievable," he mutters before sweeping me up into his arms. He doesn't give me a single second to fight him. "Don't even try to fight me on this, Valkyrie. You're in no position to walk without damaging your feet further. Only the gods know if you already contracted something from this filthy parking lot."

I cross my arms over my chest. "I didn't do it on purpose."

"I gather that you don't put your health first most of the time." He shoots me a half smile. "As your partner, I guess I'm just going to have to do it for you then, aren't I?"

Gods, that stupid fucking smile does stupid shit to my stupid fucking insides. What have I gotten myself into with him?

Nine

Are you sure you don't want to go to the hospital?" Jack asks, looking up at me from his kneeling position on the asphalt. I'm sitting sideways in the passenger seat of my truck, legs hanging out the open door.

"I'm sure," I reply, gripping the headrest as he gently cradles my foot in one hand. There isn't any pain yet, but his tender touch is sending flames up my calves. "I don't like doctors."

"Why?" He lifts the tweezers from the First-Aid kit I keep in my backseat and tightens his grip in warning before plucking out a brown shard.

My foot jerks at the pain, but Jack's grip keeps me from moving it too much. "Bad experience," I answer through clenched teeth as he yanks out another one.

He remains oddly silent as he removes two more before

moving to the next foot. "Is that where you died?" he finally asks in a quiet, soft tone.

I flinch at his words and then again at the feeling of the glass being pulled from my skin. "Mhm," I mumble. "So, I don't go if I don't have to."

"How did you die?" His tone is comforting, but the tweezers are relentless as they dig into a deep cut to find the intruder.

I swallow and tighten my hold on the headrest. "I was beaten to death," I finally answer, not quite knowing why I'm telling him this. Strangely, I feel a knot that has been sitting in my chest loosen just the tiniest bit.

He snaps his head up to look at me, eyes dark with rage. "*What?*"

Avoiding his gaze, I try to make light of it. "Well, I was beaten and then flatlined in the emergency room."

"Who? And how old were you?"

"I was fourteen," I admit, still not looking at him. "I... it was karma. I did it to myself, really."

"I don't believe that," Jack says as he fishes out the last shard of glass before setting the tweezers back in the kit. He grabs some hydrogen peroxide and pours it over each arch. I hiss in a breath at the initial burn and clench my hands into tight fists when he wipes them clean with a gauze pad.

"You don't know me, Khoury," I murmur as he delicately adds some ointment to each cut.

He scoffs at me and puts the ointment away. He then grabs long sterile bandages and begins to wrap my left foot. "There is little a young teenage girl can do that would cause that kind of karma, Valkyrie. Why do you think you fall into that category?"

Folding my hands in my lap, I tell him the truth. "When I was ten, there was a girl named Paige who used to bully me. Well, her and her friends. My family wasn't wealthy, and I was overweight. If those two weren't enough to inflict the wrath of the 'cool girls', then me being into anime and books was just the cherry on top. I was the weird outcast." I flex my calf when his fingers trail up it, his long fingers tying the bandage in place at my ankle before moving on to the next foot.

"But this girl, the ringleader, was just cruel. One day she snatched my book from my hands and threw it to the ground while calling me fat. She told me she was sorry and that she realized how mean that was. That she didn't mean it. So, to make it up to me, she invited me to play hide-and-go-seek with her and her friends. I wanted to be liked by the cool kids, I wanted to have friends. So, I agreed.

"We were all neighbors so anything in the cul-de-sac was fair game. I thought I found the perfect hiding spot, and I was ready to be the winner. It was so good they didn't find me for half an hour. But then nearly an hour went by, and I got anxious. When I came out, no one was there. I went looking for them, and they were all hanging out in her garage playing a game. They literally burst out laughing when I showed up. They couldn't believe I really went an hour before figuring it out. They then proceeded to laugh about how stupid I was." I let out a bitter laugh. "I played right into their hands, and I think that's when my trust in people broke. I was ten years old and already had to learn that hard life lesson.

"After that I was more on guard, refusing to fall into another trap. That just spurred them on for the next couple years. I was called names at every opportunity, whispered and laughed about, and had various vicious lies spread about me. At one point, one of them used to sit in class next to me and just flick me with a rubber band. I came home with welts on my skin because the teacher refused to do anything. My mom tried to get involved, but it just made everything worse.

"My self-image was completely shattered. Emotional and mental abuse that young will fuck you up. It'll distort how you see yourself for years to come." I feel his hands slide up my legs to rest on my knees, but I still can't look at him. "And I think that's why I didn't help her. Even though it had been a year of no torment, I didn't help her when she needed it."

I suck in a shaky breath. Gods, I need a smoke. "I was walking home from school after a late swim match and saw Paige get grabbed by a man. She was fighting and thrashing and doing everything she could to get free. At one point she saw me looking and screamed at me to help her, but I didn't move. I could have flipped open my phone and called 9-1-1, but I didn't. I just blankly watched her get abducted. It was only when the kidnapper's accomplice saw me watching that I ran. That's the only reason I actually opened my phone and called the police."

I finally muster enough courage to look at him. A breath lodges in my throat at the intense looks he's giving me. It's not pity, more like a mix of concern and sympathy. "Right when I pushed the call button, he was on me. He beat the shit out of me. Punches, kicks, even slammed my head into the curb. I was already unconscious when the police and paramedics came. I woke up in the hospital three days later."

Jack stands and steps between my legs. His hands cup my cheeks as he forces me to hold his gaze. "That was not karma," he says, voice deep. "That was a little girl who made a mistake. Everyone makes mistakes, Valkyrie. You owed that girl nothing. And quite frankly, I believe you were stuck in your trauma. Once you got away from the scene, I'm fairly certain you would have called the police or at least told your parents."

I blink up at him, trying to keep the moisture from my eyes. "How can you say that so surely?"

"Because you are good." He states it so firmly that I almost believe him myself.

Almost.

Pulling my face out of his hold, I turn from him. "Again, you don't know me. You don't know what I've done." He doesn't know the hundreds of people I've marked.

He sighs and runs his hands through his hair. "You're right, I don't, but I feel that you are good." He gives me one of his sly smirks. "I have a good beacon for this kind of thing, so just trust me on this."

I roll my eyes at him but wish I could believe him. "Alright, partner, enough sappy shit. Let's get back to the office and get this guy's statement." I turn and rifle through my backseat to find a pair of black flats. Finding the flimsy shoes, I drop them onto the floor in front of me and slide them on. Oh, yeah, I look so sexy with my bandaged feet and forearm.

"No," Jack takes my keys from me and slides into the driver's seat of my truck, driving the beast so my feet don't suffer further.

"What do you mean 'no'?" I repeat.

He grins at me. "Did you forget? We have a date."

"Ah fuck," I toss my head back against the headrest, ignoring the little flutters in my stomach that he remembered. Hell, I'm impressed that he even still wants to go with me looking like a mummy. "You still really want to go somewhere?"

"Yes, you're not getting out of this so easily." He puts the truck in reverse and looks at me expectantly.

"*Easily?*" I echo in disbelief. "Did you see my feet?"

"I did, which is why I'm changing the venue for our dinner." He raises a brow at me when I try to protest. "You're not winning this, Valkyrie. So, buckle up and behave."

"Yes, sir," I mumble sarcastically as I clip in my seatbelt.

"Good girl." Jack nods approvingly before backing out of the parking space.

My stupid insides flip and twirl at his praise once again. I'm so, *so* fucked.

"You clever bastard," I praise, kicking my flats off and resting my heels on the dashboard.

Jack grins as he rolls up the sleeves of his dress shirt,

hiding my blood from the waitress. "I'll admit that a Sonic isn't what I had in mind for our date, but given your feet, I figured food delivered to the truck is the closest to a restaurant."

I can't help but smile. "I don't need a fancy restaurant. A burger and a shake will win me over any day."

"I thought enchiladas were the way to your heart?" he teased.

Shaking my head, I correct him, "*Food* is the way to my heart, Detective."

He laughs, and the sound of it makes me smile. "Good. I like a woman who isn't afraid to eat."

I wave my hand at him. "I spent too many years worrying about my weight. Sometimes the insecurities still creep up on me, but for the most part, I'm a lot better with it."

A growl rumbles in his chest, making me look at him. I blush at the damn near hungry look in his eyes. "You have nothing to be insecure about, Valkyrie. I like what I see very much." The blush burns down my neck and spreads across my chest.

"T-that's very forward of you." Did I just fucking stutter? What am I, twelve?

He blinks and looks away from me, the steering wheel suddenly very interesting. "You're right. That was way over the line. I'm not used to filtering what I say."

"I noticed that," I muse. "I'm not going to lie, sometimes your blunt straightforwardness infuriates me, but it's also very refreshing. You don't sugarcoat shit and make it very clear where you stand on things. I like that." I purse my lips before shooting him a sly smile. "And I also very much like how you look."

He turns those storm-colored eyes on me, and once again, the look makes heat flare in my chest. "Good."

I lick my lips, ready to shoot back a witty response, but a knock on my window makes me jump. When I turn to look, I'm stunned to see a pissed Seth standing there. I fumble with the buttons on my door until I finally find the one that rolls down the window. "Seth?"

"Hello Val," he purrs, but the underlying note is tense. "And who do we have here? I thought you didn't do dates?"

Wow, talk about awkward. I'm about to tell him as such before Jack cuts in, leaning towards the steering wheel so he can be seen better. Or is he getting a better look at Seth?

"Jack Khoury," he says, not offering his hand. "You?" Tension crackles between them and it's almost suffocating.

"Seth Adel." He gives Jack an unimpressed once over before returning his attention back to me. "Well?"

Oh, hell no. "Not that it's any of your fucking business, but he's my partner."

"Bed partner? Or professional?" he presses.

My hackles rise. "What the actual fuck, Seth? Who do you think you are, asking something like that? Regardless of what the answer is, it's none of your business!"

"We broke up and here you are with someone new not even a week later?" Seth sneers. "We spent two months together! Did that mean nothing?"

He acts like we were dating when I made it very clear we

weren't. "Seth—"

"I wanted you to be *mine*, but you refused me everything. No dates, no personal conversations, not even a single kiss! But here you are with some random guy!"

"Raise your voice to her again," Jack warns, voice so deep and low it makes a shiver run down my spine, "and you'll wish you hadn't."

His aura faintly pulses at the warning, and I sway away from him. Seth reaches for me as I do, but Jack grabs my arm and tugs me towards him so Seth can't make contact. I look at Seth with no small amount of disgust. "I'm glad we're done, Seth. If I knew you had this possessive, crazy side I wouldn't have ever climbed into bed with you."

He narrows his eyes at me. "I could have given you the world, Val."

I cross my arms over my chest. "I don't want anything from someone who puts their ego first."

His eyes zero in on my bandaged arm then dart to my feet still on the dash. Concern flickers over his eyes for a moment. "What happened?"

"You lost the right to ask her that," Jack says, wrapping his arm around my shoulders to keep me away from Seth. "Why don't you go? It's clear you're not wanted here."

Seth's cheeks redden as I nod my agreement. "Fine," he snarls and then hits my poor, innocent truck before storming away.

I pull away from Jack and quickly roll up the window. With a groan, I drop my feet back to the mat and bury my face in my hands. "Gods, I'm so sorry you had to witness that."

He smooths a hand down my back. "Are you okay?"

"Utterly mortified, but I'll survive," I mumble and draw my hands away to look at him. "He's never been like that before. It's like he became someone completely different since we stopped sleeping together."

He hums in his throat. "Maybe you just never actually knew him. Never saw him for what he truly is."

I drop my head back against the seat. "I guess so."

I flinch when another knock taps against glass, but this time it's the waitress at Jack's window. He accepts the food from her, giving her a tip, and she glides off on her skates to serve the next guest.

"Thanks," I say as I accept my meal from him, but my altercation with Seth has left a bad taste in my mouth.

Jack gives me a pointed look. "Eat."

I take a small sip of my chocolate shake, trying to ignore his approving nod. "I'm sorry again about Seth."

He unwraps his burger and takes a large bite. "You don't have to apologize," he says after he swallows. "But I do have a lot more questions."

"More? My life story wasn't enough to scare you away?" I tease as I unwrap my own burger.

"On the contrary, I'm much more intrigued." Jack chews on a fry before his next question comes out. "Was he overexaggerating about the kisses?"

I choke on my burger, patting my chest to help it go down. Wiping my mouth with a napkin, I glance over at him.

There's no judgment in his expression, just curiosity. "He wasn't exaggerating," I confess.

His eyes widen in surprise. "Not once?"

"Not on the lips, no," I explain and then wiggle my brows at him. "Other places however…"

He lets out a soft chuckle and takes a sip of his coke. "Can I ask why?"

Ah, the question every single one of my hookups asks. "You can ask, but I won't tell you." My tone turns serious when I see him about to press me. "Jack, I've already told you more about my life than I have anyone else. I don't really understand why, but I did. This topic, however, is not up for discussion. I need you to respect that."

He stares at me for a beat, stormy eyes holding mine and searching for a truth I won't give him. Finally, he nods and turns back to his burger. "Alright then."

Surprisingly, he doesn't sound mad or pissy like everyone else has in my past. He just accepts it. I clear my throat and turn my questions on him. "What about you?"

He lifts a brow. "What about me?"

"I've told you enough about my past. Tell me something about you."

He puts his drink down in the cup holder and crumbles up the burger wrapper to toss in the bag. He hesitates briefly before turning to look at me. "Alright. My father cheated on his wife with a woman who was also married. His mistress ended up pregnant with me and went through with my birth but didn't want anything further to do with me."

I polish off my burger as he speaks, listening intently as

he continues. "My father's wife forgave him, and they decided to take me in. The husband of his mistress, my biological mother, however, was not so forgiving. In his rage, he murdered my father."

"Fuck, I'm sorry," I offer lamely. I mean, what else can I say?

Jack lets out a soft sigh as he leans forward and rests his elbows on the steering wheel. "I think that's why I became so involved with death."

I tilt my head at him. "You mean that's why you wanted to become a homicide detective?"

He blinks and looks at me. "Yes, I suppose. I wanted to have a role in convicting evil people. Sinners shouldn't get a pass just because they don't get caught at the time of the sin."

"Do you think I'm evil?" I blurt out the question before I can think better of it. At his questioning look, I drop my gaze to my lap. "I sin. I indulge in alcohol, sex, and swear like a sailor." And mark people for hell with a kiss of my lips.

He reaches out and touches my shoulder. "No, I don't. I already told you I think you're good," he says firmly. "You do none of those with an evil intent, Valkyrie. You are *not* evil. Yes, your aura is tinged with darkness, but it's not malicious. Honestly, I suspect it's from you dying."

He has no idea how close he is to the truth.

I try to push away the sudden wave of pity I feel. "Well, okay then."

Jack's smile is easy. "As far as first dates go, this wasn't so bad."

I can't help but laugh. "If you ignore the jealous ex-fuck

buddy, I suppose not."

He laughs again. "Where do you live? I'll drive your truck there, so you don't have to."

I shake my head. "And how will you get back? I'll be okay to drive so go ahead and take us back to the station."

"I wasn't offering, Valkyrie. I'm telling you I'm driving you home." He starts the truck and throws it into drive before looking at me with an expectant look. "Taylor gave me your address, but I haven't looked it up. So, where am I going?"

I sigh in defeat before listing off the directions to my apartment. "I'm across the freeway from Downtown on Martin Luther King and Alta, by the hospital." He nods and we drive in silence, but it's easy and comfortable. I realize that I like being around Jack, despite his blunt personality.

"What building and floor do you live on?" Jack asks once he pulls my truck into my assigned space.

"Eighteen and the second," I answer as I grab my purse from the backseat and throw open my door. I shoot him an exasperated look when he holds it open for me. When I see him reach for me, I swat his hands away. "I can walk!"

"No, you can't," he argues. "Your feet are all torn up. If you walk on them right now, you're going to make them worse."

"They'll heal!" I really don't want him to carry my ass all the way to my building, let alone up a flight of stairs like some prince charming.

"Why are you so stubborn?" He huffs as I slide out of my seat and tentatively set my feet on the ground. I had slid the flats back on, but there's hardly any cushion in them and I feel each cut throb in protest.

"Because I can be," I mutter.

Jack shuts my door for me and locks the truck before handing me my keys. He holds his arm out to me and I reluctantly take it, letting him take the brunt of my weight as I lean on him. I'm not ashamed to admit that I rely mostly on him to help me along the sidewalk that leads to my building. I most definitely lean more on him when I hobble up the stairs. I'm stubborn, not stupid. When we get to my unit, I release his arm so I can unlock my door.

"Um, thank you," I say awkwardly as I turn to him. "For everything."

He smiles down at me, and I feel it shoot straight down to my core. "You're welcome. It was an interesting day."

"It was," I agree with a soft chuckle.

There's a beat of silence that's thick with a mix of uncertainty and longing. I think that last one may just be me, but then he takes a step towards me, closing the distance between us. Years of denial have me automatically raising my hands between us, pressing them flat to his chest, but I don't push him away like I need to.

"I respect your boundaries, Valkyrie," he states in a soft whisper before pressing his lips to my forehead.

A pang of longing grips my heart so tightly a small gasp escapes my lips. He goes to pull away from me, but my hands have fisted in his shirt. I'm staring at the sliver of tanned skin that's peeking out from the undone buttons at his throat, my heart hammering. "Again?" I end up asking in a small, pitiful voice.

When he kisses my forehead again, I feel his smile in it. I swallow thickly and squeeze my eyes shut as his lips lightly brush over my skin before pulling back again. I force my hands to release him as embarrassment hits me hard. Dropping my gaze to my feet, I nod at him. "Thank you."

Long fingers lift my chin, and I'm met with a soft smile. "No, thank *you*. I'll see you on Monday."

Unable to form any words, I nod, and he steps back from me. With another smile, he turns and disappears down the hall. I watch him go before finally going into my apartment. After showering off the day's events and redressing my wounds, I sink into bed with my latest Patricia Briggs book. When sleep finally claims me, it does so without the help of a bottle.

Ten

*M*onday comes, and Taylor and I are making our way to my office after getting our morning coffee. We came in early with the sole purpose of discussing our weekend. I fill her in on my date with Jack on Friday, and her facial expressions are exactly what I expected them to be.

"Oh, my gods, no Seth didn't!" Taylor slams her hand down on my desk, making my cup of pens rattle. "I can't believe the audacity of that man-child!"

I take a sip of my coffee and relax back against my chair. "It was so embarrassing, Tay."

"You have nothing to be embarrassed about! That as-shat tried to be an alpha male when he's nothing more than a puppy! What a douche!" She fumes.

I laugh at her outrage. "Yeah, I'm surprised Jack stayed around after and didn't hightail it out of there. A jealous ex isn't typically something someone wants to deal with."

Taylor grins at me. "They sure don't. Unless, of course, the girl is worth it." When I choke on my coffee, she cackles. "And you're *so* worth it, Val! Jack is twice the man Seth will ever be and you know it! I bet he'd rock in bed."

I balk at her. "Gods, Tay, just go straight for the jugular why don't you?"

"I will," she says seriously before continuing. "So, I want more details on what happened after dinner."

I calmly set my coffee down on the desk. "He walked me to my door and then left."

"No, no, no," Tay interjects. "I don't believe that. What happened? Did you kiss?" At my pointed look, she corrects herself. "Okay, scratch that. I know you don't kiss people. But something *did* happen, didn't it?" When my cheeks flush, she thrusts her fist in the air with a triumphant holler. "I knew it!"

"Shh!" I shush her, glancing at my door as if everyone can hear.

"What. Happened." She leans on my desk, annunciating each word.

I look down at my coffee lid, a small smile tugging at my lips. "He kissed my forehead." When Taylor doesn't say anything, I look up at her disheartened expression. "What?"

She lets out a dramatic sigh. "That's just so anticlimactic! I was hoping you two would bang!"

I laugh as she collapses on my desk, burying her face in her arms. I pat her blonde hair while still smiling. "You don't understand what that little gesture means to me. He did it after stating he respected my boundaries. He didn't try to sneak in a kiss like so many others have tried to do. He just accepted it, and that means a lot more." Butterflies swim in my stomach as I remember it.

Taylor pouts up at me. "You still could have fucked."

"I thought about it," I admit. When she shoots me a devilish grin, I return it. "How can I not? Have you seen him?" We share a laugh and I tuck a strand of hair behind my ear. "But really, it was so tender. I didn't want to let him go. I wanted more."

"Did you tell him that?" She asks.

I shake my head. "No. I was already pawing at him like a bitch in heat. He didn't need that. I'll admit, it was nice. I'm comfortable around him." I panic as my best friend's eyes suddenly fill with tears. "Tay?"

"I knew it," she cries, wiping at her eye. "I knew he was going to be the one for you. I don't know why, but as soon as you guys met at the crime scene, I could just see you two together. He's what you need, Val."

I look down at my desk, shifting a bit uncomfortably. "I barely know him."

She smacks my desk again, making me jump. "And yet you told him your past when you haven't even gone into detail about it with *me*." There's no bite to her tone when she says this, but I know it must sting a bit. I don't want my friend to hurt, but she stops me before I can apologize. "I'm not mad. Hurt a little, sure, but it's your life and I've accepted that. It doesn't diminish our friendship, Val." She waves her hand at me. "Anyways, I'm trying to point out just how big this is for you. Don't you see?"

"I see," I mumble reluctantly. "But I'm all sorts of fucked up. What can I really offer him?"

She scowls at me. "Everything. If Seth, your past, and your kissing rule didn't have him running for the hills, I think he sees that too." A knock sounds at my door, and she stands with her coffee cup. "You underestimate yourself so much it's infuriating."

I give a noncommittal shrug but don't have anything to say in response to that. I watch as she heads to my door and sit up a little straighter when I see Jack on the other side of it. We lock eyes for a long moment, and my stomach twists in yearning.

"Good morning, Detective Khoury!" Taylor beams at him before whirling towards me with a scolding expression. "Remember what I said: *everything.*"

There are no words to describe how much I love my friend. Even when I don't deserve these kind words, she freely gives them to me. Ever since I met her, she's been like a balm to my soul. It sounds cheesy, but it doesn't change the truth of it.

"Thank you, Tay," I say, hoping my tone will convey the love I feel for her. She blows me a kiss and disappears out the door. My smile widens before I look at my partner again. "Morning."

His smile widens at my breathy tone. "Good morning,

Valkyrie. How are your wounds?"

I glance down at my forearm. The gash healed enough so that it only needed a Band-Aid to cover it. "Good. My feet still have some scratches and scabs, but they're tolerable." I eye the folder in his hand and gesture at the seat Taylor vacated. "What do you have for me?"

"Looks like we have a DNA match to our vic," he explains as he takes a seat and opens the file on my desk. "The FBI database came back with a Samuel G. North. It's a strong match for paternity."

I pick up the mug shot of the older male. "Why was his DNA in the database?"

"He was once a suspect in a murder case, believe it or not." Jack pulls out another paper from the file and hands it to me. "Better yet, I did some searching and found out his biological daughter is Janelle N. North."

Taking the paper from him, I study the image of the young woman. "Let me guess, she's been missing?"

"For almost three months," he agrees. "I wanted to wait until you were in to start making phone calls."

I nod and look at the image again. The girl is stunning. Her dark skin is smooth, eyes soft and full of life. Her black hair falls in braids around her slim but strong shoulders. Such a waste of a beautiful life. I set the paper down on my desk and lightly run my finger over the printed image. "What's the first call?"

Jack reaches across my desk and hesitates briefly before putting his hand over mine. "We'll get justice for her," he states like he can read my mind. When I nod once again, he squeezes my hand. "See? You're good."

My brows furrow as I look at him again. "What?"

"You care," Jack explains simply then removes his hand so he can rifle through the papers again. "Looks like she was officially marked as missing from Hastings, Nebraska on June 12th. She was last seen at her place of employment, The Platform Strip Club."

"Nebraska?" Moving to my computer I go to the browser and pull up a quick map of the states. "That's three states over! So now the question is if she was murdered in her state or not."

He pursues his lips together as he thinks. "You'd think someone would have seen a dead body being transported across all the state lines."

"Not if it's stashed away in a trunk." Shaking my head, I reach for my desk phone. "Well, I guess we need to actually confirm that our victim is her first. We can go from there."

Jack slides the paper over to me, pointing at the sheriff's number for the Hastings police department. I dial out the number and put it on speaker so Jack can contribute to the conversation.

"This is Wallace Anderson."

"Hello, Sheriff Anderson, I'm Detective Val Dalton from the Las Vegas Preternatural Crime Unit. Do you have a moment to talk about one of your cases?"

There's a brief beat of silence before he speaks again. *"Pardon, did you say Preternatural Crime Unit?"*

"I did," I agree. "I believe my partner and I may have

found one of your missing persons. Do you have a minute?"

"*Uh, yeah. Sorry, give me one second to get my computer going.*" We glance at each other as the sound of shuffling papers comes through the speaker followed by a series of keyboard clicks. "*You all have your own department for monsters?*"

I blink at the disbelief in his tone. "Yes," I begin. "We're one of the many police departments taking part in the new division."

"A lot of the larger populated cities are creating the unit," Jack adds. "I know Los Angeles is in talks with the city council about it."

"*Oh,*" Anderson says with a small tinge of disgust. "*I guess that makes sense.*"

I shoot Jack an eye roll. "Yes, so, the case."

"*Right,*" he grumbles into the phone as he taps on his keyboard some more. "*Okay, what do you have for me?*"

"Well, we have a Jane Doe in our morgue, and I think she might be one of your missing persons. Her prints aren't in the system, so we had to run some of her DNA through the FBI database. We had a familial match and traced her back to your town. Does the name Janelle North ring a bell?"

"*You found Janelle?*" He's just as surprised as we are. "*In Las Vegas?*"

"We believe so, but we can't be certain without more information from you." Jack cuts in. "We found her missing person's flier online, but we can't actually match our Jane Doe to the pictures."

"*I-is she beat up that bad?*" Anderson whispers.

I shake my head, even though I know he can't see it.

"No, Sheriff. Her head is missing entirely." The line goes silent, and I frown at Jack. "Sheriff?"

"*What do you mean her head is missing?*"

"I'm not sure how much clearer I can be." I keep my tone kind.

"*No wonder the monster cops were called in for it,*" he hisses. "*Who else would do that to that poor girl? Better yet,* what *would?*"

"Sheriff, I should warn you that both my partner and I are these monsters you seem to resent so much." Jack's warning is subtle but clear. "We are doing what we can on our end to find out what happened to Janelle North and would greatly appreciate your help."

Anderson sputters over his words. "*Of course, I meant no disrespect.*" He clears his throat before continuing. "*So, we need to make sure that your Jane Doe is actually Janelle?*"

I flip through the file Latisha gave us and pull out an image of a monarch butterfly tattoo. I set it down on the desk and tap it to get Jack's attention.

"Correct," Jack states, looking at the photo. "Are there any definable characteristics on her body? A tattoo, or birthmark?"

There's more typing through the phone before the sheriff speaks again. "*Looks like she has a black and orange butterfly tattooed on her hip. Also, a mole on the back of her shoulder.*"

I find the photo in the file and show Jack. "Looks like it's a match," I state.

Anderson sighs through the phone. "*How did she get all the way to Las Vegas?*"

"We aren't sure. Her body was frozen at some point so

we can't properly determine the time of death," I explain.

"*Frozen?*" He breathes. "*What the hell kind of perverse thing is that? Is it a monster thing?*"

Jack takes over the call before I can snap. "There were also traces of Natron in it, which is a type of salt. Any chance you have a local stash of it?"

He snorts. "*This is Nebraska. We use Natron to dry out our fish and meat. There's loads of it here.*"

"That's what I assumed," he says and looks at me. "We still can't assume she was murdered there."

"How would you keep a body frozen from Nebraska to Nevada? A freezer truck?" I suggest.

"It's not impossible." Jack agrees.

"*Do you have any leads at all? I have to tell her family something.*" Anderson says with another heavy sigh.

I frown at the speaker. "It's an ongoing investigation. We had another victim that was killed in the same manor a few days before we found Janelle. So, we—"

"*Wait!*" Anderson shouts suddenly. There's a furious tapping of keys before he sucks in a gasp. "*Holy shit. Let me guess, decapitated head and ripped open chest? No heart?*"

I balk and look at Jack. "That's right. You have something similar?"

"*A few days before Janelle went missing, a county over found a body like that. They ran her through the FBI DNA database, but nothing came back. The only reason I know about it is because it was on the local news.*"

Jack's intense gaze holds mine. "Three victims make a

serial killer."

"Fuck," I curse and run my fingers through my hair. "Sheriff, do you know of anywhere else this may have happened? The only reason we knew to call you was the DNA match from the father."

"*No*," he rumbles unhappily. "*She's still unidentified and was buried as such.*"

My heart aches at the thought of her never getting a proper burial, of her family never knowing what happened to her. "We'll find who's doing this."

"*I hope you do. Janelle's family is going to want to have a funeral for her.*" The Sheriff says with a brief tone of anger. "*Solve this so we can bring her home.*"

"We'll do our best. Thank you for your time, Sheriff." I press down the receiver and end the call. Turning to Jack, I add, "We have to stop them before they kill again."

"We're going to try our damn hardest." He knows better than to make that kind of promise. In our line of work, it's almost bad luck to make that kind of vow.

"I know." I turn back to my computer and start googling news articles that correlate with our scenes. I'm going to catch this bastard if it's the last thing I do.

Eleven

After three more days of researching and calling other police departments, we have a total of six victims. There's a very strong possibility that there are more, but if there wasn't any media coverage it's like finding a needle in a haystack.

Jack stands next to me in front of a white board, the victims' locations taped in place. Once again, they are all female and have yet to be identified. "The only thing we know they have in common is that they're female." He sighs. "That, and the fact that five of them showed up in cities they're not from. Well, what we assume is a fact. There are no missing persons reports that match the Jane Does that appeared in their city."

I nod, running my hands through my hair in frustration. "If only we knew who they were. Maybe that would at least give us something else to work with."

He rubs his forehead. "What made Stephanie Browne different?"

Shaking my head, I catch on to his line of thought. "I've been thinking the same thing. She's the only one that was killed and left at the scene. Why was she an exception?"

"What if she wasn't? What if they were just interrupted?" Jack cocks his head at me. "What if you scared them off?"

I blink at him. "Me? I doubt that. She was killed so publicly."

"We don't know that the others weren't," he points out. "Remember the camera interference? We both agreed it was magic. What if it applied in person as well?"

The blood drains from my face. "That's a terrifying thought. You think a powerful warlock could be behind it then?" As the words fall from my mouth, I instantly think of one person. No, there is no way Seth can be involved. I left him at his apartment the night Stephanie was killed. It would be highly unlikely that he would have beat me to the club or showed up after without me knowing. Relief sags my shoulders.

Jack shrugs and reaches for the suit jacket draped over his chair. "It's a thought. Either way, it's clearly a very strong individual."

I watch him slide his jacket on, eyes lingering on the flex of his shoulders. I blush when he turns to me and catches me ogling him red-handed. Looking away, I begin mindlessly straightening papers on my desk. "Time to go already?"

"Yes, and we're going out to dinner."

I whip my head back towards him at the statement. Amusement lifts my brow. "Oh, are we?"

"Yes." He's so smug and sure of himself. "I believe I still owe you enchiladas." When I visibly perk up, he lets out a laugh. "That's what I thought. Grab your coat."

A small part of me wants to bristle at the order, but a bigger part of me wants enchiladas. We're not going to talk about the other part that wants to please Jack.

Jack smirks at me as I follow him to my office door. "What? No fighting me on this?"

I lift my chin in an air of defiance we both know is fake. "You mentioned enchiladas. You'll learn that I'll fight you very little when it comes to Mexican food."

He presses his hand to the small of my back, and I feel it throughout my body. "I look forward to learning more about you," he all but purrs.

"You suave bastard," I mumble, cheeks flaming as we head to the elevator. A smile spreads my lips when Taylor rushes to meet us. "You out of here too?"

She scoffs as we file into the elevator. "As soon as it's 5:30, I'm out."

"Hot date with Bryan?" I tease.

She shakes her head with a smile. "I'm meeting him tonight at the pack house. We're doing a pack run in the desert."

"Well, that sounds like fun. I know you enjoy those," I

comment.

Her grin turns coy. "What about you two, hm?"

Jack gives her his charming smile. "I'm taking Valkyrie to get her enchilada fix."

She claps her hands together as the elevator lands on the first floor. "Good man! Treat her well Jack, or I'll cut off your balls. Have fun you two!" She blows us a kiss before practically skipping out of the lobby.

"Well, the lady has spoken," he muses as he leads me to the parking lot.

"She may be cute and cuddly, but don't underestimate her. If she says she'll cut your balls off, she probably will." I laugh as I follow him to his car.

"Ah, now I see why you two are friends," he teases.

I wiggle my brows at him before slipping into his dark grey SUV. Once I'm in the plush leather seat, I look around the car. It's a pretty standard SUV interior with a touch screen dash. "I kind of expected you to be in something more manly."

"I think your truck is manly enough for the both of us," he says with a smirk as he starts the car.

"You're not wrong." I laugh and buckle up when he backs out of the spot.

"I'm rarely wrong, Valkyrie," he states without smugness.

"Gods, I fucking love enchiladas," I coo before taking

another bite of my food. "Mmh!"

Jack is staring at me with a strained expression. "You make eating almost erotic."

I choke on my food and quickly drop my fork in favor of covering my mouth. Once I manage to get it down, I stare at him incredulously. "Excuse me?"

"No, you aren't excused." His voice drops to a dark, sensual tone. "I enjoy listening to your little moans."

Heat spreads across my cheeks before darting straight down to my core. "Maybe if you play your cards right, you'll hear a few of your own," I tease.

He shakes his head and leans over the table, dropping his voice another octave. "There will be nothing *little* about our time together."

Holy fucking shit.

"Gods, Khoury." I laugh, wiping my mouth with a napkin to try and hide my embarrassment. It usually takes a lot for me to get so flustered, but this man is something else.

He blinks and leans back a little. "Is it too much?" he asks, tone unsure.

I shake my head and look down at my plate. "No, I like your honesty. I was just curious as to when you decided to pursue me."

"I've wanted you since I met you," he states casually and without shame. "But our date changed things."

I can't help but agree with him. Still, I want to know what exactly happened to change it. "What about it did?"

"The fact that I told you about my parents," Jack explains. "I think you trusting me enough to talk about yours helped me do the same. Also, I can't deny the feeling I get when I touch you." His hand reaches for mine, and I don't hesitate to slide my fingers across his palm. Heat licks up my arm. "I always seem to find reasons to touch you."

I nod. "It's a fire that doesn't burn." Our eyes meet across the table, and a mutual understanding of the feeling clicks into place. We both feel this heat. My brow furrows slightly as I consider why that may be. "Is it because of what we are?"

His thumb brushes over my knuckles. "That depends on what we *both* are, doesn't it?"

He wants me to tell him; I know he does. The confession is on the tip of my tongue, but then a waiter approaches our table, asking if we need anything. "A shot of Jose with salt and lime please."

Jack holds up two fingers. "Make that two."

When the waiter leaves to put our order in, the courage to tell Jack that I'm a hellhound disappears. "I'm scared to tell you," I admit in a small voice.

His black brows knit together. "Why?"

"I don't want it to change your opinion of me." I bite my lip, fingers twitching in his hold.

"I doubt anything can change that, Valkyrie." He squeezes my hand. "But I'll admit I'm also nervous to tell you what I am for the exact same reason."

I let out a humorless laugh. "Hopefully we prove both of us wrong?" My voice hitches, making it a question instead of a statement.

"Hopefully," he murmurs as his eyes stare into mine.

They seem to trace over my face, taking in every small detail and imperfection, before they look off to the side and narrow in anger.

"What is it?" I ask, turning to look over my shoulder. The color drains from my face when I see Seth sitting at the bar, sneering at me. There's a pretty blonde sitting on the stool next to him, her body turned towards him as she talks. He doesn't seem to be listening to her, his attention wholly on us.

"Is he stalking you?" Jack asks, his voice just above a growl. "Do you want me to handle him?"

He moves to stand, but I tighten my hold on his hands. "I doubt it. Although we never came here together, we both eat here sometimes. I'm sure it's just a coincidence. Let's just finish our meal and leave, okay?"

He scoffs before relaxing back in his seat. "Looks like we won't have to."

Glancing over my shoulder again, I see Seth helping his date from her chair. With another cold glare in our direction, he leads her out the door. I sigh in relief once he's gone. "Well, at least he didn't try to make a scene again."

Jack takes one of the shots as the waiter drops them off. He lifts one up, and when I do the same, he clinks our glasses together. "Cheers to that."

Twelve

*A*fter dinner Jack asked me if I wanted him to drive us back to the station so I could get my truck. I didn't ask him to take me home, I demanded it.

But now that we're here, I'm nervous. My hand shakes as I unlock my door, and I feel like a gods damn virgin sneaking her boyfriend into her parents' house.

"We don't have to do anything you don't want to, Valkyrie." Jack says softly, his hand lightly landing on my shoulder.

I manage to get my door unlocked and turn towards him with a raised brow. "Tapping out, Detective Khoury?"

He closes the door behind us and quickly whirls me around so I'm pinned against the hard wood. He runs the tip of his nose along my temple. "Never. I just want to make sure you're committed to this." His nose brushes across my cheekbone before his teeth gently nip at my ear. "Because once I start, I'm not stopping until you're boneless with satisfaction. Not until I'm sure you'll walk with a limp tomorrow. A limp that'll force you to remember all the things I'm going to do to you tonight."

Liquid heat pools between my thighs, and I have to stifle a groan at his words. "Fuck, Jack."

A low growl rumbles in his throat, and he cups my jaw. "Say it again."

There's not a single piece of me that wants to disobey him. I've never really been one to be submissive, but something about Jack makes me want to drop to my knees.

"Jack." I moan as he places hot, wet, open mouth kisses along my neck.

"Good girl," he praises and presses his hard body against mine, pinning me harder against the door. When I run my hands down his back, he releases my jaw in favor of pinning my wrists above my head in one hand. "Me first. If you behave, you'll be rewarded."

Fucking shit, *yes*.

I squirm in his hold as he ghosts his free hand down the length of my throat before tracing my collarbones with his fingertips. He grazes down my torso before slipping under my shirt. His fingers leave a trail of fire along my skin as he snakes up to one of my breasts. His large hand encases it through the lace of my bra, and I let out a soft, little moan.

Jack bites my shoulder at the sound and releases my wrists. When I move to touch him, he shoots me a look that makes me freeze. "Not yet." He jerks his chin towards the only hallway in my apartment. "Bedroom."

It takes more willpower than I'd like to admit to not scurry down the hall. Instead, I shoulder past him with a haughty expression before slinking towards the hallway, an extra sway to my hips. Feeling him close behind me, I rip off my V-neck shirt and toss it over my shoulder before he can stop me.

"That was for me to do," he growls in reprimand. I can feel him reaching for me by the flare of heat heading towards my back. I skip out of reaching distance while undoing my slacks. "*Valkyrie*," he warns.

I ignore him as I slip into my bedroom, letting my pants shimmy down my thighs. Kicking my feet free, I turn towards him in just my bra and underwear.

Jack slowly stalks towards me, storm-colored irises almost swallowed by his pupils. He lifts his hand and brushes his knuckles across my ribs, making me shudder. "That's not behaving," he scolds me.

"I find it hard to behave, Detective," I coo oh-so sweetly. "Is that going to be a problem?"

"Not at all." He slides his hand down to the front of my bra, fingering the clasp there. Instead of freeing my breasts like I want him to, he jerks me forward by the material. Once again, our bodies are flush against one another, but much to my dismay, he's still clothed. "I will enjoy punishing you just as much as you'll like disobeying me."

My pussy clenches at the promise in his words. "Is that so?" I taunt.

"You'll see soon enough." His hands caress down my

spine before continuing to my ass. He easily lifts me from the ground, but instead of letting me wrap my legs around his waist, he tosses me onto the bed.

I land with a single bounce before he's on me. He hovers over me, keeping my body under his. His kisses down my sternum towards my bra. Again, instead of undoing it, he moves towards one of the cups. His tongue flicks over the edge of the black lace, following it all the way along the curve. He repeats the movement on the other side before giving the bottom edge the same treatment.

Jack finally unclasps my bra, my breasts now free from their confinement. His pupils dilate as he zeros in on the titanium bar in each nipple. "I like these," he rumbles with approval as he flicks the tip of his tongue over one of the piercings.

With hooded eyes, he nuzzles the swell of my breast and palms the other. He doesn't knead or grip it, simply holds it in his hand while his tongue traces circles around the outside of my nipple, toying with the bar.

My core is already drenched, but it's not enough. "More."

His eyes dart up to meet mine. He pulls back slowly and blows along the wet trail he left around the nipple, making it harden almost painfully. "Is that anyway to ask for something?"

My jaw clenches as his fingers flex around my breast teasingly. "Please."

"Good," he praises right before his grip shifts, thumb and pointer finger pinching my nipple. His mouth closes

over the other, teeth lightly nipping at the sensitive flesh between suckles.

"Fuck," I moan, closing my eyes as he worships my
chest.

After thoroughly licking, biting, suckling, and pinching,
he leaves my swollen nipples to lick down my stomach, tracing my pawprint with his tongue on the way. My abs tighten
with need as he nears the top of my lacy thong. A frustrated
breath huffs past my lips as he once again trails his tongue
along the edge of the material. He licks across my groin and
runs his teeth over my right hip bone. I jump at the feeling,
but he's already moved on to trace the material that runs towards the inside of my thigh. He licks the side of my crotch,
and my breath hitches with anticipation.

But then he starts all over on the left side.

"*Jack*." It comes out as a whine, and I don't care.

He's back at the crotch of my panties, and I can feel
him smirk against the damp fabric. I'm soaked for him, and I
have no doubt that he can feel it. With gentle teeth, he bites
at my mound. Before I can ask him to do it again, he licks
hard along my folds through the lace. My back arches off the
bed as I finally get *some* contact there.

"Again?" he asks coyly, fingertips running along the top
of the thong.

"Yes." When he pauses his movement, I rush to add,
"*please*. Yes, please."

"That's my girl," he all but purrs, and my stomach does
a little flip. He gives me another hard swipe of his tongue

before his thumbs hook on the sides of the lace. Way too slowly, he slides my underwear down my legs. Tossing the scrap of material to the floor once they're off, he begins to kiss his way up my leg. His lips brush along my ankle, calf, and inner knee before he sits back.

I bend my legs up on either side of him and watch as his eyes instantly fall between my thighs, staring at my pussy hungrily. Fuck, that's hot. In one swift movement, he pulls off his shirt, throwing it to the side. I swallow thickly as I take in his dark golden skin, my eyes tracing each dip, outlining his pecs, abs, and the sexy V that disappears beneath the waistband of his slacks.

"Please let me touch you," I whisper, lifting my hands towards him.

"Since you asked so nicely." He chuckles, but it's deep and breathless. It's good to know he's as affected as I am.

I waste no time in sitting up, my hands immediately skating over the bronze skin of his chest. My fingers trace over the same lines my eyes did, and I bite back a groan at how hard his muscles are. His skin is nearly scalding, and I want to burn against it.

"You're perfect," I breathe, leaning closer to him so I can skim my lips over his collarbone. "You're like a god."

A growl rumbles in his chest as he presses my body back against the bed with his. "And you're like the warrior you're named after. Allow me to worship your body."

I prop myself up on my elbows and watch as he lazily trails down my body once again, placing random kisses and nibbles on his way. When he gets to my core, he shifts his body so he's lying flat on his stomach, head between my thighs.

"Keep your eyes on me," Jack commands.

It takes everything in me to hold his gaze as he slowly runs his tongue up my center. My eyes threaten to flutter shut when he repeats the movement, only this time his tongue stops to toy with my clit.

My breath hitches as he licks me slow and long twice more before truly feasting on me. There is no way I can keep my eyes open as his mouth attacks me like a man starved. He's all tongue and a bit of teeth as he kisses, sucks, and nips at the tender flesh.

"Oh, my gods, Jack," I moan, fingers sliding into his silky black locks to cradle his head. I may have also pressed his face to me a little harder.

"I'm not your god yet, Valkyrie," he growls, his breath puffing hot air against my core before he returns to his meal, a long finger slipping in to join the action.

My hips buck, encouraging him as he slides in a second finger. His thumb finds my clit, rubbing firm circles into it as his mouth moves to the inside of my thigh. My legs start to tremble on either side of his head, thighs threatening to close as my orgasm begins to build. My stomach tightens and clenches, that tingle growing and growing until I'm also there. I'm seconds away, almost there—and then he completely pulls away.

"Why did you stop?" I ask in a bewildered tone. "I was

right there!"

Jack smirks down at me as he sits up. "Oh, I know you were. That's why I stopped."

I stare at him as if he's suddenly grown a second head. "What the fuck? Why?"

His hand goes to the fly of his slacks. He undoes the zipper and pushes both his pants and his boxer briefs down his strong thighs. He shifts to the side so he can take them off, leaving him completely bare. My mouth literally waters as I take in the sight of him. I barely get a glimpse of his impressive erection as he strokes it before he climbs back over my body, my legs bent on either side of him.

"Why?" he hums as he brushes a kiss below my ear. "Did you forget you disobeyed me earlier? That was your punishment."

I whine, hands sliding up his arms to rest on his shoulder blades. "You sadistic bastard," I mumble without heat.

Jack lets out a huff of a laugh, and the hot air against my neck sends a shiver down my spine. "Perhaps, but I did warn you."

"You did," I breathe as he presses our bodies together, his hips caging mine. A wanton whine escapes my lips when I feel the length of his cock rub against my slick folds. "How long are you going to tease me?"

He bites at my neck. "Tell me what you want."

"I want you to fuck me," I demand, shifting my hips to try and get his dick to slide in. Swallowing my pride again, I add the word I know he's waiting for. "*Please*."

Jack smirks against my neck, and I know he's pleased.

He pulls back just enough to reach between us, and a second passes before I feel the head of his cock breach my entrance. My breath hitches and gets stuck in my throat as he surges forward. He eases out and pushes back in a few times, sinking a little deeper each time as I adjust to his size. When he finally bottoms out, I moan at the slight burn of him stretching me.

He groans as I clamp down on him, a hand falling down to my thigh and gripping it tightly. "You fit me perfectly," he rumbles and hikes my leg higher over his hip. "I knew you would."

My nails rake down his back and cause a shudder to ripple through his body. "*Fuck me.*"

With a growl he does just that. He withdraws to the tip before slowly thrusting back in, still letting me adjust to him. He does this a few more times before *really* moving. Soon he's pounding into me with hard, quick thrusts, my breasts bouncing with each one. His hand drops my thigh in favor of squeezing one, fingers pinching the nipple around the metal bar. I squeeze my eyes shut as pure pleasure completely overtakes my senses. My body knows nothing but Jack and the ecstasy he's bringing it.

With a parting suckle to the neglected nipple, he shifts back onto his knees. He grabs my calves and yanks me closer until my knees are hanging over his hips. With a firm grip on my thighs, he swiftly fills me once again before starting a relentless pace.

The new angle hits that sensitive spot, and I'm crying

out before I can stop myself. "Fuck!"

Maybe he knows I'm teetering on that edge, but he growls out, "Not yet." His grip turns almost bruising as he slams harder into me. "Not until I say so."

He's fucking crazy if he thinks I can stop this with what he's doing to me.

"I can't—"

"You *will*," he commands, but it's almost drowned out by the wet sound of our bodies slapping against one another. I bite my lip, trying to hold out on my orgasm, but it's like trying to hold back a flood with a piece of paper. He grunts, his thrusting almost turning frantic. "Almost, Valkyrie."

I whimper in response. Actually fucking whimper. "Jack." Somehow his name comes out as both a curse and a plea.

"Say it again, and you can come." He reaches between us, his thumb strumming my clit.

"*Jack!*" I cry out as my orgasm hits me hard, hips jerking in his hold and legs trembling.

"Fuck!" His growl is loud enough to shake my already quivering body. With a few spastic thrusts, he buries himself deep and follows me over the edge.

Thirteen

*J*ack's body collapses on top of mine, our sweaty bodies slick against one another. I run my hands down his back as he buries his face in my neck, trying to catch his breath. My fingers ghost back up his spine, relishing in the smoothness of his skin, before sinking into his hair.

"Well done, Detective," I tease, voice still a little shaky.

He huffs out a laugh and leans up on his elbows to look down at me. My hands fall from his hair, giving it more of the tousled, just-fucked look. His eyes dart to my mouth, but when he dips his head, he brushes his lips along my cheekbone.

Disappointment hits me hard, but I know it can't be any other way.

Jack sits up and slowly slips out of me with a groan. Instead of flopping down next to me on the bed, he stands and grabs his boxers. "Can I get you anything from the kitchen? Water? Coffee?" He lifts a brow. "Alcohol?"

"I can get it," I insist, sitting up and moving to the edge of the bed.

He comes over and lightly pushes me back against the bed. "No, I'll get it. I want to take care of you after that."

A blush heats my cheeks at the earnest tone. "Um, okay. I have a bottle of green tea in there if you don't mind?"

"Of course." He leans over me to press a kiss to my forehead before standing. I try to grab him, but he swats at my hands with another laugh. "Patience, Valkyrie. I'm not done with you yet."

Almost instantly I feel my inner slut perk up at the idea of a round two. When liquid pools between my legs, I assume it's arousal, but the gush gives it away. I quickly stand from the bed, grabbing the closest article of clothing on the ground to catch his cum as it drips out of me. I blink when I realize that in our lust induced haze, we didn't use a condom.

"Fuck," I curse under my breath and hobble to the bathroom. I shut the door behind me and sit on the toilet to pee. It takes a few bundles of toilet paper to wipe up the rest of his mess. After flushing it all down, I remain seated. With a heavy sigh I rub my face, trying to sort out all my facts.

One: I'm on birth control so that should hopefully have me covered.

Two: I haven't been with anyone but Seth in the past two and a half months, and we always used protection. I knew he had other partners, and I didn't want to be a part of that.

Three: Typically, wereanimals can't catch diseases.

Four: Jack and I aren't wereanimals.

Five: I don't know anything about Jack's sexual conquests.

"*Fuck*," I mutter again.

There's a soft knock on the door followed by a soft,
"Valkyrie?"

Standing, I head to the door and open it. At his concerned expression, I give him a tentative smile, but it doesn't
seem to appease him. I sigh softly again and take my green
tea from him when it's offered. "We didn't use a condom," I
point out.

He tilts his head at me. "I know. What concerns you
about it?"

I take a small sip of my tea, a bit miffed at his question.
"Why aren't you concerned at all? You don't know if I'm
carrying something or not."

Jack hums and leans against the door frame. "You're
right, I don't. It was a mistake on both our accounts, but I
should have been in better control than that. I can tell you
that I'm clean if that makes you feel better. I haven't been
with someone in a while."

I blow out a soft breath. "It does. I'm also clean. It's
just, I know wereanimals can't catch diseases like that, but
we've both acknowledged that you and I don't fall into that
category."

He nods. "I can see why you're worried. I'm sorry I

wasn't up front with you about it."

I look down at my drink, twisting the cap back and forth. "Thank you," I murmur. "For not making a big deal about my concerns. For not making me feel silly about them."

Jack closes the distance between us, tilting my chin up with his pointer finger. "You don't have to thank me for simply listening to you. If there's something bothering you about us and I can do something to fix it, I will. I respect you, Valkyrie."

I just stared up at him, mouth floundering for something to say in response. Really, who is this man? How could he be so perfect in so many different ways? Everything he says to me is what I want, what I *need*, to hear. He makes me feel normal. He makes me feel accepted.

I don't know how it happened, or when, but my lips are on his. They're warm and soft and exactly how I imagined they'd feel. I'm clumsy with my kiss because I don't know how to do it. The ones I give my marks are pecks, a simple press of lips against lips.

At the reminder of my marks, I tear myself away from him with a gasp. No, no, no! I stumble away from him, covering my mouth with my hand in absolute horror. What have I done? What did I just do? How could I? My eyes brim with tears as he reaches for me. "*No!*" I choke out.

Jack holds his hands up as if I'm some spooked, rabid animal. "Hey, it's okay. Calm down. Tell me what happened just now."

Gods, he's so fucking reassuring and he has no idea what

I just did to him! I have to do something to fix this. I have to! Ignoring the confused Jack, I whirl towards the mirror, glaring at the black pawprint below my breasts.

Take me to Cerberus. I demand. When nothing happens, I rub hard at the mark, snarling in a panic induced rage. *Take me to Cerberus! Now!*

"Val?" Jack asks softly, using my nickname to get my attention.

I see him approaching me in the mirror and shake my head. "I'm going to fix this, Jack. I promise."

His brow furrows. "Fix what? What is going on?"

My bottom lip trembles, but I break my gaze from his in the mirror and sneer at the pawprint again. "Now, damn it!" As soon as the command leaves my lips, I'm tilting sideways to the ground. I can see Jack rushing to catch my body, but my soul has already sunk through the floor.

I crash onto the sands of the Styx, still completely nude. I leap to my feet and whirl around until I see Cerberus. The triplets are standing in almost a straight line, crimson eyes staring at me in a blank expression.

I close the distance between us and grab the lapels of the one in the middle. His gaze turns questioning, as I stare up at him with wide pleading eyes. "I didn't mean to mark him," I rush out. "I take it back!"

"You cannot just take back a mark," he replies. "It

doesn't work that way."

Tears sting my eyes again. "Please, Cerberus. I had a moment of weakness. It's not his fault!" I shake him, my desperation mounting.

"This man you are with," another begins, doing nothing to rebuke me from their triplet. "He is not what you think he is."

I blink. Do they know what Jack really is? It doesn't matter. Not right now. Shaking my head, I press on. "It doesn't matter. Please take back the mark. *Please*."

Cerberus stares down at me, mouth tightening so that his lips are pressed in a tight line. "You should stay away from him."

Anger punches my gut at the warning. Who are they to tell me who I should be with? "Fat chance of that." I sneer up at him. "I don't care what you think of him. Of us. I just need you to get rid of the mark I placed on him."

His red eyes narrow slightly before they all wave a hand simultaneously. "He is not marked."

I blink, lips parting in surprise. A part of me didn't think they would actually do it. "Really?"

"Yes." They answer blandly as the one I'm holding pries my hands off his lapels.

"Thank you," I murmur.

"There is nothing to thank," they say as the middle one straightens his suit jacket. "You may go back."

Before I can reply, they wave their hands again and I'm back in my body.

I gasp loudly, sucking air greedily into my lungs. I thrash

for a second until strong arms tighten around me. It takes me a second to realize I'm in Jack's lap, cradled in his arms. Blinking rapidly, I look up at a seriously pissed off detective. "Jack?" I ask in a rough voice.

"Where?" He demands with bite in his tone. "Where did you go?"

Swallowing at the hard look in his eyes, I try to sit up, but he holds me firmly in place. "What do you mean? I didn't go anywhere. I just passed out, that's all. It happens sometimes."

His lip twitches up in a silent snarl. "Don't lie to me. I felt your soul leave your body, Valkyrie. You were just a husk." When I glance away, he grabs my chin and forces my face back towards his. "No more lies. Tell me the truth."

I lick my lips nervously but can't look away from him. "I had to fix what I did."

His brow creases ever so slightly. "I don't understand. What did you have to fix?"

"I marked you," I whisper, forcing myself to break eye contact as shame and guilt resurface. "Your soul, rather."

"That's not possible," he says, but I refuse to look at him to truly determine what his tone means. I can't tell if it's disbelief or certainty.

"It is," I mumble. "I'm…"

"A hellhound," he supplies at my hesitation. I jerk my head up and look at him with wide eyes. He doesn't look disgusted or afraid. He looks almost amused. "I haven't met one before, but once you said marked it all made sense."

"You know about hellhounds?" I ask, still astonished.

"Yes." His knuckles brush along my cheek. "And I'm telling you that it's not possible to mark me."

"But Cerberus said he—" I cut myself off, replaying the interaction with the guardian. That fucker! He never said he took back the mark, did he? He just said Jack wasn't marked. Gods! Why didn't I catch that?! "He said you weren't marked."

"Exactly." He cups the back of my neck and lowers his head towards mine. "I should have known what you were when I saw the figurine on your desk. Especially when you wouldn't kiss anyone. I can't believe I didn't put two and two together."

He's talking, but I'm too focused on what he said before that. I shift in his lap so that I'm facing him, thighs on either side of his. "I really can't mark you?" I ask seriously, hope and longing rising swiftly up inside me. "You swear to me? You know for certain that I can't? I need you to be absolutely sure."

"I swear," he rumbles, looking up at me. "You don't have to fear—"

I swallow the rest of his words as I press my lips hard against his. It's awkward because I still have no idea what I'm doing, but pure elation fills me. The fact that I can freely kiss this man without any consequence is overwhelming. My lips begin to tremble as I'm finally able to have something I've been denied for a decade.

Jack's hands cradle my face, thumbs brushing away tears I wasn't aware fell. When I pull back, he looks me in the eye and gives me a small, knowing smile before tilting my head a little. Then his lips are back on mine, kissing me deeply. He lets me enjoy this simple version before his tongue coaxes my lips apart.

I instantly obey, eager to learn more about this simple act I could never enjoy. When his tongue touches mine, my stomach flutters and desire shoots straight to my core. I hesitantly rub my tongue back along his, and his rumbling growl encourages me. I frame his face in my hands and delve deeper, determined to lick every inch of his mouth. I want to devour him.

When we finally part for air, I do so with a suck to his bottom lip. My chest is heaving as I trace his glistening lip with my pointer finger.

Jack nips at my finger and pushes his hips up against mine. I feel his hard length press against me, and my desire turns to liquid heat. We share a brief look of mutual need before our lips collide together once again.

"Wait," Jack breaks the kiss and looks at me with utter seriousness despite his panting. "Do you want me to get a condom?"

In response, I reach between us and free his cock from his boxers. I stroke him a few times until he growls against my mouth. Giving in to both our need, I raise up my hips and slowly lower myself, inhaling sharply as each delicious inch sinks into me. Once I'm fully impaled on him, I'm forced to break lip contact as a breathy moan escapes me at the full feeling.

Jack groans and bucks up, driving his erection deeper into me. "Ride me, Valkyrie. Take your pleasure before I rip it from you."

My nails dig into his shoulders as I do just that. I rock my hips against his, lifting myself up and down to fuck myself on him. I kiss him between moans and pants, not getting nearly enough of his lips.

"I have a new firm demand," I breathe against his lips.

"Hm?" He looks up at me as his hands grip my hips.

"Now that I have this, you can't take it away." I grab his chin, holding it firmly. His pupils dilate at my hold, and I can't tell if he's thrilled or feels challenged. Does he want to take control? "Don't use kisses as punishment."

Jack's eyes soften, and he slides his hand up my body until they're cupping the lower part of my jaw. "I wouldn't do that. I can see how much it means to you."

I nod and welcome his lips as they meet mine in a tender caress. "Thank you," I whisper once we part.

"You don't need to thank me," he says against my lips before he presses another soft kiss to them.

Before I can return the kiss, he grabs my waist and switches our positions. My back hits the cold tile of the floor, and Jack's hot body between my thighs only enhances the shiver that runs down my body. He leans over me, bracing his forearms by my head before driving into me with new vigor. My back arches, thrusting my tits towards his face. He rumbles his approval and flicks his tongue over one of my hardened nipples before sucking it into his mouth.

Gods, this man.

When my back rests against the tile once again, one of his hands fists in my hair and tugs it to the side, exposing my neck to him. His mouth latches on to the skin there, lips, tongue, and teeth marking it as his.

"Valkyrie," he groans against my neck before releasing my hair. When our eyes meet, his pupils are nearly swallowing the grey of his eyes again. "Play with your breasts in my stead."

I don't think twice before obeying his command. I slide my hands to my chest and cup each one before giving them a light squeeze.

"Do you think that's how I want to touch them?" He asks, stilling his hips so that his cock remains nestled deep within me.

A whine pitches in my throat when he stops his thrusting. I clamp down hard around him, trying to get him to move, but I'm only rewarded with clenched teeth for my efforts.

"Do I need to repeat myself?" Jack slowly begins to slide out from me, and I shake my head.

"No," I quickly say before grabbing my breasts harder and kneading them. They're sensitive from his earlier treatment of them, but damn does it feel good.

"Don't forget those pretty pink nipples," Jack says as his

eyes track each movement of my fingers.

I pinch them between my thumb and forefinger and watch as Jack's nostrils flare once I do. I moan at the pure ravenous look in his eyes. It spurs me on to roll the buds between my fingers, plucking at them.

"Good," he praises in a rough voice. "Now be a good girl and hold on to them as I fuck you. Don't let them go."

Before I can acknowledge his command, he slams back into me, making me gasp. "Fuck, Jack!" I can only hold on to my own tits as he pistons his hips hard against mine. I tighten my grip as my pleasure mounts with each hard thrust from him.

"You can come when you like," Jack grunts out between clenched teeth.

Good girls say thank you, don't they? "Thank you," I breathe. "*Sir.*"

His eyes flash at the title, a possessive glint in those grey pools. With a growl that would impress a werewolf, he jerks my ankles up to his shoulders and bends over me, all but pinning my hands to my chest.

The new angle hits deeper, and I cry out at the intensity. It's just on the border of too much. "*Jack.*" It only takes a few thrusts for my orgasm to take me. I squeeze my eyes shut as the wave crashes over me, a breathy moan escaping my throat.

He bares his teeth, his face taking on a pure feral look, and slams in a final time. I feel his body go taut for a few long moments before relaxing. He kisses each of my ankles before guiding them off his shoulders and carefully lowering my shaking legs. His eyes fall to my hands, and he gently pries my fingers off my breasts.

"This is my fault," Jack says softly, tracing his fingers over the red marks along my sensitive skin. "I shouldn't have had you hold them."

I look down at the marks and shake my head. "This was all me."

"Do you like pain?" He asks without judgement.

My brow furrows. "No, I don't think so. At least, not like this. It didn't hurt. I mean, if it did, I didn't feel it during sex. I think it just heightened the pleasure you were giving me."

He hums. "Good to know." With a gentle, soothing kiss to each breast, he slowly slips out of me, making us both release a tiny groan. "Stay," he commands before standing and walking over to my towel rack. I watch his shapely ass as he grabs a hand towel and walks over to the sink. He turns on the water, waits a few seconds, then submerges it.

"Thanks," I say as I sit up and reach for the towel.

He holds it out of my reach and gives me a stern look. "I clean up my own messes, Detective."

I can't help but laugh. The movement causes his so-called mess to make a dash towards the exit. As soon as I part my legs, Jack's hand is there with the towel. I wince at the warm, damp cloth, my pussy a little oversensitive from not one, but two fuck sessions. My cheeks heat with a mix of embarrassment and surprise as he lightly wipes the area clean.

"I don't think I've ever had someone try to take care of me like this after sex," I murmur as he folds the towel to the clean side and wipes off his dick.

Jack tosses the towel in the sink and turns to me with a frown. "That's disappointing. You deserve to be taken care of. Not just after intense sessions like that, but in all things." He picks up the plastic bottle of tea I dropped earlier and hands it to me.

When I grab it, he swings me up into his arms and carries me back to the bedroom. I would have protested, but my legs still feel like jelly. He gently sets me down on my side of the bed and gestures for me to drink. I do as told but track him as he makes his way over to the other side of the bed. A new self-conscious, anxious thought bubbles up inside me.

No one has ever slept over before. I always kicked them out after sex, even Seth. I was too afraid someone would end up marked somehow.

"Y-you're staying?" I ask, hating how high-pitched my voice sounds.

His hands freeze on the blankets he's pulling back. A small flash of uncertainty flickers across his gaze. "Do you not want me to?" He straightens and scratches the back of his head in a nervous gesture. "I can go if you want me to, Val."

That nickname. I hate it in his mouth.

"No, I want you to stay." And I do. "I've just—well,

you'll be the first."

He blinks at the confession before a small smile curves his lips. "I feel honored then," he says lightly as he climbs into bed next to me. He props his head up on his hand and grins. "Don't worry, I'll tell you if you snore."

"We'll see who snores." I scoff and set the bottle down on my nightstand. After sinking under the covers, I turn towards him. His eyes meet mine and nerves tighten my stomach. My toes curl with uncertainty until he chuckles and shifts onto his back, an arm open towards me.

"Come here." It's not a command this time, but an invitation.

I wiggle closer to him until I'm in the crook of his arm. He pulls me flush against his side, but I'm tense and awkward. He simply pets my hair until the nerves fully dissipate, my body finally melting against his.

With a sudden thought, I lift my head and look up at him. "Will you kiss me goodnight?"

Jack's eyes soften at my request. He lifts his head and presses a soft, tender kiss to my lips. "Good night, Valkyrie."

Warmth spreads across my body. I lower my head back to his chest and curl in closer to his body. "Night, Jack."

Fourteen

*T*he sweet, sweet smell of liquid life pulls me from my sleep. I blink groggily at the clock next to me and see that it's close to seven in the morning. Sitting up, I rub my eyes before looking over at the other side of the bed. It's rumpled state quickly reminds me of Jack and what happened last night.

He was so...attentive. To everything. My pleasure, my mental hang ups, and the other needs I have.

Smiling, I climb out of bed, and my inner slut all but purrs at the subtle ache between my thighs. Spotting his shirt next to my feet, I tug it on. The hem falls to my upper thigh, just barely covering me. After finger-combing my hair, I make my way to the kitchen but stop when I see a shirtless Jack. He's only wearing his underwear and my, is it a delicious sight.

My eyes greedily take in the expanse of his back as he reaches up to grab two coffee mugs from the cupboard before I shamelessly ogle his ass. When he turns towards me, he does a double take. My cheeks heat as he slowly drags his eyes down my body then back up, a small smile curling up his lips.

Setting the mugs down on the counter, he stalks over to me. He cups my face in his hands and sensually caresses my lips with his. I close my eyes, a soft hum of pleasure echoing in my throat as I kiss him back.

"Good morning, Valkyrie," he rumbles when we part.

"Good morning, Jack," I whisper against his lips.

He smirks and presses another quick kiss to my lips. "Coffee?" he asks as he grabs the pot of freshly brewed coffee.

"Yes, all the liquid life," I say, walking over to join him at the counter. When I reach for a mug, he lightly smacks my hand away.

Jack sets the pot back down before grabbing me by the waist to sit me down on the counter. He looks me over, eyes lingering on my thighs, and nods his approval before going back to the coffee. "How do you like it?" he asks casually, as if he didn't just put me on display for him.

I chuckle. "There are a few flavored creamers in the fridge. I'll take a healthy pour of whatever you pick."

Jack takes my mug with him to the fridge and pours in the caramel flavored creamer. When he brings it to me, he makes a point to spread my legs more so he can stand between them. We're very close, and it feels remarkably intimate even though we're both just sipping our coffee.

"How do you feel?" His free hand lightly skims up my thigh to my hip, lifting the shirt as he does. "I noticed these this morning when I woke up."

I follow his line of sight to the faint bruises along my skin. "They don't hurt, if that's what you mean. I don't mind a few marks if they were worth getting. Plus, they'll be gone tomorrow."

Jack's eyes dart to my throat before meeting mine. "And was it? Worth it?"

"Very much so, Detective Khoury," I answer, lifting my brows suggestively as I take a sip from my coffee, never breaking eye contact.

His eyes hood in response. He dips in and presses a soft kiss to my neck before backing away from me. At my questioning gaze, he points at the microwave clock. "If I don't get away from you, we're going to be late for work."

I sober at the reminder of work. At the zero leads we have for all those headless women. "Fuck," I mumble and rub my face. "I can't believe I forgot."

"To be fair, I think I thoroughly distracted you." Jack runs his hand through his disheveled black hair. "Speaking of that, we need to talk about last night. You told me what you were, but I didn't get a chance to tell you about me." A smirk tilts up his lips again. "Someone kept my mouth busy."

I hum in satisfaction at the reminder. "I did." Hearing my phone ringing from the bedroom, I set down my mug and hop off the counter. "Hold that thought because I'm dying to finally hear this," I tell him before hurrying down the hall, I snatch my phone up from the nightstand and blink when I see an unfamiliar number. Deciding to go the professional route, I answer it as I would a work call. "This is Dalton."

"*Is this Val?*" comes an uncertain masculine voice.

"It is. Who's this?"

"*Bryan, Taylor's intended.*"

I raise my brows in surprise. "Oh, hey, what's up?"

"*Taylor gave me your number a while ago for emergencies,*" he begins, the tremble in his voice making my hackles rise. "*By chance have you seen her?*"

"Taylor?" I clarify unnecessarily. Who else can it be? "I haven't seen her since work, why?"

A whine begins to come through the phone before he clears his throat and cuts it off. "*She never showed for the pack run. It's not like her to miss a run, let alone without telling me or the alpha. I thought maybe you guys might have had a call last night?*"

Panic coils in my belly. "No, we didn't get called to a scene if that's what you mean." I say, looking up at Jack when he walks into the room with a curious expression. "Have you heard from her at all?"

"*Not since she got off work. She called me like she always does and told me she was going to go home and relax a bit before the run. I had to work later than her, so I was going to meet her at the pack house.*"

My stomach clenches. "And you haven't heard from her since?" I ask.

His breath hitches a bit. "*No.*"

I'm trying not to panic, but the fluttering feeling begins

to creep up from my stomach to settle in my chest. "I'll let you know if I see her at work. If not, we'll go from there. I'll make sure to let everyone know and tell our lieutenant as well. We'll have everyone looking for her."

"Our alpha is also going to contact the nearby pack alphas if she doesn't show by tonight," his voice lowers as he continues. *"I'm scared, Val. This isn't like her."*

"No," I agree quietly. "It's not. Still, we can't assume the worst. We have to stay positive." I tell him this, but my mind can only see the pictures of headless bodies stuck to my office whiteboard.

"Will you please text me when you get to work and let me know?" he asks.

"Of course, Bryan. I'll go straight to the lab first, I promise," I say, trying to keep my face neutral as Jack walks over to me.

"Thank you," he replies before hanging up.

I pull the phone from my ear, but keep it clutched tightly in my hand. Looking at Jack, I keep my tone flat. "Taylor is missing."

Jack's brow furrows for a moment as he takes in this information. "That was her fiancé?"

"Intended mate." I correct robotically. When he reaches for me, I skitter away. "Don't," I warn. It comes out as a hiss and I can see the small flash of confusion in his eyes, but I know damn well that if he tries to comfort me right now, I'll succumb to my panic.

He rakes that hand through his hair instead, not pushing me. "You know I will do what I can to help you find her."

"I know," I state and straighten my spine to hide behind

my bitch persona, using it as a shield. "We should get ready for work."

He nods once, but I can see the uncertainty there. "Alright."

The drive to work is awkward and I'm entirely aware that it's my fault. I built up a wall to keep the panic in and accidentally succeeded in keeping Jack out. Even when I saw the hickey on the hollow of my throat, I simply pulled on a turtleneck sweater instead of commenting on it.

Guilt finally brings out my words. "It's not you." I can feel him look at me even though I'm turned from him, eyes staring out the windshield as my hand dangles out the window, cigarette between my fingers.

"I know," he says quietly.

"I'm trying to be strong," I murmur.

His voice softens further. "I know."

"If I let you comfort me, I'm going to break down. I'm going to *break*," I whisper, breath fogging up the window.

"I know," Jack repeats for the third time without judgement. "If it comes to that, I'll be here for you. I'll put you back together."

Those words alone make my eyes water, but I bite my lip harshly in reprimand. No. No crying. Taylor is fine. She's the bubbly to my cynical. She *has* to be fine.

I rub at my nose as we pull into the parking lot of the station. I get out of Jack's car and stub out my cigarette as I wait for him to grab a fresh button-up from the back seat. He pulls it on over the plain tee he found in his car this morning and buttons it up to right below his throat. He shoots me a reassuring smile before gesturing to the building.

My eyes scan the parking lot for Taylor's car, but it's not in its usual spot. Still, I search for the blue bug with no luck. Trying to stay positive, I walk in through the front doors with Jack, dropping my cigarette butt in the trash as I do. He leads our way through the access door and to the elevator. I'm biting on my bottom lip the entire way up. It's only a floor up, but it feels like it takes hours to get there.

I all but sprint down the left hall once the elevator doors open. I dodge two people in lab coats before rushing through the door. Speeding my way towards Tay's cubicle, I tell myself she's there over and over again.

Except, when I do reach her station, it's empty.

A whine threatens to climb out from the back of my throat at the empty chair. I whirl towards the cubicle next to hers and hone-in on her coworker. "Have you seen Taylor?"

The girl has the fucking nerve to blink at me. "Who?"

"*Who?*" I snap incredulously. "Taylor! Your coworker that sits right here every fucking day? Ring any fucking bells?"

She ducks her head. "I-I'm new," she squeaks out. "It's only my second day."

A snarl twists up my lip, and I'm about to lay into her when Jack wraps an arm around my shoulders and pulls me away from the cowering woman. "Stupid fucking incompetent piece of shit."

"Stop," he chides, quickly pulling me out of the lab. He

doesn't stop until we're in my office. He lets me go and closes the door behind us. Before I can say anything, he grabs my face and forces me to look up at him. "You can't be self-destructive right now. That's not going to help her."

"I'm not!" I bite out. "I asked her a question and the dumb ass didn't even know—"

Jack covers my lips with his, silencing me. "Attacking your coworkers isn't going to help either," he says, breath fanning over my lips. "I know it's hard right now, but you need to try to remain calm and logical."

He's right, I know he is, but anxiety doesn't listen to reason.

I take in a deep, shaky breath. "I'm trying," I murmur. "It's hard."

"I know," he soothes. "But if anyone can find her, it's you. And I'll be with you every step, okay?"

I can't do anything but nod, my words now tied up in my throat. Right as I lean towards him, my office door flies open. There's a surge of hope that it's Taylor, but it's immediately crushed when I see Scott standing there instead. Surprise lights his features as he looks at us, no doubt taking in how intimate our position is.

Jack drops his hands from my face and turns to our lieutenant without an ounce of shame. "What is it?"

Scott shakes off the surprise, his face becoming grim. "We have another body. Same style."

My breath wheezes out of me. My mind floods with images of Tay's headless body lying on the ground in a puddle of blood. I can clearly see her picture joining the rest of the

Jane Does on my whiteboard.

I must have made some pitiful sound, or maybe Jack just saw the cord of my resolve snap, because his arms are around me, one of his hands cradling the back of my head. "Shh, Valkyrie. We don't know if it's her."

I shamelessly cling to him, absorbing the strength he's freely giving me as my eyes sting. "What if—"

"No," his voice is sharp. "None of that. Not until we know for certain."

Scott clears his throat forcefully to get our attention. "What is going on?" he demands. "Dalton, it's not like you to get choked up like this."

Jack's chest rumbles with a protective growl. "Taylor is missing," he bites out, shooting our boss a look that could wither him where he stands.

Scott's lips part in shock. "Meyers? When? Why wasn't I notified?"

I press my face to Jack's shoulder as he relays the information to Scott. In this moment, I've never been more thankful for anyone. I'm barely holding back the floodgates, but I know if I talk about it, I'm going to snap, and I can't do that.

Not yet.

Fifteen

ou ready?" Scott asks as we stand outside the yellow
crime scene tape. The body is on the other side of
the k-rail on the west side of the I-15 freeway, close to the
Flamingo Road exit. Since Jack caught him up on the Taylor
situation, he's been nice. Which is weird for us.

"Do you want me to go in first?" Jack offers as he slides
on a pair of plastic gloves.

I shake my head and snap on my gloves. "No, I need
to do it. It's still my case." I take a deep breath in and slowly
let it out. As I do, I mentally check out, forcing my personal
feelings to step back from the situation.

When I duck under the tape, I do so as Val the detective
instead of Val the worried best friend. Jack is close behind
but not close enough to suffocate me. Just enough to let me
know he's there as both my partner and my support. When

exactly did he become both?

I squat down next to the headless victim, making sure I don't step in any of the blood pooled around her. "This time the victim was killed here. She wasn't dropped off at a club." I state, pointing at the blood staining the dirt beneath her. The body is also lying frontside down, limbs in awkward positions as if she were thrown down. "She's not like the last Jane Doe."

"Does anyone happen to know who she is?" Jack asks an officer standing nearby.

"No, sir. The person who found her happened to have a flat tire on the freeway and pulled over. I have his statement but told him to standby until you guys got here," he replies. "And we haven't checked the body. We were waiting for you to arrive. The only thing we've done is let the crime tech take pictures."

Jack nods and reaches for the pockets of our victim's jacket. He finds a phone and clicks the center button, but he hands it off to a technician to bag as evidence when it asks for a passcode.

"Let's roll her," I say, trying not to assume it's Taylor even though the body type seems very similar from behind.

Jack looks at the crime scene technicians. "You guys have everything you need?" When they nod, he looks at me then down at the body. "On the count of three."

Jack counts down and together we very carefully roll the body over onto its back. The heavy, suffocating knot in my chests dissipates when I get a clear view of the torso. Small breasts and no crescent moon tattoo under the collarbone.

It's not Taylor.

I'm so relieved I could vomit. Clearing the emotion from my throat I look at an expectant Jack. "It's not her," I whisper. "It's not Taylor."

The fact that he also visibly relaxes warms my decrepit heart to him more. He understands what she means to me. "I'm glad."

I take a shaky breath and nod before focusing in on the poor woman who wasn't so lucky. Frowning, I take a closer look at the ripped open chest cavity. I don't know why, but this seems to be messier than the others. Yes, the others had been torn open, but this one seems to have been done with rage.

I point to a suspicious puncture wound by the torn flesh. "Does this look like it was done by a fang to you?"

Jack leans in to get a better look. "Or a claw." He agrees and looks at me. "You think it was a wereanimal of sorts?"

I shake my head and stand. "But that wouldn't explain the magic."

"No, it wouldn't," he answers, standing as well. "Perhaps there are two of them."

"I hope not." That would make it twice as hard. I pull off my gloves and jerk my head towards the officer who talked to us upon arrival. "Let's go question the guy who found her."

"Let's." Jack follows me over to the officer, pulling off

his gloves as well.

When the officer takes us over to the witness, I stop several feet away when I see a familiar blonde sitting on the ground. "Seth?"

His bright green eyes meet mine, a relieved smile curling up his lips. "Val! I was hoping it would be you," the warlock says as he jumps to his feet.

Hearing a growl at my back, I whirl around and put my hands flat against Jack's chest to keep him in place. "*Don't*," I warn. "This isn't the place. We have to be professional."

"You don't think this is suspicious?" Jack asks with a hiss, glaring at Seth from over my head.

"I think it's a hell of a coincidence," I clarify. I lightly dig my nails into his chest to make him look down at me. "You should stay here while I question him."

"Like hell," he snarls. "I don't trust him. I haven't gotten close enough to him to truly read his energy, but I have a bad feeling about him."

I shake my head and slip my fingers into his breast pocket to pull out his tiny notebook and pen. "You're letting my situation with him cloud your judgment, Jack."

The tension in his face relaxes marginally at the use of his name, but his next words still have bite. "Maybe *you're* the one letting it affect *your* judgment."

I bristle at that. "If you must know, I was leaving his apartment the night Browne was murdered." Something in me heats at the way his eyes narrow in a mix of jealousy and possessiveness. "There's no way he could have beat me to the club, let alone kill her."

Jack runs his hand through his hair. "Fine," he grumbles. "But if he makes you uncomfortable or tries to man-handle you in any way, I'm going to stop him."

Does he think I'm completely incapable? I understand he's being protective, but I can't help but feel insulted. "I can handle myself, Detective Khoury."

He sighs at my icy tone. "That's not what I mea—don't walk away from me. Valkyrie!"

But I'm already doing just that. I approach Seth, who, based on his sour expression, watched the exchange between Jack and I.

Ugh, men.

"So, I hear you found the body," I begin, flipping open the notepad. "Can you tell me why you were down here on this side of the freeway?"

A flash of something ugly flashes across his face. "I'm great, Val. Thanks for asking."

I press my lips in a hard line and push down my irritation as I mentally count to three. "Seth, this is my job. In said job, I am a *professional*. A *professional* trying to figure out who is going around killing women in this manner. So, I'm going to keep this *professional*. Do you understand?"

He works a muscle in his jaw. "Yes," he spits out.

"Wonderful," I drawl. "Now, if you could answer the question?"

He lets out a heavy sigh. "I got a flat tire while driving to work. I must have hit something in the road, so I swerved off to the side before I could do any more damage or hit someone." He rubs his jaw. "I don't know how to put on a spare, so I called AAA to come help me out. I was leaning against the k-rail as I waited for the truck, and that's when I saw her on the other side."

I jot down some notes before continuing. "And the tow truck driver can confirm that?"

I know Seth well enough to expect a sassy remark, so I shoot him a look warning him against it. His lip twitches with a repressed sneer, but he nods all the same. "Yes."

"Alright. Prior to pulling over, did you happen to see anyone else nearby? Any vehicle stopped or driving away on that side?" I ask.

Seth shakes his head. "No, but I also wasn't really paying attention to my surroundings after the tire popped. I was focusing more on safely pulling over."

"What about after you stopped? See anyone or anything you would consider abnormal or suspicious?" I ask.

He gives me a deadpanned look. "Yes, a dead body."

I almost crush the notebook in my hand in agitation, resisting the strong urge to grab my gun and shoot him in the dick. Does he not realize how serious the situation is? "I'll take that as a no."

Seth jerks his head towards the body. "So, this is the killer you mentioned a while ago?" He asks. "Looks like it's a serial killer after all."

I'm about to nod but stop when I think about his words.

"Why do you say that?"

We haven't released any information to the press yet. Honestly, we purposefully keep any preternatural crime quiet to prevent the backlash from the human side of society. Is it fair? Probably not, but mass panic fueled by hate only leads to more crime and murder.

However, when it comes to confirmed serial killers, we have to say something to the public. It's to help keep people safe more than anything. That being said, Scott is scheduled to have a press conference later today.

Seth's eyes meet mine, and an eyebrow lifts in question. "This is at least the second body, right?"

Again, relief eases my chest. Damn, Jack has me suspicious for no reason. "Three bodies make a serial killer," I clarify as I tap the pen against the paper. "Anything you want to add before we let you go?"

He reaches out and lightly wraps his hand around my bicep. "I miss you."

I feel Jack's aura flare out before it hits us. It doesn't hurt me, but Seth's eyes widen with shock. Instead of letting go, his hand tightens its hold.

My lip lifts in a silent snarl. "Let go of me before I break your hand."

Seth glances over my shoulder, no doubt at Jack since I can feel him coming towards us, before staring down at me with a look of pure disgust. "You made the wrong choice," he whispers before jerking his hand back and stalking towards his car.

I watch him go, hackles raised from the exchange. I feel heat behind me before Jack's hand glides down the back of my neck, almost as if he knows how riled I am. My body relaxes at his touch, and it pisses me off. I don't like to be placated like a small child.

I shrug off his touch and step away from him. "I'm fine."

"I didn't say you weren't," Jack points out. I whirl towards him, and he crosses his arms over his chest, looking at me with a neutral expression. "I told you if he tried to grab you, I would intervene."

"And I told you I can handle myself, Detective." I slap his notepad against his chest, making him uncross his arms to catch it.

His storm-colored eyes harden as he steps closer to me, notepad crumpled in his fist. "I know you can. That wasn't the point."

"Then what was?" I ask, turning away from him to head to my truck. He follows me, much to my own annoyance, but I ignore him as I open my door and pull out my pack of smokes. I briefly realize I haven't been smoking as much as I normally do, but the sudden urge can't be ignored. As soon as I lift it to my lips and start to light it, Jack rips it away.

Uh, I think the fuck not.

"Excuse me, who the fuck do you think you are?" I demand as he crushes it in his fist.

"Smoking isn't going to help the situation." Jack says,

eyes narrowed at me.

"*You're* not helping the situation!" I shout and ignore the glances from the officers nearby. "I'll do what I want, when I want. Do you understand that, Detective Khoury? We fucked. Yay for us. But that's all it was. You getting your dick wet doesn't warrant you a say in my life, understand?"

A flurry of emotions flash across his eyes before I can read them, but the lingering one I understand all too well.

Anger is one of my best and longest friends.

He opens his mouth to say something but seems to think better of it. He audibly snaps his mouth shut, shoots me an angry glare, turns, and makes his way towards Scott. Which is good because I don't think I can drive him back to the station without sucker punching him.

Pulling out another cigarette, I light it up and take a deep inhale before sliding into the driver seat of my truck. I send Scott a quick text saying I'm taking the rest of the day off before throwing the truck in drive and heading to Taylor's house.

Sixteen

*I*t's almost midnight when I finally step back into my apartment, dripping wet from the sudden downpour. I toe off my soggy flats and leave them by the door before hurrying to my bathroom for a shower, trailing water as I go. As I wait for the water to heat, I peel the soaking turtleneck off my body before struggling to pull off the slacks suction-cupped to my legs.

Finally free of my wet clothing, I slip into my shower and groan in bliss as the hot water pelts down on me. Closing my eyes, I stand there for a few moments and soak in the comfort the heat provides. Then the day catches up to me, and the pushed down emotions slam into me all at once. My knees feel like they're about to buckle, so I lower myself to the floor before they can give out. Wrapping my arms around my legs, I press my forehead to my knees and finally let the tears come.

I couldn't find Taylor.

I met up with Bryan after leaving the scene this morning, and together we searched for her. Las Vegas is so densely populated, it's harder than trying to find a needle in a haystack. Still, we went to all her favorite places, talked to her family, and even went to some of the casinos with her picture.

Nothing.

Five to seven people a day go missing in Vegas, more than two hundred people a month, and the rate of finding them is abysmal. I refuse to let Taylor be part of that statistic, but I'm also at a loss for what to do next. We tried tracking her phone, but it's off.

The tiny spare time I had not thinking about Taylor was divided between the case and Jack. Okay, it was *mostly* Jack. Every time I tried to think of the case and the new victim, Jack popped up and took over my thoughts.

I was mean to him. I know I was. I didn't mean it when I said that it was only a fuck. We both know there's more than just attraction between us. It's not love, I've only known the guy for two weeks, but there's a connection I can't deny. A pull that makes me yearn for him.

However, I stand firm on the part where he doesn't have a right to dictate anything in my life. I'm a grown ass woman who can make her own decisions.

Still, I can acknowledge that I was a bit harsh by snapping at him. The case, Taylor's disappearance, Seth, and then Jack just completely undermining my ability to defend myself just set me off. The suppressed stress and buildup of emotions didn't help, and they all came out at once in the wrong way. At perhaps the wrong target, too. A part of me wants to apologize to Jack, but another stubborn part wants him to come to me.

A fresh wave of tears come, and I press my forehead harder against my knees. The sob that was about to escape my throat turns into a startled gasp when my shower curtain is flung open, the metal rings holding the fabric screaming in protest.

Standing there, looking so relieved, is sopping wet Jack.

I want to scream at him. Scream at him for breaking into my apartment and scaring me. For undermining my strength and ability to take care of myself. For seeing me so vulnerable right now.

I want to scream about the injustice that my best friend of all people is missing. That it's not fair, and that it should be me instead of her. That I'm terrified she's going to be one of the girls on my whiteboard.

Instead, that sob finally breaks free.

This frustrating man that has me all tied up in knots climbs into my bathtub still fully clothed. Not fazed by the hot water, he sits down and pulls me into his lap. I don't even try to fight him.

"I'm here," he says, voice strained.

I cling to his soaked shirt, bury my face in his neck, and cry harder. He cradles the back of my head, his cheek resting on my wet hair. Never once does he ask me what's wrong or push me to talk about it and that in itself means a lot to me.

We stay there for a while, him holding me until my sobs

turn into sniffles and my skin begins to prune.

"You scared me," he finally whispers, the sound almost drowned out by the water.

I adjust myself in his lap so my head is leaning against his shoulder. "What?"

The arm around my waist tightens while the fingers of his other hand tangle in my hair, gripping it just a little tighter. "I couldn't find you."

My brow furrows. "What do you mean?"

"After you left this morning. I thought you would go back to the office, but you never did." He lets out a small sigh. "After your altercation with Seth, our victims, and with Taylor's disappearance, I assumed the worst."

I move so I'm facing him, my legs on either side of his hips. "Didn't Scott tell you I took the rest of the day off?"

"Not until later," he replies, gaze holding mine. "But even afterwards I looked for you. I drove past your apartment three times, and your truck wasn't there. When I saw it just now, I couldn't help it. I had to make sure you were okay."

"So, you break into my apartment and scare the shit out of me?" I tease, trying to lighten the heavy mood and erase the worry lingering in his eyes.

His cheeks pink in response. "Well, when you put it like that it sounds creepy."

I manage a soft, weak laugh. "Just a little."

He cups the back of my neck, thumb brushing along my jaw as he presses his forehead against mine. "I'm sorry."

I close my eyes at the contact, allowing the comfort to

wash over me. "For what?"

"For upsetting you," Jack replies. "It wasn't my intention."

I sigh and pull back so I can look at him again. "I can take care of myself."

He holds my gaze and nods. "I wasn't trying to say you weren't capable of doing so. I know that you are strong. I know very well that you can handle yourself." When I remain stubbornly quiet, he tightens his hold on the back of my neck. "But you shouldn't have to. I want you to understand that it is my pleasure to defend you. I want to be the person who stands up for you, who scares off anyone who dares to talk down to you."

"Your pleasure?" I ask, a small smile curling up my lips as a flutter hits my stomach.

He slides his hand around my throat and runs his thumb over my bottom lip. "*Distinct* pleasure," he repeats seriously.

I can't help it, I laugh. "Is that so?"

He smiles at my laughter. "Yes. And this isn't something I feel the need to do for everyone, Valkyrie. I want to snarl at anyone who even looks at you without respect." His face becomes somber once again, a glimmer of confusion in his eyes. "And as childish, weird, and overbearing as it may seem, I want to wrap you up in my arms, cover you in my scent, and scream to the world that-" He swallows as he pauses. "-that you're under my protection."

I have a strong feeling that wasn't what he was going to say initially, but I don't want to know what the original words are. Instead, I close the distance between us and press my lips against his. It's weird how quickly I've become comfortable with the act of kissing him. A part of me feels like it's the first time each time, but also familiar enough that I'm comfortable and confident doing it.

Jack's hand slides up so he's cupping my jaw, holding it firmly in place while his tongue delves into my mouth. My tongue slides against his, but his pushes back, the two soon fighting for dominance. When I moan in my throat, he slides his other arm under my ass and lifts us both.

Once my feet are on the ground, I rip his shirt open, sending buttons flying against the tile. He shrugs out of the ruined shirt and peels off the plain tee underneath. A devilish thought takes over as I break away from our kiss. He's forced to release my face as I dip my head down and press kisses to his wet skin, my tongue lapping up the water.

He hisses in pleasure as I bite one of his nipples before dropping to my knees, kneeling before him like he's my own personal god. He sucks in a shuttered breath as I do. When I look up at him, fingers working at the buckle of his belt, he's looking down at me with a strained expression.

"Valkyrie—" he begins but bites off his own words when I lick him hard from groin to belly button. I kiss back down to the waistband of his slacks and deftly slide down the zipper, being careful of his straining erection.

I fight with the material clinging to his strong thighs until I finally have his pants and boxers down far enough for his cock to spring free. I take him into my hand, relishing in the groan that escapes his lips.

I lightly stroke him as I lean in and flick my tongue

around the base of him, but not the actual shaft. I kiss my way to his inner thigh, teeth lightly nipping at the soft tender skin there. With a soft squeeze, I lift his dick towards his stomach and run my tongue along the seam of his balls before making my way across to his other thigh where I resume my kisses and nips.

Hearing a bang, I look up along the length of his perfect body to see him bracing himself against the wall. His arm is straight out in front of him, hand pressed hard against the tile as he watches me with needy anticipation.

I look away from him and smile against his heated skin before resuming my kisses and licks. Satisfied that I tasted my way around his cock, I pull back and focus directly on the glistening head. I hear him take in a shuttered breath as I flick my tongue over the slit, lapping up a mix of precum and water.

It's impossible to keep the smirk off my face as I release him and stand up. A small, teasing laugh escapes me when he looks at me with incredulity and no small amount of confusion. I walk my fingers up his chest but keep my eyes on his. "You're not the only one who can delve out punishments when someone misbehaves."

Jack's eyes flash. There's so much in that look that I can't dissect it all. All I know for certain is that he likes my tease, but he's about to make me pay for it. He only proves me right when he whirls me around so that my chest is flush with the wall, the cold tile making my nipples tighten almost painfully.

One of his hands slides down between my thighs, fingers tracing the wetness gathered there. If he's checking to make sure I'm ready for him, he needn't bother.

"Brace yourself," he growls in my ear as he kicks my legs apart.

"Don't like the taste of your own medicine, *sir*?" I coo innocently, but I do as told and press my palms flat against the tile.

His growl is so deep I feel it vibrate against my back as he presses against me. "On the contrary, Valkyrie, I'm going to make up for upsetting you."

I feel a hand on my hip, holding me in place as his blunt head nudges at my entrance. I moan as he slides in and buries himself to the hilt. He lets me adjust to him in this position for a few seconds before beginning to move. His thrusts are hard and quick, forcing me further against the wall.

His fingers slide into my wet hair before fisting it tightly, yanking my head back and forcing my spine to bow as he powers into me. "I want you to come, Valkyrie," he says before a sharp slap meets one side of my ass. He rubs the sting out of it even as a throaty moan escapes me. "But *that* is for scaring me."

"Again," I beg shamelessly.

He releases my hair, letting my body relax, and slides his hand down my spine before gripping my hip once again. "Is that how you ask for things?" he asks, purposefully thrusting into me harder to make his point.

"Please," I whisper.

"Please, what?"

I give him what he wants because I want what I'm asking for so much more. "Please spank me again."

Jack's hand caresses the swell of my ass. "Good girl," he

praises before delivering another smack.

"Fuck!" I cry out, my orgasm already starting to build. His hand is rubbing at the place where he spanked me, but little tingles remain. And I swear I can feel them in my clit.

He groans when I push my hips back against his, meeting him thrust for thrust. He bends towards me, teeth nipping at my shoulder as his hand finds one of my breasts. He plucks the nipple before his fingers trail down my stomach to my clit.

A wanton whimper escapes my throat as he rubs the over sensitized bundle of nerves in hard, firm circles. My hips jerk in reflex, and I lose our synchronized momentum. It's impossible for me to match his thrusts as he toys with my clit, each stroke making my mind go blank and my body spasm.

I'm almost there, ready to fall into the wave of ecstasy when his hand retreats. A frustrated whimper turns into a cry when his hand slaps my ass for the third time. My orgasm hits me hard. It bows my spine, flinging my head back against his shoulder. His hand cups my throat, holding me against him as he fucks me through each wave of pleasure.

It's not long before Jack follows me over the edge with a grunt. He slams into me a final time and stills, his hold on my neck and hip tightening for a second before he relaxes with a groan. His arm drops and wraps around my waist, holding me to him as we stand there panting. Once we recover, he eases out of me and backs us up towards the now lukewarm stream of water.

I turn and face him as the water pelts down on his back.

I laugh at the sight of his slacks still bunched around his thighs. "Get those off and shower with me."

"So bossy," Jack responds with a soft chuckle as he wrangles his pants off.

"Damn right I am," I respond, ducking around him so I'm under the water. I lather up my loofa with body wash, but it's tugged from my fingers before I can start scrubbing my skin. A smile curves my lips even as I shake my head. "I can wash myself, Jack."

"I certainly hope so," he teases before gliding the loofa down my arm. "But I'm going to do it. Do you remember the conversation from last night?"

I hum. "You mean the one about taking care of me?"

"Exactly," he says as he brings the loofa across my chest to my other arm. "So be good and let me do this."

And so, I do.

Seventeen

*A*fter showering, I sit on my couch in an oversized shirt, carefully sewing Jack's buttons back onto his shirt. My legs are draped over his lap, and I can't help but smile as he trails his fingers up and down my bare skin.

"Sorry again about this." I say, slipping the needle through one of the tiny four holes in the button. I'm still surprised I found them all. I expected at least one to have gone down the drain.

"It's just a shirt," he answers, but his eyes remain on the exposed skin of my legs. His fingers slide up my thigh, a growl rumbling in his throat when he reaches the hem of my night shirt. "No bottoms? You're a tease."

I laugh as his fingers press into the meat of my thigh. I've always had thicker thighs, despite the rest of my body being somewhat toned. I used to fret about it, but now it's just a part of me.

Plus, Jack seems to like them just fine.

"I have underwear on!" I protest. "Which is more than what I can say for you, Detective Khoury."

He glances down at the fluffy grey towel still wrapped around his waist. "I didn't have a choice, unlike you, Dalton." We had to throw his clothes in the wash after our shower together, and now they tumbled in the dryer.

I grin but keep my attention on the button. "Maybe I just want to keep you on your toes."

He scoffs, but his fingers relax and start to trail back down my leg. He looks at me and nods to my hands. "When did you learn to sew?"

I remain silent as I hesitate, flashes of my family coming to mind. "My mom taught me." My voice is soft as I answer him, the familiar sadness welling up at the sensitive topic.

Jack's fingers stop. "Oh?" He asks, and I know he's asking me to continue without pressing.

I nod once. "Mom was really handy with this kind of stuff. I can sew a button and patch a hole, but she could *really* sew. She used to make me and my sister Athena's Halloween costumes every year. And they were always so much better than that retail bullshit." A small smile curls my lips even as my eyes get a little glassy with longing. "She used to drive my father crazy with the sewing machine. She'd be up all night trying to finish whatever project she was working on. Whether it was our costumes or making new curtains. She'd always make new ones for each holiday and season. She hated routine."

Jack is quiet for a moment, letting me get my emotions under control before asking exactly what I knew he would. "What happened to her?"

A bitter, self-loathing scoff escapes me. "Nothing. I mean, nothing like what you're thinking. She's alive and well. Her and my dad live in Summerlin."

"You talk about her in the past tense," he points out with confusion.

"Because I haven't seen my family in years," I say as I tie off the thread and snip it free. I set the scissors and needle down on the coffee table but keep the damp shirt in my lap as I look at him. "I pushed them away. I didn't want them to be caught up in the fucking mess that is, well, me."

Jack hums and starts to stroke my leg again. "You should cherish your family while you have them."

I sigh and look away again. "I know I must sound like a petulant child to you, especially given how you lost your dad, but I had to do it. After I was turned into a hellhound, I was a totally different person." I delve my fingers into my hair, fiddling with the wet strands. "The Monster Movement had already happened, obviously, but I'm a different kind of monster. No one really knows of hellhounds. And even those who know of them, don't *actually* know any. We're like the shapeshifters that were wiped out, except we don't seem to really exist."

Jack meets my gaze as I look at him again. "Trust me

when I say that I understand how you feel, Valkyrie. Finish your story, and I will tell you mine."

I nod, eager to know his tale since we were interrupted this morning. "I told you before that I became obsessed with Greek mythology after Cerberus sent me back. I studied all the gods but really focused on the ones of the underworld." I drop my hands to my lap and stare down at them. "My mom," my voice wavers, turns watery. "She was so supportive of my new passion. Every time we went to any thrift store or Goodwill, she would get me anything related to Greek mythology. Books, toys, paintings, all and everything. She never questioned me."

I clench my hands into fists. "But my dad was a bit concerned that I kept looking into the underworld gods. My family goes to church every Sunday, but my dad has always been the more religious one because he was raised that way. So, anything related to hell puts him on edge. When he asked me about my new passion, I told him I met Cerberus when I died. He didn't like that. He refused to believe it because if he did, to him, that meant his daughter was evil enough to end up in hell."

Jack shakes his head. "That's not how it works," he growls. "Mortals have such a black and white picture of what happens after one dies."

"I know the different realms of Greek's underworld, but my dad doesn't." My shoulder lifts and falls with a shrug. "Some people are blindly led by their religion."

Jack's fingers suddenly tighten on my thigh again. "Is

that why you believe you are evil? Because your father said so?"

I swallow. "It didn't help deter me." Jack's fingers twitch against my leg, but I continue. "Especially when Cerberus pulled me back into the underworld a few months later. I was scared of him, them, whatever they prefer to be called. It was the triplets plus the three fates, all circled around me as they explained my position.

"They told me what my kiss would do to people and what they expected me to do for them. For the underworld. The kiss of death is what they called it, even though the people I marked don't immediately die. But, when they do, they arrive at Styx instead of anywhere else." I gingerly press my fingertips to the pawprint hidden under my shirt. "I was officially marked as a hellhound and given the power they made me have. Do you know how terrified I was? I was fourteen and had the power to determine where a person's soul would go. What if I messed up? What if I marked someone who didn't deserve it? And then the worst and biggest fear: what if I doomed my family? My friends?"

Jack's hand leaves my thigh and tucks my short black hair behind my ear. "That's when you pulled back." It isn't phrased as a question.

I nod. "My family's love language is touch. Hugs and kisses primarily. I stopped both. If I was close enough for a hug, I was close enough for a peck, and I refused. It broke my mom and dad's heart and gave my sister a complex. After a month of it, my dad came to me and apologized. Damn near cried as he told me he didn't think I was evil. That his little girl never could be. I smiled and told him I forgave him, but it crushed him when I patted his shoulder when he tried to hug me."

His thumb brushes over my cheekbone, wiping away a tear that fell. "It must have been hard for both of you. *All* of you."

I press my cheek harder into his hand. "More so for them when I began to spiral. Even at fourteen, I tried to do what I could to numb the pain. It hurt me that I wounded my family, as well as the friends I abandoned without warning. I hung out with the wrong people, and even then, it was only because I knew they wouldn't look for any deeper connection with me. Plus, it was the easiest way to get alcohol." My mouth tightens. "It's also when I lost my virginity. Taken advantage of when I had a bit too much to drink." When Jack growls, low and vicious, I shake my head. "If I said no, I think he would have stopped because when I told him not to kiss me, he didn't. Still, everything went so fast. Even now I don't really remember a lot of it, but I know it happened."

"Did you even have a chance to say no?" he asks, his voice like ice. "Drunk consent is not consent, Valkyrie."

I swallow and drop my hands back to my lap, clenching them tightly together. "It doesn't matter. It happened and it's over with. Please let it go."

He huffs out an angry breath, and the fact that he's mad on my behalf comforts me. "Alright, go on."

"My parents were concerned when they found a bottle

in my room, but they thought that was it. They didn't know that I binged on the weekends with these so-called friends. I started to fight them when they tried to ground me to stop me from going out. I would curse and scream at them and say the meanest things." I let out another sigh. "And then it got worse when I finally got my first assignment.

"I was sixteen and things between my family and I were tense and awkward. I stopped acting out as harshly but still stayed away from home as long as I could. Whether it was sleeping over at a friend's house on the weekend or working late at my part-time job." Unclenching my stiff hands, I stare down at the crescent shapes I dug into my palm. "I had to mark my English teacher.

"He was known to leer at girls, staring a little too long at their chest or ass, so I was hoping to use that against him. I waited until after class and pretended to have a question regarding an assignment. I was so fucking nervous that I was sick to my stomach and almost didn't go through with it. Still, I mustered up the courage and approached his desk after everyone left. I was shaking and stammering, but he took it all in stride. It was like he was getting off on the thought that I liked him. That a student half his age wanted him. Which is just, ugh, gross. But I let him think what he wanted so long as I got the job done.

"As soon as I got the chance, I pressed my lips against his and drew back just as quickly. I saw flashes of girls he'd hit on and cornered as well as his underage conquests, so I took that as my confirmation that I did the job. I tried to leave, but he caught me. I kicked him in the dick and ran from the room, but one of my so-called friends was outside the door. She watched the whole thing through the small window beside the door and took a picture." I trace one of the cuts. "She took the picture to the principal, and my parents were called."

Jack's hand leaves my face, his fingers sliding along the damage I inflicted on my palm. "How bad was it?"

"*Bad*," I answer. "I ruined my teacher's career, not that he didn't deserve it. My parents insisted I was a victim, but I told them that I initiated it. They were stunned and said they didn't know who I was anymore. They didn't understand why I changed so much, why I was making all these terrible choices. They wanted me to go to counseling to get help for my drinking and promiscuous behavior, and I told them to go fuck themselves."

A weak, bitter laugh escapes me again. "When I said that, my dad was livid. He looked me in the eye and said that maybe I was evil after all. I know he said it in the heat of the moment, but I didn't care. I just agreed with him. The more my parents hated me, the safer they were.

"But I was given two options by my dad: shape the fuck up or get the fuck out. I didn't have anywhere to go so I played by their rules for two years. They moved me to a new school. So, I kept my head down and counted down until I could go away to college and get away from them. I still drank but tried to limit it to the weekends unless I came back from a mark. My mom and I spoke as briefly as possible, my dad and I ignored each other, and my sister just looked at me with such…confusion."

His fingers thread through mine and I squeeze our hands together. "I studied my ass off, making up for the two years before that. I graduated from high school with a scholarship to a college I didn't even want to go to. I only cared that they paid for my dorm to get me out of there. But I remember my parents being so proud, and I was confused. Why were they proud of me? Why did they even go to my graduation? They went to my college graduation too, and I didn't even tell them about it! I thought I succeeded in making them hate me, and yet there they were supporting me."

Jack's thumb traces a circle on my skin. "Parents are supposed to love their children unconditionally. Yours are no exception."

"They should be," I point out and finally look back up at him. There's nothing but understanding in his gaze. No pity, no judgment. Just acceptance.

I don't know if I want to throat punch him or kiss him.

"I was—*am* horrible to them, Jack. Even now, my mom and dad call every holiday and birthday. Send cards full of love and silly gifts. I keep the conversations short and never reply to the cards, but they keep coming. I was mentioned on TV for helping solve a case last year, and they called to tell me how *proud* they were. Why?" My stupid eyes fill up with stupid tears again. "I don't deserve them."

Jack slides his arm around my waist and pulls me onto his lap. When I press my face into his neck, he rests his chin on my head and strokes my back. "Of course, you deserve them; they're your parents. Not just that, but you deserve to be loved. Being a hellhound doesn't take that away from you."

"But it does," I argue.

"No, it doesn't," he rebukes. "Just because we are creatures of the afterlife doesn't mean we are not entitled to the indulgences of the heart."

I sniffle and rub at my nose before tilting my head back to look at him. "We?"

He gives me a small smile. "We."

I hold his gaze, the color of his irises still reminding me of Styx. He said he's also from the underworld, is that why his eyes remind me of the river of souls? Is that why I've felt pulled towards him since our first meeting?

Jack opens his mouth to speak, but the dryer cuts him off with a chime, announcing that his clothes are done.

I scoot off his lap and make a shooing motion at him with my hands. "Go get your panties on, Detective. Then I want to hear everything about you."

"They're boxers," he clarifies indignantly. He rolls his eyes at my snicker and stands from the couch, holding the towel in place as he makes his way down the hall towards my stacked washer and dryer.

As I hear him rummage through the dryer, I pick up my phone from the coffee table with hopes of seeing something from Taylor or Bryan, but there's nothing. With a sigh, I set my phone in my lap and rub tiredly at my face. Jack distracted me from my stress, but now it creeps back up onto my shoulders with just as much weight.

I miss my best friend.

It may have only been a day, but somehow knowing that she is missing makes the void in my chest grow wider. I never had to worry about this shit when I was keeping people away from me. But then Taylor wedged her way under my skin and permanently embedded herself there.

"You're frowning," Jack comments.

I look up and see him walking into my kitchen, dressed in his slacks. His wide chest is still on full display, letting me admire the toned, bronze skin. "I'm thinking about Taylor." I admit, tearing my eyes from him so I'm not distracted by his body again.

"We'll find her," he states confidently before turning to the fridge. He pulls out a jug of juice and turns back to me with a lifted brow. "Apple juice?"

I cross my arms defiantly. "Problem?"

"Are you a small child? Do you know how much sugar is in this?" He asks, a tilt of a laugh on his words.

"Yes, and?" I say, trying to keep my own lips from twisting into a guilty smile. "I like my sweets!"

He sets the jug down on the counter and shakes his head. "You're not a hellhound, you're a sugar hound."

I can't help it; I laugh. "Wait until you see my candy stash above the sink."

Jack does just that, opening the cupboard that holds

my two greatest weaknesses: sour candy and alcohol. "Gods Valkyrie!"

I laugh again, covering my mouth to try and stifle it at the disbelief at his tone. "I can't help it!"

"Wait, what is this?" he asks, his tone losing its humor.

Clearly, he disapproves of the seven different liquor bottles I have stashed in the cupboard. A flash of embarrassment heats my cheeks. "You already know I have a problem," I murmur. It occurs to me that saying this to him is the first time I've probably admitted out loud that I may have a drinking problem.

"No. What is this?" His voice is deeper now with an edge of ice.

I stand from the couch and walk over to him. I can see him from the living room but not what he's looking at. I make my way to him but keep a couple feet away as his aura pulses. Smoothing down the hackles his energy rose, I look at my guilty pleasure cupboard. "What's what?"

He gestures at the items, but at my confused expression, he grabs the copper chalice Seth left behind and all but shakes it at me. "This!"

I blink at the vehemence of his tone and cross my arms over my chest, trying to hide the apprehension I feel. "Calm down, Jack."

A growl escapes his throat, and his lip lifts with a baring of teeth. He's never looked more canine than in that moment. Is he also a hellhound then? "Answer the question!"

Defiance rises in me as he suddenly reminds me of Seth

and his outburst. "Keep fucking yelling at me like that, and I won't say shit." His nostrils flare and his pupils dilate, but I go on. "So, you'll go off on anyone who disrespects me, but you're allowed to do so? I think the fuck not."

He jerks like I slapped him. "No, I didn't mean—"

"Didn't you? Your aura is still pressing on mine, trying to push me into submission. I give you control in the bedroom, but that's where it ends."

His power instantly shrinks back, but the hair on the back of my neck is still standing. He runs his hand through his hair and lets it fall to the back of his neck, gripping it tightly. "I'm sorry."

I rub my arms and look away from him. "Maybe you should go."

"Don't push me away again," he says, voice soft. "I'm sorry I lost my temper, but you don't understand. This is important."

My brow furrows with irritation. "It's just a fucking cup!"

"No," he stresses. "It's not. Please, just answer the question."

I don't want to talk about Seth. And I really don't want to give in and answer his question after he shouted at me. It feels a little childish, but I don't want him to think he can get away with talking to me like that. "Push the topic and leave or drop it and stay the night with me."

Jack hesitates, and that's all the answer I need.

My arms drop to my sides, and my face falls into a neutral expression. "It's from Seth. He left it here the night I ended things between us. The wine he made is in there too if you want to question that as well. Why don't you take both on your way out?"

"Valkyrie—"

I cut him off. "I'll see you at work on Monday, Detective Khoury." I turn and walk away from him, just like I did at the crime scene. Was that really just this morning? Fuck, it feels like days ago.

I feel his eyes on me as I walk to the living room and retrieve my phone. They continue to follow me down the hall to my bedroom until I shut the door behind me, blocking his view. I press my back to the door and hold my breath as I hear him shuffling around my small apartment. I can sense him near my door, so I close my eyes tightly and hold my breath, not sure I'll have the willpower to send him away a second time.

Turns out I won't need to.

With an audible sigh, he retreats from my bedroom door. After a few moments I hear my front door open and click shut. I wait a few more seconds, just to make sure he's really gone before letting out a groan and pushing away from the door. I make my way to the side of my bed and sit down, barely feeling the mattress dip as my head reels with what just happened.

I was wrong, this isn't like the crime scene at all. My lashing out at him had stemmed from my stress and anxiety, this time it came from hurt. He made such a big deal about others respecting me but then acted like a total fucking alphahole. Not just that, but I had just got done spilling my bleeding heart to him.

Yanking open the drawer of my nightstand, I pull out the bottle of whiskey and frown at the small amount left. After unscrewing the cap, I flick it off and let it soar across the room without another thought. Crawling up closer to my pillows, I lean back against the headboard and lift the bottle to my lips. I take a hearty gulp and remind myself that this is exactly why it's so much better when I don't let people get close to me.

Eighteen

I jerk awake when a chorus of meows fills my ears. Fumbling for my phone, I knock over the empty whiskey bottle before finally answering Scott's call.

"Hello?" My voice is barely more than a grumble.

"Get your ass up, Dalton," Scott says in lieu of greeting.

I pull my phone from my face to look at the time, wince at the bright light, and then groan at what I see. "It's three in the morning on a Saturday. What exactly am I getting my ass up for?"

When I hear his heavy sigh, I already know what he's going to say. *Fuck*

"We've got another one." He sounds just as tired as I am.

"Are you kidding me?" I lurch upright and fling back the covers, whatever little buzz I had before sleep clearing away.

"We just had a body yesterday morning. This is insane."

"*It's definitely not good,*" he agrees. "*The press conference didn't go well either, so I need you down here ASAP. It's, uh,*" My brow furrows at his pause. "*It's different from before.*"

"Different?" I echo. "Different how?"

"*You'll see when you get here. We're in a small industrial parking lot next to the Rio.*"

"Did you call Jack?" I ask, standing on shaky legs before stumbling towards my closet to find something to wear.

"*Oh, Jack, is it?*" Scott muses, but his voice sounds hollow. "*Don't think I didn't see how close you guys were yesterday. I think this is where I'm supposed to give you the 'don't date your coworker' speech.*"

My cheeks heat, but I shoot him a scowl he can't see. "Shut up. It's nothing." Tucking the phone between my cheek and shoulder, I angrily tug on a pair of yoga pants and curse as I trip in the process.

He scoffs disbelievingly in my ear. "*Right.*"

"Get the fuck off my case and text me the address, will you? And tell Khoury!" I snap and hang up on him before he can retort. After sliding my phone in a pocket, I put on a bra and snatch a red hoodie from the ground before pulling it on.

"Please don't be Taylor, please don't be Taylor." I mumble on repeat as I step into some worn, black tennis shoes. Hurrying to my kitchen, I grab my wallet and slide it into my hoodie pocket. When I finally locate my keys, I rush out of my apartment and lock the door before running to my truck.

I'm not sure what I'm staring at, even with the lights the crime scene techs put up. I mean, it's definitely the remains of our first male victim, but other than that, I'm not sure what to make of the pure carnage before me.

Innards are strewn across the pavement in a splattered pool of blood. The intestines and stringy, red, fatty tissue look like they were both dragged and thrown across the ground. The head is missing like the others, but theirs had been broken off all at the same vertebrae. Not this one. A chunk of the spinal column stands above what's left of the neck, the white of the bone standing out in the vast sea of red like a beacon.

Crouching down next to the tattered remains of the torso, I examine the exposed rib cage. The previous victims all had their ribs torn outwards, flayed out on either side of the sternum, but these are snapped down. Not down inside the body, but down towards the hips. Glancing at the top of the rib cage, I notice that the skin is tattered and ripped. What remains of the sternum also has a very distinct gouge.

I angle my head, trying to mentally put together the torn skin running along the outside of the shambled rib cage. I hover my gloved hand over the wound and spread my fingers out. Hooking the tips of them forward like claws, I mime the action of slashing my hand down his body.

"Oh gods," an officer mumbles before he gags and vomits off to the side of the scene. The putrid, acidic smell hits my nostrils, and I have to press my nose into my shoulder for a second to push down the impulse to sympathy puke.

"A wereanimal?" Scott mumbles.

Taking a deep breath of my detergent, I move my face away from my hoodie. "Or some sort of other beast? I don't know what else could cause this." I admit as I look at the other bruises on the man's body. I point to his hands, specifically the various puncture wounds and scrapes. "These look like they were made from teeth."

"There's no way an alpha would allow a member of their pack to do this," he grumbles disapprovingly. "But I suppose it could be a packless wereanimal. Did any of our other victims have defense wounds like these?"

I shake my head. "No, it's a first. This is also our first John Doe. And, like the last victim, he was killed here and not dumped at a club. The only thing that matches is the missing head and heart. Why the change?" The fact that it's our first male victim is extremely concerning to me.

Scott rubs his chin. "I just had the press conference last night. You think it's a copycat?"

"Doubt it. Plus, there's still the magic from the first scene to account for." I pull off my gloves and take out my phone, taking close up pictures of the wounds to show Jack later. Speaking of which. "I can't believe Khoury isn't here." I mumble and tuck my phone back in my pocket, trying to smooth down my rising panic that this is our first male victim and Jack isn't here.

Scott lifts a brow at me. "Lover's quarrel?"

"So help me, kitten, I will take out your fucking knee-caps if you don't stop pestering me about this," I threaten before nodding to the crime scene techs when they gesture at the body.

He scoffs and follows me as we step away from the scene, letting the techs do their jobs. "That's not a no."

I scowl at him. "Can you let it go?"

"This is why you don't date your coworkers. This right here." When I spin around to face him, his brows are raised expectantly. "Tell me otherwise. Tell me you two didn't get into a fight. Give me another reason as to why he's not here."

I put my hands on my hips, defensiveness bubbling up inside me for his shitty image of Jack. I may be angry at him and concerned for his safety, but he doesn't deserve to be talked about like this. "Don't talk about him like that. Do you think Jack would really abandon his duties because of a fight? That he would ignore a call about our case because of something so damn trivial? Like, really Scott? If you think so low of him, you probably shouldn't have hired him."

Scott's sudden grin throws me off. "Wow, you must really like him if you're defending him. Do I hear mating vows?"

I toss my hands up in exasperation. "Go snort some fucking catnip!" I snap. With a huff at his snicker, I turn and stomp towards my truck. When I get to my beautiful beast,

I pull off my holster and put it back in the center console before sliding into my driver's seat and letting my head fall back against the headrest.

Fucking men. Maybe I need to start sleeping with women again.

The thought disappears as quickly as it comes. Jack, like Taylor, has burrowed himself under my skin, and part of me hates it. I question this connection we seem to have over and over again. Is it because we're both from the underworld? Or am I only finding something in him simply because he can give me something I've been denied for a decade?

With a heavy sigh, I pull out my phone again and try calling him. When he doesn't answer, worry curves my lips down in a frown. A cramp twists my stomach when I'm reminded of Taylor once again.

Again, Jack, *like Taylor*, is missing.

Without Scott here to act as a buffer against my panic, it hits me like a tidal wave crashing against the shore. I press a hand to my chest, feeling my heart pounding in protest. Now that we have a male victim, all I can think about is how Jack isn't here with me. How he didn't answer Scott's call and isn't taking mine. How it's very concerning and suspicious that both people I care about are missing from my life while there's a murder running around. It's hard not to find it personal.

I don't know if I can handle both of them disappearing on me.

I hang up when the call goes to voicemail and quickly

type out a text to him. *At least let me know if you're okay.* I bite my lip and tack on two more words. *In person.* Not letting myself second guess it, I hit send and drop the phone into my cupholder.

There's no way I'm going back to sleep tonight, so when I throw my truck in gear, I head straight to McDonalds to get some cheap ass coffee and fries. Unless breakfast is served this early, then maybe one of those biscuit sandwiches. Either way, I plan on staying up to work on the case so I can be both productive and distracted.

Mostly distracted.

Nineteen

*I*t's still dark when I pull into my parking spot and slide out of my truck. I balance my coffee and phone in one hand, tuck my small bag of food under my arm, and push the truck door closed with my hip. With my free hand, I press the lock button on my keys and then begin my trek towards the complex. I grumble in irritation when I notice that the lights that illuminate a few of the buildings' stairwells are still dead. With how much we all pay for this shit, the office shouldn't bat an eye when it comes to putting in a request to fix the lights.

"Cheap fucks." I murmur as I follow the sidewalk that leads to my building.

When I near building eighteen I stop, assessing the grassy area to my right. I know that some of the lights are out, but with my heightened senses, I can usually see in the dark without straining to do so. But not now. I sharpen my eyes, scowling at the darkness next to me for an explanation to the dense blackness.

I feel the surge of energy before I see the hunched form a few feet from me. My hackles shoot up in warning and I react on instinct, taking a step back. Two golden orbs snap my way, and my breath catches in my throat at the crazed look in them. Adrenaline doesn't seep into my veins; it shoots into them like a bullet. I gasp at the sudden energy my body shoves at me, my heart hammering and pulse thrumming. But I know that the moment I move, this thing will come at me.

How utterly dumb of me to keep up with the bad habit of leaving my service gun in my truck's center console.

It takes a step toward me and then another, a rumbling growl filling the air between us. My eyesight sharpens again, and I can just make out a reptilian-like snout pointed in my direction. Almost like a lizard. But that doesn't make sense. Its body is too high off the ground. When it takes another slow, predator step, I can make out the fur surrounding its neck. Like a lion's mane? What the fuck is this thing?

Run.

I hear the triplets' voices in my head, my pawprint burning along my sternum at the same time, and it spurs me into action. My feet stumble in their haste to retreat, and the monster takes that opening to charge at me. I chuck my coffee at it and hear a gurgled hiss as the hot liquid hits, but I don't wait to see if I damaged it. I take off towards my apartment, whirling my keys in my hand so that one sticks out between each finger like Wolverine's claws.

When I reach my stairwell, I jump up to the fourth step and thank the gods that the wall lights are working. I let a pained scream when something sharp clamps at my calf and jerks my leg out from under me. My chest and chin collide with the stairs, blood filling my mouth while the breath wheezes out of me. I make myself turn on my side, kicking my free foot at the monster's face.

And it most definitely is a monster.

I've seen pictures of chimeras before, but this is a sick, twisted one. Its face is that of a crocodile. A fucking *crocodile* that has its jaws clamped around my calf like a bear trap. One of its lion paws bats at my shoe, trying to get me to stop kicking its face. Fat chance of that. It's wide, powerful legs kick off from a step, releasing my calf to snap at my face. I swing my head back, cracking it against the concrete step. I'll take a split scalp over a mangled face any day, thanks.

I jab my hand at its throat, embedding my keys in its neck. It hisses out a howl and swings its head back. My keys come away covered in black blood, but I barely spare it a glance as I prepare to strike again. It rears back like a horse, giving me a clear view of its elephant-like legs. Or maybe a hippo? I don't have time to ponder it longer, not with those claws coming towards me.

"Stop!"

Jack's bellow startles me, but the flare of his aura seems

to scare the monster. Its paws land on my shoulders, pinning me to the stairs, but the massive head swings to the side, looking for the source of the voice. It finds Jack standing at the base of the stairs and growls. Its attention focuses back on me, and I bare my teeth at it in a sneer. It snaps its jaws at me and lunges for my face again, but it never makes contact. Jack has the mane fisted in his hands, keeping the snout from reaching me. With a vicious snarl, Jack yanks the monster off me and throws it down to the base of the stairs.

Struggling to sit up, I look at Jack as he stands with his back to me, staring down the beast. I can't see his face, but I can feel his warm energy radiating from him with the cadence of a rapid heartbeat. The relief that surges through me knocks the breath out of me. Thank gods, he's okay! He's not missing! He hasn't been taken from me.

My attention is drawn back to the beast when it snarls. It snaps its jaws at Jack as he flares his aura again, but I can clearly see the tail tucked between its grey legs in submission.

What the hell?

I struggle to stand up, but my leg gives out on me. Scrambling for the railing, my keys clank and *shink* against it, the metal-on-metal screech echoing in the stairwell. Jack whirls around to look at me, and it takes a lot to not flinch back at the intense, cold gleam there.

I swallow the blood in my mouth. "Jack?" I whisper uncertainly, clutching the railing tighter.

His gaze softens minutely as our eyes meet. At the sound

of scratching nails on concrete, he quickly turns back to the beast as it flees. "Ammit!" he snarls, moving to chase after it.

What's he going to do, hunt that thing down? Did he not see the same beast that I did?

"Jack!" I quickly reach for his shirt, fisting my hand in the material to keep him here with me. Where it's safe.

He once again turns to me, and the desperation I see there is confusing. He glances to where the beast disappeared then back to me as if torn on what to do. As if he doesn't know if he should stay or go after it.

"Don't," I plead and wipe at my lips as blood dribbles out of the corner of my mouth. I bit my tongue when I hit my chin and the fucker is bleeding like a bitch.

Jack's eyes hyper focus on the blood I probably just smeared all over my chin. They then travel to my leg, and his nostrils flare. With a last fleeting, longing glance in the direction the monster disappeared to, he reaches for me. He steadies me on my feet and loops an arm around my waist as I sway with dizziness.

"What's wrong?" He asks as I stumble up the next step.

Everything. "I hit my head," I mumble back.

His hand delves into my hair, fingers running along my scalp. I suck in a breath when he finds a sensitive spot. When he pulls back his hand, I'm not at all surprised to see blood coating his fingers.

"Damn it." Jack mutters under his breath and sweeps me up into his arms.

I don't even try to fight him this time. Not when a wave

of exhaustion hits me so hard my eyes droop. He jostles me, and I open my eyes to see we're at my door already. Damn, did I black out? With difficulty, I unclench my keys and try for the door. When I miss the lock three times, Jack gently sets me on my feet.

"Sorry," I whisper, a little embarrassed as he takes my keys and unlocks the door, all the while keeping a steadying arm tight around my waist.

"It's fine," Jack replies tensely.

A familiar pang of disappointment swells in my chest. He's mad at me. Is it because I kicked him out a couple hours ago? Or because I stopped him from chasing that beast? Or is it all of it? Has he finally realized I'm not worth the effort? It's probably about time.

I swallow again, glad there's less blood this time, and try to push out of his hold after he walks me inside the apartment. His grip tightens as he leads me to the couch, but I continue to try and squirm away from him.

With a growl of frustration, he releases me, and I topple back onto the couch. I look up at him, but quickly look away at the anger in his eyes.

"*What*, Valkyrie?" he snaps. "What now?"

I blink and furrow my brow, but I don't look at him. "Nothin'."

Jack's aura flares briefly with his irritation. "Don't fall asleep," he orders before stalking away from me.

I assume he's leaving and that makes the hurt and anger battle within me. How did things go so wrong with us? Maybe I shouldn't have been so stubborn last night. Maybe I should have just told him then and there, but I don't deserve to be yelled at. I'm not going to lower my self-worth by allowing that.

A gentle touch to my cheek startles me, my eyes snapping open. I'm met with Jack's grey gaze, concern softening the furrow between his brows. "I said not to fall asleep," he chides, but it doesn't have any bite of attitude from a few moments ago.

"Sorry," I mumble, unable to look away from him.

He shakes his head, dismissing my apology. "If you have a concussion, I don't want you to sleep yet." When I simply nod in response, he presses a cold bundle of ice to my head. "Hold this."

I do as told, holding the towel to my wound as he sits down on my coffee table. I worry my bottom lip between my teeth as he gently takes my leg and sets it on his lap. He rolls up the fabric of my legging, but my eyes are focused on his handsome face. When his eyes narrow into a glare, my calf muscle flexes in his hand with tension.

"Stay still." His hand tightens around my calf as he gives me another order.

"You don't have to," I protest when he picks up a damp towel and starts to clean my leg.

With a heavy defeated sigh, he rests the towel on my leg and hangs his head. After a few tense seconds that sends my heart galloping, he speaks. "*What* is the matter, Val?"

Gods, I really hate that fucking nickname on his lips.

"You don't have to stay and do this. I know you're angry," I say softly.

"I'm not angry," he responds, but his words are tense once again.

"You've been angry since last night." I pull the sleeves of my hoodie down past my hand, balling it in the fabric as I hold the makeshift ice pack. "Why do you think I didn't answer your question? Why I made you leave?"

When he finally lifts his head again, his eyes look almost tormented. "You're right. I am mad." I look away from him, but he continues. "But only because you keep pushing me away."

My eyes snap back to him, my own irritation rising again. "Bullshit."

His eyes flutter shut, his jaw working. "It's not. Last night you kicked me out because I asked you a question. Now a few hours later you're *physically* pushing me away from you even though you asked me to come here. Your muscles tense when I touch you." His brows slant down again. "As if you can't stand to be touched by me anymore."

I blink at him, my annoyance dissolving just like that. "That's not true."

His steely stare holds mine. "Explain to me how it isn't."

"Someone's bossy tonight," I murmur. "It's not that I don't want you touching me, Jack. Of course, I want to be touched by you. I just don't want you to feel like you must. You seemed put out to have to haul my ass to my apartment. Like it bothered you to do so. That's why I said you don't have to. You don't have to stay and take care of me if it's upsetting you to do so."

Jack leans forward, effectively eliminating any small space that is between us. "What did I say the other night?" When I remain quiet, a low growl rumbles in his chest. He possessively cups the bottom of my jaw. "Answer me."

The thrill of obeying him flares. "That I deserve to be taken care of."

"In all things," he adds, running his thumb over my bottom lip.

I hate that I'm disappointed that he didn't praise me. I clear my throat and find my footing again. "I don't need you to take care of me."

He lets out a frustrated huff and drops his hand from my face. "I *want* to. Don't you understand that by now?"

My head tilts, and I curse as it makes my vision swim. I reach out to steady myself and Jack's hand finds mine. I close my eyes tightly, trying to get the room to stop spinning. "Why?" I grit out.

"You looked like you needed an anchor," he responds, going to release my hand, but I wrap my fingers around his.

"No, Jack," I start. "Why do you want to take care of me so badly? Am I like a wounded animal you feel you have to take pity on?"

"This pity party isn't like you, Valkyrie," Jack says, but

when I look up, I see a small smirk tilting up the corner of his lips. "I have no explanation for you. I told you it's not something I feel the need to do for just anyone. Something about you calls to me. It has since I met you."

I mull over his words and blink, trying to focus on which of the two is the real Jack. "Because we're both from the underworld?"

He shrugs. "Possibly, but does it really matter? I like how I feel when I'm with you." His voice drops an octave. "And when I'm inside you."

My toes curl and I nudge his stomach with the leg still in his lap. "Don't use your sexual prowess against me right now. My head hurts too much for that."

His face becomes serious again. "I'm sorry you got hurt. How are you feeling besides the pain?"

"I just got really fucking dizzy," I answer honestly, closing my eyes again.

He takes the ice pack from my hand and gently prods at the tender spot on my scalp. When he pulls back, only a few specks of blood are on his fingers. "Good, it seems to be healing quickly. Why don't you lay back on the couch while I tend to your leg?"

I try to look at said leg to assess the damage done to it, but my vision goes a little blurry. With Jack's help I managed to swing my legs up on the couch, lying along the length of it. After he puts another hand towel down over my useless decorative pillow, I rest my head against it and look up at the ceiling.

"How does it look?" I can't help but ask as he resumes cleaning it. When he doesn't immediately answer, I try to squint down at it, but it doesn't help.

"Like you got caught in a hunter's trap," Jack responds, gently pushing my shoulder back down so I'm flat against the cushions once again. "You're lucky the bone didn't break."

Another wave of exhaustion hits me, and my eyes slide shut. "Yeah," I try to say, but it comes out more as an exhale. My eyes flutter open when I feel his fingers poke and prod at my calf, but I can barely feel the pain as my body starts to shut down for sleep.

"I'm glad I stopped her in time," he whispers.

I hum my acknowledgment that he spoke, but the void of sleep finally pulls me under.

Twenty

When consciousness comes back to me, I'm lying on familiar fine, pale green sand. Rolling over onto my side, I see a massive three-headed black dog beside me. Each set of ears is perked up in alert and facing a different direction. Their noses twitch occasionally, scenting the air for something, but what?

"Cerberus?" I ask softly, getting to my knees.

All three heads swing my way, studying me. With a wisp of black smoke, he separates into the three identical triplets I'm used to. "Valkyrie," they greet.

My brow furrows in confusion as I look at them. "What's going on? Why am I here?"

"For protection." One of them says as he approaches me, the other two crossing their arms over their chests to watch.

"Protection from what?" I look at the one who squats down in front of me. "What are you doing?"

He touches my calf and I wince. "Your soul is reflecting the wound on your human body, like I thought."

"What? What are you talking about?"

He stands and cocks his head at me. "The thing that bit you, the bite is reflected on your soul."

"Look at your leg," another prompts.

I do as told and look at my leg. Jack wasn't kidding when he said it looked like I stepped into a trap. All the way around my calf are almost perfectly spaced holes. No, "holes" isn't the right word. They're puncture marks; *teeth* marks. Just like a shark...or a crocodile. The night catches up to me. and I rub at my face.

"The thing that bit me."

"Yes. You should have run sooner," they all say with disapproval, red eyes narrowing into a glare.

"I get that," I deadpan. "Again, protection from what?"

The triplets standing off to the side clasp their hands behind their back. "As we said, the creature that attacked you is from the underworld."

I blink and look at my leg once again. "I've never seen a chimera like that before." A shiver makes the hair on my arms stand. "It was terrifying."

The Cerberus who examined my leg nods. "That's because there is only one of her kind."

My arms cross over my chest as I rub at the chilled skin.

"Where does she come from? Here? The Greek side?"

They tense and glance at one another before one of them speaks. "We don't speak of *other* factions."

I pick up on their emphasis. "So that's a no." Their following silence is answer enough. "Can I ask why you don't speak about each other?"

They shrug simultaneously, once again acting as a single entity in three different bodies. "It's an agreement that we have come to. In essence they are our competition. You must understand that most of us have a counterpart in other domains."

"Even you?" I purse my lips together, trying to think of examples. "Would that be like Satan and Hades? Osiris? Dis Pater?"

They nod. "Yes, those are all gods of the underworld. And yes, even we have counterparts."

"But you said this thing that attacked me is one of a kind. Does that mean it doesn't have a counterpart in any other underworld?" Bringing the question up makes my calf twitch with an echo of pain.

"Correct," one of them says.

"All underworlds have their own beasts and monsters. Their own different types of demons," another adds in.

The third one's eyes stay on mine, and he tilts his head as I bite my lip. "You have another question."

"I do," I agree, looking at my leg again. The bite marks remind me of those on John Doe. "Is this thing the one causing my murders? The thing you told me to mark?"

Again, they fall silent and look at each other in question. I've never seen Cerberus like this before, and it's both amusing and concerning.

"The answer is both yes and no," they finally say. "We cannot explain more, but you are welcome to ask more questions."

They're giving me a chance to get more information.

I rub at my bottom lip with my thumb, staring down at the silky sand as I think. I know better than to ask about Taylor. They can't tell me about souls that have passed here, so instead I focus on my whiteboard. All the pictures of the headless, heartless women laid out based on a loose timeline.

"This creature has been killing for a while," I surmise. When they just stare at me expectantly, I keep going. "The bodies that appeared were sporadic before they came to Las Vegas, but now that they're here they're escalating. Why?"

"Control is a fickle thing," they muse. "It isn't always so easily held."

Their words have a double meaning, and it takes me a second to realize what it is. It's something Jack and I commented on a few days ago. "There's two of them?" When they stare at me, I rub my face in disbelief. "Fucking shit! This is insane. We're not any closer to figuring out who it is!"

"You are closer than you think," one of the triplets says, the other two giving him a sharp, reprimanding look.

I look at him in surprise then back down at my leg. "It *did* attack me, but why?" I press my palms to my eyes and groan in frustration as I play back my attack. A startled breath gets caught in my lungs when I remember Jack showing up and pulling it off me. I had been so fucking worried that he had gone missing, that something had happened to him, but he showed up at my apartment completely fine. And then the beast had *cowered* at Jack's aura. Why? Not just that, but it had seemed like every part of Jack wanted to chase after the beast. Was it because he knew it was related to our case? Or because he lost control of it?

And was he cursing at it, or calling it—*her* by a name? And I now remember that he did in fact address it as a female.

"Ask," Cerberus presses.

"Is this beast's name Ammit?" I whisper. Every part of me is pleading for them to say no. Or say that they don't know. Or that they can't tell me. I need something besides a confirmation.

"Yes."

Gods fucking damn it!

I feel my chest constrict, the air wheezing from my lungs. I pull my hands from my face and look down at them as if they hold all the answers. Jack knows about Ammit. Has he known this whole time that she was part of the murders? Is he the one controlling her?

"You warned me to stay away from Jack," I murmur and slowly lift my head to look at the triplets. "He's not from our underworld, is he?"

They seem almost disappointed by my question but shake their heads. "No."

I swallow thickly as doubt skitters down my spine. What are the chances that a body would be discovered the same day Jack started his job at the LVPCU? That it would be his first case?

Cerberus gives a soft sigh and waves their hands at me. "Perhaps you need to ask him more questions. He's angry we took you away from him. We just wanted to make sure she did not take your soul while you slept."

I'm about to ask him what he means, but my soul slams back into my body. My back arches as I gasp in air, my eyes flying open.

"I've got you." Warm hands cradle my face, thumbs brushing soothing circles along my cheekbones. "It's okay, I've got you."

I blink several times until I can focus on the handsome face staring down at me. As Jack's hand moves to smooth my hair back from my face, I notice my head is in his lap. Gods, I hate how comforted I feel by him.

His eyes soften as his knuckles brush along my cheek. "I hate that he does that to you," he comments, oblivious to my rising panic and fear.

My heart pounds against my ribs as I stare up at him, trying to harden my resolve against the man who wormed his way into my life and for maybe the worst reasons. I have to remember that he may very well be the killer of so many women. Not to mention a liar.

"How do you know the beast?" My voice is quiet as my amber eyes meet his.

His hand stills, eyes widening slightly. "What?"

I smack his hands off me, disgusted by the potential of his touch, and lurch into a sitting position. He leans back in time to avoid the collision of our foreheads. "You heard me," I hiss, standing from the couch and trying to ignore the twinge in my calf and the way my vision swims.

Jack fluidly rises from the couch, but his shoulders are tense, jaw tight as he looks at me. "What did Cerberus tell you?"

Scoffing, I put distance between us and slowly limp back towards my bedroom. My service gun is *still* stupidly in my truck, but I have a Glock in my nightstand. I want to think that Jack won't hurt me. But then again, I also never thought he could be a murderer either. "I didn't need him to figure it out. I may have hit my head, but I remember you calling her name. At first, I thought you were cussing at her, but you weren't, were you? Her name is Ammit, isn't it?"

He quietly follows me with a pinched expression. "Yes."

I quicken my pace at his admission and rush to my drawer. I push aside two mini bottles of vodka and wrap my fingers around the grip of my gun, flicking off the safety and loading the chamber. When I whirl back around, I level it at him. Jack's hands shoot up in surrender, but I can see the surprise in his eyes.

Is that a glimmer of hurt I see in there too?

The audacity. As if he's the one in this situation that is hurting. That's been betrayed. That's a *murderer.*

"How could you?" I ask, my words coming out with a harsh bite.

"No, it's not what you think, Valkyrie," he says slowly as if speaking to a child that needs placating.

"It's Val," I snap childishly, knowing damn well how much I hate hearing him call me by my nickname. But honestly, I'm terrified my resolve will fail if I keep hearing my name on his lips. Gods, what did this man do to me? Was this all part of his plan?

"*Val,*" he amends. "Please, let me explain. I'm not sure what Cerberus told you, but it's not like that."

"You're not from *my* underworld, and neither is Ammit. But you two are from the same one, aren't you?" When he reluctantly nods, my lip trembles. "Which one?"

His face crumples in defeat, a sigh escaping his nose. "Egypt," he answers softly.

"Why?" I hate that my voice cracks as my emotions build up in a chaotic mess. "*Why?* I trusted you."

Jack shoves his hands into his hair and grips it tightly with frustration. "This is not how I wanted any of this to come out. I was going to explain everything to you."

I tighten my grip on the gun as my hand shakes a little. "Oh, were you? Was that before or after you fucked me,

Jack?"

He looks like I sucker punched him, and a grimace twisting his expression. "It's not like that."

A harsh vibration buzzes along my thigh, and I almost pull the trigger out of surprise. Stupid fucking phone. I smack my free hand against it, trying to get it to stop. "Or maybe you wanted to make sure I was wrapped tightly enough around your finger first?"

The color blanches from his face, the rich tan skin turning pale. "Never," Jack whispers, but his tone is firm. "If you would just *listen* to me."

My phone stops, the call going to voicemail, but a few seconds later it's vibrating once again. I try to ignore it as I keep my eyes on him. "You sure? You weren't trying to get the pitiful detective to fall for you so you couldn't possibly ever look guilty? What better way to cover your tracks, am I right?" This hurts way more than it should. He never should have gotten so close.

Those sensual lips part in surprise. "*Guilty?* Just what do you think I did, Valkyrie?" He blinks at me as if finally putting together what I figured out. Finally, I can see the embers of anger flare in his gaze. "You think I'm responsible for all the deaths? For mutilating all those women? Have you lost your mind?"

When he takes a step towards me, my fear spikes. I steel my spine and tighten my stance. "Stay back!"

"No, you need to—fuck!" He shouts and grabs his

shoulder, grunting with pain. He looks at the blood bloom-
ing around his hand and turns a bewildered glare on me.
"Did you just *shoot* me?"

I did, and the lingering regret angers me more.

"I warned you." My chest is heaving, hand shaking harder. My phone starts vibrating again, and I almost pull the
trigger a second time.

He eyes the gun warily before meeting my own with a
scorching stare. "If you shoot me again, I'm going to slap
that ass of yours so hard you'll be feeling it for days."

I gape at the calm, serious manner he said that in. Did
I shoot the common sense out of him? "Really? You think
this is the fucking time for that?" I seethe, narrowing my eyes
at him even as my whore body responds to his crass words
and the promise in them. "You're not going to distract me."
Once again, my phone stops vibrating only to vibrate one
more time after. This is dangerous for both of us. "Don't
move," I warn him and pull the phone from the pocket of
my yoga pants.

"Yes, ma'am," he says, squeezing his shoulder tighter.

I scowl at him before finally looking at my screen. The
world promptly slips out from under me. My knees wobble,
and I have to lock them in place to stop myself from melting
into a puddle of despair. "Taylor," I cry, staring at the picture. "No, no, *no.*"

My beautiful friend is lying on her side, hands bound
behind her back and ankles tied together. Her blonde hair is

matted with dirt and dried blood, bruises discoloring parts of her pale skin. I'm whimpering, I know I am, but I can't stop it.

"Valkyrie? What is it? What's wrong?" Jack asks.

I hate how authentically concerned he sounds. As if I didn't just shoot him. As if he isn't a fucking a murderer who stabbed me in the back.

Hardening my heart, I angrily thrust my phone out at him as all reasoning leaves me. "What the fuck is this? Where is she, Jack?!"

He holds up a hand when I raise the gun once again. When had I lowered it? "Don't," he pleads. "I don't know anything about Taylor. I would never do anything to hurt her. I know what she means to you. To hurt her would be to hurt you, and I would never do that. Who sent the picture?"

Gods, I'm so emotionally fucked right now I didn't even check. All I saw was the picture and hyper focused on it. I click on the picture and open the text. The name I see there sends a wave of nausea over me, my stomach clenching and roiling.

"Let me guess," Jack begins, but again his voice is soothing and calm. "Seth?"

My head snaps up to look at him, but I can't even muster a glare. "How…?"

"The chalice," he replies, pulling his bloodied hand away to look at the bullet hole in his shoulder. "It's why I was so adamant about getting an answer from you."

I clutch my phone tighter. "I don't understand. What

does that have to do with anything?"

"It's from my homeland." He raises his head and looks at me. "When I saw it, I thought that you were the one behind the murders. That maybe you were the one who helped Ammit escape. It wasn't farfetched, especially since you're a hellhound. It's why I was so angry. I suspected you just like you are suspecting me."

"I have every right to suspect you, Jack! The bodies started landing as soon as you showed up! You know Ammit! You're from the same underworld as her! How am I not supposed to think otherwise?!" The tone of my voice rises as hysteria teeters on taking over.

Jack's eyes soften again as he watches me. "I know how it looks, but it isn't me." He gestures at my phone. "What else did Seth say? Or did he only send the picture?"

Swallowing, I scroll down and look at the text under Taylor's picture. "Maybe this will be an incentive to answer your phone," I read.

"It's been Seth since the beginning." Jack takes a tentative step towards me. "The chalice confirmed it."

"It's just a cup," I whisper, not ready to believe it.

"It's not," he stresses. "This chalice is Egyptian made. Not just that, but it is very, *very* old. It's the kind that was left in crypts and at the base of alters. It's impossible for anyone other than a god to have it."

This doesn't make any sense. "But he was with me the night Browne was killed." I repeat, trying to find any excuse that it wasn't Seth. "I mean, I left him to go to the club, but he would have had to follow me there and kill her without me seeing him."

A possessive growl rumbles in Jack's chest. "You may have been with him, but that's not the issue. Ammit is the one killing people; Seth is the mastermind."

"You can't be certain that it's him." It can't be true. I couldn't have been sleeping with a murderer. Oh gods, had I been fucking two of them? When I focus on Jack again, he's standing less than an arm's length away from me. I quickly lift my gun again. He doesn't try to stop me when I press it against his chest, right over his heart. "How do I know you're not just like him? That all three of you aren't in on this together? That I wasn't just a pawn to you?"

"You are not a pawn to me, Valkyrie." His fingers loosely wrap around my wrist, but he doesn't push the gun away. "You were an unexpected surprise, but one that I am very grateful for."

This is all too much.

The emotional rollercoaster is rapidly draining my energy, leaving me tired and wary. "I don't know what to believe," I whisper.

"Believe me," Jack pleads, his thumb rubbing circles into the soft skin of my wrist. "Or, at the very least, believe that Seth is who you need to focus on. He's the one that has Taylor."

Taylor.

I look at my phone again, tears pricking my eyes as I

take in the battered form of my friend. Before I can ask anything, the phone starts ringing, a picture of Seth with his signature cocky smirk appearing on my screen. Panicking, I look to Jack for help. He nods to the phone, his fingers sliding towards my gun. I don't let him take it from me, but I do take it away from his chest as I answer the call.

"*Ah, I thought that would get your attention.*" Seth's mocking voice says as I press the warm glass to the side of my face.

I push down my panic and latch onto the anger, letting it boost my confidence. "Why do you have Taylor?"

"*Why?*" he mocks. "*Because you love her.*"

My feet move without thought, causing me to pace across the room with a stagger in my step. I can feel Jack watching me, but I don't look at him. I'm still not sure what to make of him or if I can even trust him. "Of course I love her. She's my best friend."

"*Exactly,*" he hisses. "*You dropped me like I was nothing so I thought I would return the pain.*"

"That's not fair," I protest. "She has nothing to do with us." Feeling Jack approach, I whirl towards him, gun already lifting. He holds up his bloodied hands before gesturing at the phone and then to his own ear. Understanding, I put the phone on speaker.

"*No, she doesn't,*" he agrees with an edge of humor. "*But that doesn't matter. You hurt my feelings and so I wanted to lash out.*"

My anger flares with the sheer childishness of his statement. "Is this a joke? Are you fucking five?"

A soft growl comes through the speaker. "*I would be very*

careful how you talk to me."

"Seth—"

I'm cut off by his laugh. *"Seth? Did your dog not tell you who I am?"* His laugh fades into a contemplative hum. *"Unless of course, he hasn't figured it out yet."*

"Why don't you enlighten us?" I grind out through clenched teeth.

"Us?" He echoes. There's a mix of bitter jealousy and amusement in his tone. *"I suppose I shouldn't be surprised. My, my, I must say, you're not a very good guardian, are you? Letting your coworker escape like she did."*

My eyes snap to Jack's, apprehension snaking down my spine again. Guardian? Coworker? Just who is Jack? *What* is he?

His gaze holds mine unwaveringly, but I can see a flicker of dread in his eyes. Despite what he's feeling, he doesn't let it show in his voice as he replies to Seth. "She wouldn't have escaped if you hadn't helped her."

"But what fun would that be?" Seth coos. *"Ammit needed a vacation. She's having quite the fun."*

Jack suddenly snarls, startling me into taking a step back. "So much fun that she attacked Valkyrie. Or was that also part of your plan? To rip out the heart of the woman you seem to want so desperately?"

There's a beat of silence before Seth speaks again. *"She wasn't supposed to,"* he states in a low, cold tone. *"She was instructed to retrieve my cup."*

"Did you really expect that to pan out?" I cut in. "Especially with how you're obviously losing control over her?"

Seth sighs as if it's nothing but an inconvenience. "*A temporary issue, I'm sure. Maybe merely sensing the guardian sent her into a panic. She clearly prefers one god to another.*"

"God?" I repeat, eyes widening as I stare at Jack. He does nothing to rebuke that statement and that terrifies me.

"*Oh yes. I did tell you that your chose the wrong one, remember?*" Seth hums in self-satisfaction, but I barely hear him.

My overloaded brain quickly finds all the pieces and shoves them together in my head.

Egyptian.

A dog.

A guardian.

A god.

"Anubis?" I whisper in a tight voice. My throat closes up on me as I stare at Jack with wide, disbelieving eyes.

A muscle in his cheek clenches and twitches before he gives me a single, tense nod.

The phone slips out of my hand and drops to the carpet with a muffled thud.

Twenty-one

*S*eth's cackle comes through the speaker, jarring me from my shock. *"Well, the jackal is out of the bag, isn't it? When you're ready to come to me and make the right choice, you know where to find me. Taylor and I will be waiting, Val!"* He has the balls to make a kissing sound before hanging up.

The sudden silence is suffocating.

My knees finally give out from the overload of emotional turmoil. Ja—*Anubis* reaches for me but stops when I manage to make a protesting grunt in response and lets me sink to the floor with my gun loosely cradled in my lap.

A fucking god. My eyes widen. Holy shit, I *fucked* a god.

Two of them, according to Seth.

And then I shot one.

At my choked wail, Anubis takes a tentative step forward. "Valkyrie?"

"I shot a god," I mumble. When I hear his soft chuckle, I look up at him. No wonder his grey eyes remind me of the river of souls. Doesn't Anubis judge souls? Deem them worthy of the afterlife? "I shot Anubis."

"I don't know whether to be concerned or amused that that is what you decided to fixate on." There's a soft humor in his voice, but his brow is still furrowed with uncertainty.

"I shot you," I repeat more firmly, staring at the bloody hole in his shoulder. "With a gun."

"You did," he agrees. "And it hurt."

My cheeks flush when he kneels in front of me, a protest on my lips. "Don't. I mean, a god shouldn't kneel?"

He gives me a forced, strained smile. "Many gods wouldn't."

"Then why?" I ask, sucking in a breath when he touches my cheek and cradles it.

"Because I want to. Because I can." His voice gentles. "Because I don't want you to treat me any differently, Valkyrie. The man you know would kneel before you without question if you freaked out. I am still that Jack."

"Jack," I say and then slap my hand to my forehead. "Short for jackal."

He pulls my hand from my face and gives me a sheepish grin. "I thought it was clever."

"You're an asshole," I snap my mouth shut with a clack of teeth, realizing I probably shouldn't be insulting a god, but when I look at him, his grin has widened.

"There's my girl," he rumbles approvingly.

I hate how both my heart and core clench at that. "*No.*" Knocking his hand from my face, I lift a finger in warning. "No. You don't get to use your sexy god voice on me." His lips tilt up in a smirk, but I pretend not to notice. "Not after you lied and led me on for your own gain."

The smile abruptly vanishes. "I did not use you," he argues, seemingly affronted by the idea. "Nor did I lie."

"Omitting the truth and withholding information is still lying, Ja—*Anubis*—fuck!" I shout in frustration and rub hard at my face with the heel of my hand.

"You can still call me Jack." I let him take the gun from me when he tries to ease it out of my grip. What good will it do against a god anyways? He takes my hands into his and holds them firmly when I try to tug them away. "I tried to tell you, Valkyrie. So many times. But we either got interrupted or it wasn't the right timing."

I stare down at our hands, his tan skin a stark contrast to my paleness. "Any of the times I bled my heart out to you would have been the right time," I murmur.

He takes in a slow breath. "Perhaps," he begins. "But in the beginning, we both had reservations about telling each other what we are. When you told me, I was going to tell you in return, but you were so happy to finally kiss someone that I didn't want to ruin that moment for you. You deserve to be happy."

I bite my lip, recalling how he had tried to say something

before I slammed my mouth against his for the second time. "And after?"

"Then Taylor went missing," Jack reminds me in a gentle tone. "And then there was our fight, and the fiasco about the goblet."

"Taylor," I repeat, the image of her battered body flashing before my eyes again. I forcefully pull my hands out of his and climb unsteadily to my feet. Once again, I ignore the rush of dizziness that comes with standing. "I need to get her."

Jack fluidly rises with me. "Seth has her."

"I know," I hiss and make my way to the kitchen, looking for my keys. "And I'm going to get her back."

Jack puts a hand on my shoulder, but I shrug him off and ignore the growl he gives me. "It's a trap, Valkyrie. He wants you to come to him."

"I'm not going to let her suffer anymore because of me. It's not fair to her! Stop trying to stop me!" I snap when I whirl on him.

With another growl, he lurches forward. I step back, but he follows, rapidly eating the distance between us until I'm backed against the counter. He throws his arms out on either side of me, caging me in. "Listen to me," he demands, his voice low and dangerous. "He is a *god*, Valkyrie. He has hidden his aura from me, so I don't know who he is exactly, but he is still a god. You can't just go in blindly."

I stare up at him defiantly. "I can't just leave her. I won't."

"I'm not asking you to," he bites out. "I'm asking you to

be smart about this. We need to make a game plan."

"We? I don't remember asking you to tag along, *Anubis*." His lip twitches with a sneer at the way I hiss out his given name. "Don't think I've just forgotten and forgiven you. You may be a god, but you still deceived me."

His nostrils flare with anger and I flinch, suddenly very aware that I pissed off a god.

I don't realize I've shut my eyes until I feel his hand cradling the bottom of my jaw, three of his fingers resting against the side of my throat. His touch is soft as he tilts my head up, voice tender when he sighs my name, "Valkyrie." When I open my eyes again, I see his are damn near blazing. "Don't be afraid of me." He lowers his voice until it's almost a whisper. "Not you."

My chest tightens at his tone, and my resolve cracks. "You hurt me."

"I know, and I'm sorry. I wanted to tell you everything." He bends until his forehead touches mine, lashes dark against his skin as his eyelids drop. "I didn't know how to explain my fuck up. How I let one of the most dangerous creatures in the underworld escape to the mortal world on my watch."

His breath fans against my lips as he talks, and I fist my hands in my hoodie to keep from grabbing him. "What is she?"

"Ammit devours the souls of the unworthy," he explains. "If a soul fails the heart weighing ceremony, she wipes them out of existence. They will have no afterlife."

A shudder runs through me. "How long has she been

missing?"

"A while," he responds. "I've tracked her by the number of souls she's decimated. When she devours a soul, Thoth and I know." At my pinched brows, he explains, "Thoth records all results for the heart weighing ceremony, whether they're devoured or go on to meet Osiris. He's been doing my job as well while I'm here."

"Osiris is the God of the Underworld?" I ask, but I know the answer even as he nods. My brow furrows when I think through what he's told me. "Wait. You've been tracking her through the souls she's devoured? Since she escaped?" When he nods, I growl and push at his chest. "Then you knew that all the victims we found, even those from across the states, were her work?"

He sighs and pulls back to look down at me once again but doesn't let me push him away. "Yes, but it's not that simple." When I struggle against him, he tightens his hold on my jaw and presses his hips against mine, pinning me to the counter. "Will you stop being so damn hardheaded and listen to me?"

"Yes, *sir*," I sneer sarcastically. "Whatever you say, *sir*. Or shall I call you God? If sir gets you all hot and bothered, I wonder what calling you God will do?"

A growl rumbles in his chest as his gaze shifts to my lips. "Watch that mouth of yours, pet, or I'll punish it."

"Empty promises are useless," I snarl back. "Just like your lies."

His nostrils flare again as his gaze locks with mine.

Holding me in place, he presses his lips hard against mine. It's punishing, almost bruising. "If only we had time for me to prove you otherwise," he breathes before tracing my bottom lip with his tongue. "But there's too much to say and do."

"Then start talking," I demand in a harsh whisper, hating how my body reacts so strongly to him.

"Yes, I knew all of these women were Ammit's doing, but I didn't know how she was doing it," Jack begins. "By the time we knew she devoured a soul, it was too late. We can only feel it in the Hall of Maat because my powers are stunted here. When a soul blinked out from existence, I would rush to that town, but by the time I got there, Ammit was nowhere to be found.

"I would hunt for her, follow whatever trail was left behind, but the god helping her is very good at masking them. I can't stay out of the hall for extended amounts of time, and they must know that." He releases my jaw, letting his hand fall loosely around my throat, his thumb lightly stroking my rapid pulse. "I didn't realize they weren't killing their victims in the same town they took them from until I started working with you."

"But you *know* them. You know the Jane Does on my board?" I press.

He shakes his head. "No. I don't know their names, Valkyrie. That's part of the problem. Yes, we know when Ammit destroys a soul, but without it being done in the Hall of Maat, they simply get recorded as 'Unknown'. We need the heart weighing ceremony for that."

My gaze drops to his chin as I stubbornly refuse to look at him. "There are more victims than what we found, aren't there?

Another sigh, albeit this one is more reluctant. "Yes, including one that happened here before Browne. It's why I knew to come here. The soul was devoured three days before Browne was." At my horrified expression, he continues. "That's why I need to find her. Seth, or whomever he is, is losing control of her, and she's throwing the world out of balance."

"How?" I ask, twisting my hands in the fabric of my hoodie as I try to keep my fucking sanity in the absolute craziness that is happening.

"Osiris, as well as the other underworld gods, is upset," he explains. "Not only is she taking souls that aren't meant for our underworld, but she's also destroying innocent souls that should be granted an afterlife."

"Stephanie Browne was supposed to be ours," I murmur. "I went to the club that night to mark her for Cerberus. That's why I found her."

Jack nods. "That explains why you were there that night. I can only imagine that Cerberus is feeling the heat from Hades for all these souls getting loose."

I didn't think of it like that. "Probably."

"Now that Ammit has had a taste of innocent souls,

I'm concerned with what that means for us. I need to get her back to the hall before it's too late." He finally pulls away, dropping his hands to his sides. "Unless it's already too late for her."

My fingers continue to worry the fabric with anxiousness as I look up at him. "You had a chance to get her." His eyes meet mine, but he doesn't say anything. "When she attacked me," I clarify. "You stopped her, ripped her off me." My stomach bottoms out when he continues to hold my gaze without remorse. "That's why you hesitated. That was your chance to grab her. Why didn't you?"

"You were bleeding. Terrified. Did you really think I would leave you?" Again, his hand raises so his fingertips can trace over my cheek. "As if I could?"

I shudder at his tone but force myself to jerk my cheek away from his touch. I can't fall for this. I can't let myself slip into this being, this god. My head has to stay clear and focused for Taylor. "Don't." My voice is softer than I like. "This is all too much for me to handle. I thought you were missing, then assumed you were a murderer, and now I find out you're Anubis? I can't deal with this."

Jack lets me shove past him but turns to watch me as I head to the living room to put my shoes on. "I know it's a lot."

"A lot?" I laugh humorlessly. "No, a lot was when we got our first male victim, and I thought you were next since you had vanished. This is extreme. This is *too much*." I finally locate my keys and snatch them off the coffee table. "I'm getting Taylor back from your fellow god, and then I'm going to raise hell. If Ammit ki—" My voice cracks on the word so I change it. "If she hurts Taylor, you're next on my list, god or not."

I feel Jack at my back as I stalk out of the apartment with a limp. "That's fine," he says in a quiet tone. "I'm going with you, so I'll be within reaching distance of your wrath."

Shoving the key in the lock, I turn the tumbler then yank the key back out. "Fine." I bite out and storm past him towards the stairs. "I'll take a page from your book and use you to get Taylor back."

My only response is a soft sigh and following footsteps.

Twenty-two

*T*he drive to Seth's is tense.

Jack's sitting in the passenger seat next to me, not making a single sound or movement. It's making me more aware of my anxious breathing, makes the drumming of my fingertips seem almost deafening. But I can't stop it. I'm nervous to confront another god, especially an unknown one to Jack, but I'm mostly terrified for Taylor.

How much has Seth hurt her because of me?

My fingers stop tapping against the leather and wrap tightly around it instead. When did Seth become so obsessed with me? How did I fail to see it? I really thought that when I broke things off between us it would be amiable. I should have known better after he ruined my date with Jack.

Jack.

Anubis.

I glance at him from the corner of my eye. I still don't

know how to wrap my mind around everything I've learned in the past hour. I wasn't lying when I told him it was too much, but it's not just for the reasons I told him. Those very much come into play, yes, but I'm also trying to work out the knots in my stomach and chest about us.

This stupid god means something to me.

Whether it's because I completely opened up to him or because of this connection we have, he's become important to me. But is the connection real? Does it only exist because of what he is? Did he use any of his prowess to lure me to him? Or is it because we're both hounds of the underworld?

"Is everything between us fake?" I whisper.

Jack doesn't hesitate to answer, and it makes it that much harder to decide if it's a lie or not. "No."

"How do I believe you?" Easing the truck to a stop at a red light, I wring my hands around the steering wheel. "How do I know that this isn't part of your power? Your plan?"

"You keep insisting you were part of my plan when I've told you that you weren't." He turns his head to look at me, but I don't have the balls to meet his gaze. "You were a surprise. I'll admit that you were also a distraction, but one I can't seem to fault or regret. I thoroughly enjoyed our time together, Valkyrie." When my brows furrow, he quickly adds, "and I don't just mean in the bedroom."

I don't answer Jack but take his answers and add them to the pile of 'what the fuck' topics in my mind. The light turns green, and I press down on the accelerator a little harder than necessary, the engine growling its excitement in response as it lurches through the intersection. When we finally pull into the parking lot of Seth's apartments, my pulse is pounding against the side of my neck.

Jack turns his body towards mine. "Remember that most gods are egotistical," he begins. "From the phone call, I can tell Seth is no exception."

"Why tell me this?" I ask, still not looking at him.

"Get him talking," he clarifies. "I'll have my phone recording it so you can take it to Scott."

I don't like the finality in which he said that. "What do you mean?"

He runs a hand through his silky black hair and sighs. "When I get closer to him, I should be able to tell who he is and from there I can assess how dangerous he is. Either way, our powers are stunted in this realm. I won't have all my strength to take him down, but neither will he."

Once again, my brows knit. "What the fuck are you saying, Jack?"

Our eyes meet. "That I don't know what's going to happen, but I'm going to have to take him to the underworld as soon as I can. So, get him talking before I take him away. A recorded confession to help your case."

"*Our* case," I correct. "It's still both of ours."

He gives me a faint smile. "Just get him talking."

I reach out and grab his forearm, his muscles instantly bunching and tensing under my touch. "What exactly am I supposed to tell Scott if you vanish?"

He looks down at the fingers wrapped around his arm.

"Hopefully the recording will be enough." He gently removes my hand and gives it a soft squeeze. "But you can tell him the truth if you need to."

I watch him slink out of the truck before grabbing my service Glock from the center console and follow suit. Locking my truck, I tuck my keys and phone into the front pocket of my hoodie. I shove the Glock into the back of my Yoga pants and cover it with the hoodie before leading Jack to Seth's apartment door. It's physically a short journey from the parking lot to the unit, but it feels like it takes hours to get there.

When I'm finally standing in front of the door, I hesitate for a second. I'm about to face off against a god who has my best friend captive because I broke up with him.

What in the actual hell? How did it come to this?

"I'm here, Valkyrie. You're not alone in this." Jack's soothing rumble comes from beside me.

I nod, which is a terrible thing to do with my blazing headache, and try to swallow down the despair and anxiety choking me. Pulling out my gun, I click off the safety despite knowing that it'll probably be as useless against Seth as it was against Jack. With a shaking inhale, I knock on the door. When Seth doesn't answer, I twist the handle and, finding it unlocked, push it open.

I cautiously poke my head in, scanning the living room that the entryway faces. Stepping in, I cradle the gun in both hands while trying to keep my posture relaxed. "Seth?" I call out. "Taylor?"

"In the kitchen, Val!" Seth calls merrily.

Jack has masked his aura, but I can feel him close behind me as I limp through the apartment towards the kitchen. I've been here countless times since Seth and I started seeing each other, but it has never felt as foreign as it does now. My eyes dart and scan everything, taking in the decorations and furniture with a new critical eye.

When I approach the kitchen, I reel back from the stench of blood, rot, and fruit. Scrunching my nose in a pitiful attempt to get rid of the stench, I step onto the tiled floor. Jack stays behind, his back pressed against the wall next to the kitchen entry.

"What is this?" I ask, looking over the chaotic kitchen.

There's fruit strewn across the counters. Some of it is fresh and bright, the others are overly ripe with dark green fuzzy spots on them. Small gnats fly over the piles of spoiled fruit before landing on them. Various colorful glass bottles are haphazardly tossed on the counter, some lying on their sides and spilling out suspicious dark liquids.

"Making wine, of course," Seth explains with a smile from his spot in front of the sink. He's standing there with a black butcher's apron, his hands twisting a bar-like knob on top of a wooden bucket. Small planks make up the bucket, almost like a barrel.

"Wine?" I echo, taking a small step forward.

"Yes, it is what I do, after all. Or did you forget that in

our weeks apart?" His tone is light, but his smile is mocking and cruel as he steps away from his wine press. He grabs a tattered towel from the counter and wipes at the dark red stains on his hands. He *tsks* when he turns to me and sees my gun. "Now, now, there's no need for the gun, Val."

I give him a disbelieving look. "No need? You kidnapped my best friend!" Remembering Jack's phone recording this, I go on. "Taylor doesn't deserve this, Seth."

He hums as he picks up a short, sharp knife and grabs a handful of strawberries, a mix of fresh and spoiled. "So, you said," he says. "But *you* do. I've never been rejected before, Val. You wounded me and then my pride when you chose a dog over me. Quite rude."

"I thought we had an agreement," I respond bitterly. "We were just bed buddies, Seth. I told you I didn't want a relationship."

The blade snaps down hard on the wood cutting board with a loud *thunk*. "And yet you went on a date with the guardian. Two of them at least."

"He's my partner," I stress, keeping the gun trained on him. "We're investigating the murders going on in town." My eyes narrow into a cold glare. "But you'd know all about them, wouldn't you?"

Seth hums noncommittally. "I believe we already discussed this."

"No," I shoot back. "We didn't. You went on and on about Ammit." I remember what Jack said about his ego and start to poke at it. "Or was she the one controlling you? After all, you were left to clean up all her messes, weren't you? A god reduced to an errand boy, it seems. First you lose the girl, then your supposed control. What a pity."

I don't realize he's thrown the knife at me until it sits buried in my thigh. Fuck that was fast. Way too fast. Maybe I pushed the god's buttons a little too hard. When I look down at the handle protruding from my flesh, the pain hits me and I try to muffle the groan. My fingers wrap around the handle, but then Seth's hand is around mine.

He takes the gun from my other hand as he grips my fingers tight around the handle. I spasm with pain as he moves it just a little towards the inside of my thigh. "Val, Val, *Val*," he chides in a disappointed, sad tone. "Why did you make me do that? I don't want to hurt you."

Anubis' aura flares wide and heavy at those words. I flinch but keep my eyes on Seth's as a cruel smirk twists the corner of his lips up. "There he is." He bares his teeth in a mockery of a grin. He tilts his head back and calls for Anubis in a louder voice. "Surely you know I felt that, jackal! Come on out!"

Jack steps into the kitchen with a growl rumbling in his throat. I look at him, but his raging, storming eyes are fixated on our hold on the knife in my thigh. "Let her go."

"No, and you're going to stay right there, dog. I could so easily slide this a little further inside her thigh and nick that femoral artery. I wonder how long it'll take a werewolf to bleed out," Seth says, forcing my gaze back to his. "But I don't want to kill you, Val."

"Y-you killed all those other women," I stammer through the pain and grit my teeth. "What's one more?"

He scoffs at me again and has the audacity to pet my hair with his free hand. "I didn't actually kill them; Ammit did." His eyes darken with anger. "But make no mistake that I chose each and every one of those women. I made the decision, not her. I am the mastermind, not that beast! Do you understand?!"

My free hand flies to his forearm when he moves the knife again, but I swallow down the cry of pain that tries to rip free from my throat. "Y-yes." I'm smart enough not to comment on the fact that Ammit killed a man a few hours ago. Definitely not one of Seth's choices since he specifies *women*.

"Good," he praises and pets my hair again. "If I didn't want you so badly, I would kill you just to piss off Anubis. It would bring me great joy to see him so angry. To take and destroy what he deems as his."

Jack lets out another deep growl, but it turns into a dry laugh. "Tell me, what are you more upset about? That she chose me over you, or that she kissed me?"

There's a tense beat of silence before Seth's aura explodes out of him like a bomb. I would have stumbled away from him at the sudden impact, but Seth's hand has tightened painfully in my hair. His blazing green eyes lock onto mine as he bares his teeth in a savage snarl.

"So, you did kiss him," he snarls low and dangerous. "I've waited for your kisses for months and yet you give it so freely and quickly to this—"

"Shezmu," Anubis suddenly states in an amused tone. "I should have known with all the missing heads."

Seth snaps his head towards Jack with bewilderment. "You baited me," he hisses, his grip easing on my hair but not my hand.

"You have always been one so easily riled," Jack muses and then cracks his knuckles. "But your fun is over. Summon Ammit, and let's go back home."

Seth tosses his head back and cackles. "Go back? Why would I ever do that?"

"Because Ammit is throwing the world out of order with her mindless killing," Anubis growls. "And you will be punished for aiding her escape."

He lifts a brow at my partner. "Exactly. So, tell me again why I would willingly go back?"

Is there any chance they can have this conversation without a knife stuck in my fucking leg? Every time Seth talks I'm terrified he's going to hack through my femoral artery.

I must make a small noise of protest because Seth turns his attention back to me. "And what do you think, Val?" Again, his tone is mocking and condescending.

"I think," I breathe through my nose to help manage the pain. "That I'd like this knife out of my leg. Then I'd like to get Taylor and go home."

Shezmu blinks at me before laughing. "Silly me, I completely forgot about your friend!" He lets go of my hand, but mine remains locked around the knife, fingers numb and stiff from his hold. "I'll go get her."

"She better be in one piece, Shezmu," Jack warns. "Head intact."

My stomach drops at that visual. "Why would you specify something like that?" I ask anxiously then look at Seth with desperation. "Why would he say that? Why would you remove her head?"

"Our victims," Jack reminds me.

I keep my stare on Seth despite the nausea rising in me. "What is with the missing heads?"

He shoots me a grin that used to leave my panties discarded on the floor, but now all it does is make me shudder. "For the wine press, of course."

I blink at him, refusing to comprehend what he's saying. "The...wine press?" I repeat slowly. "I don't understand."

His grin widens as he pets my cheek with his red-stained fingers. "Oh, I think you do. But, in case you really don't, let me give you a history lesson." He clears his throat dramatically and gestures at the barrel in the sink. "I am Shezmu, God of Wine and Blood. I'm also a deity of oils and perfumes."

Anubis snorts. "He is a demonic god, a lesser deity."

Shezmu snarls at the insult. "I was once called the Executioner of Osiris! He is the one who told me to use the heads of the wicked for my wine press!"

"Before you started giving your wine to other gods to increase their power," Jack sneers. "Then he forbade from you doing it!"

"Forbade?" Seth rolls his eyes. "The other gods love the power boost it gives them, and I love the favors they owe me. Why would I stop?"

My stomach hollows out again. "Wait. You make wine from *heads*?"

"Yes, the best blood is there, in my opinion," Seth says as a matter of fact.

My throat tightens and convulses with the need to vomit. I'm scared to ask the next question, but it's tumbling out of my lips before I can stop it. "And the wine you had me try?"

He grins at me again. "Which one?" He laughs and playfully taps my chin. "Just kidding." When my face relaxes with relief, his smile turns into a cruel smirk. "It was all of them."

Oh *gods*.

I've drank blood from pressed heads.

I cover my mouth with my free hand as I gag. Oh my gods, did that include the heads of my victims? "The bodies we've found? Their heads?" I manage to choke out the question even as my stomach roils with disgust.

"Of course. I can only keep them frozen for so long. Plus, it takes two to three weeks to ferment it all properly. The last bottle I left at your house was the second woman you found. I still have your first victim's head in the works," Seth muses.

"Stephanie…?" I murmur, remembering the woman I found at the strip club.

His hand cradles my face tenderly. "Oh, my Val, you look so pale. Don't worry, a little bit of wine will add some color to your cheeks. Good thing I have plenty."

I can't help or stop what's coming. I turn my head from his hold and stumble against the counter, throwing up onto the mess that was already there. The few fries I managed to wolf down earlier come out half-digested and settle onto the rancid fruit. I have to brace against the tile as I upchuck another violent wave. Seth's hand is on my back, rubbing circles along my sweatshirt, but his touch makes me vomit again.

"I was going to use that fruit," he chides softly. "But oh well."

"Why?" I croak, squeezing my eyes shut. "Why are you doing this?"

"Because it is my nature," he hums.

"Disgusting." I spit out and wipe at my mouth with the sleeve of my hoodie.

Seth's hand slides into my hair and yanks it back again. The knife shifts in my leg, and I cry out, the pitch drowning Jack's furious growl. "Stay back, Anubis! I'll hack her leg off if you step any closer!" There's a brief pause before he returns his attention to me. "You weren't complaining when my tonic helped your cramps, were you?"

I bare my teeth at him. "Are those also made from people?"

"Some," he admits. "Just depends on what it is."

I take in a shaky breath through my nose. "And Taylor?"

"Right, right, I keep forgetting about her." Seth slides his fingers through my hair as he releases it. He looks down at the knife in my leg and glances at my partner. "You should really be careful taking it out."

I gape at him as he all but skips from the room, as if he wasn't the one who had stuck the knife in me. As if he hadn't warned Jack to stay away from me this entire conversation. A swell of pain and utter repulsion hit me, and it forces me to close my eyes again as I breathe heavily through my nose.

"Valkyrie."

When I open my eyes, Jack is standing in front of me with a pained expression. "Get this thing out of my leg," I demand through gritted teeth.

He moves to my side. "Hold onto to me."

I do so without hesitation, all doubt and insecurities about us momentarily forgotten. When I press my face to his shoulder, he holds it there while his other hand wraps around the handle. One heartbeat passes, and then a second. When the third starts, there's a sickening wet sound as he swiftly pulls the knife out.

I bite down on his shoulder to stifle my scream. He doesn't move to stop me, just holds me tighter to him as he tosses the knife onto the counter. When I finally pry teeth off him, he squats down in front of me to look at the wound.

"How bad...?" I breathe, bracing my hands on his

shoulders as a different pain throbs throughout my leg and across my body.

"You'll need stitches," Jack states before he takes off his shirt and proceeds to tear off a portion of it. He loops it around my thigh and looks up at me in warning.

"Fuck," I curse and grip his shoulders tighter. "Okay, *okay*. Just…do it." No sooner do the words leave my mouth that the fabric tightens painfully around my thigh. I stifle another scream and dig my nails into his bare skin.

Jack gives me a few seconds before he stands and gently removes my hands from him. He holds them in his own and stares down at me. "No matter what happens, I need you need to remember what I said about us."

"What?" I breathe, squinting at him through my pain.

"Nothing was fake," he stresses. "Everything was real. If there's only one thing you believe from all of this, let it be that."

My gaze finally focuses on him as I meet his eyes. "Jack?"

He presses a quick, hard kiss to my lips before stepping back, putting a wide distance between us once again. Before I can ask him anything, Seth comes back to the kitchen, all but dragging my best friend behind him.

"Taylor!" I shout and try to move towards her, but my leg twinges in pain, unable to withstand the abuse afflicted to both its thigh and calf.

"Yes, yes, your precious friend," Seth taunts. He whirls Taylor around so that her back is to his chest.

My eyes well with tears as Taylor's normally bright blue

eyes meet mine. Both eye sockets are bruised, but one eye has a broken blood vessel, the white stained with swirling red. Her lips are chapped, the bottom one split and bleeding. Her face is pale, making the bruising along her cheekbone look almost vibrant.

"Val," Taylor whines in a quiet, broken voice and my heart feels like it splits in two.

This is all my fault.

"Tay, I'm so sorry. I am *so* sorry." The tears fall from the corner of my eyes. "It's going to be okay. I promise."

Seth grabs the same knife Jack threw onto the counter and presses it to Taylor's throat. I make a protesting, strangled cry and step towards them, but Seth shakes his head at me. "You shouldn't make promises you can't keep, Val."

"Seth, please—"

"Call me by my real name, Val. I want to hear it on your lips."

I lick my dry lips and force my eyes away from Taylor to look at him. "Shezmu," I begin. "Please let her go. I'll do anything you want."

"*Valkyrie,*" Jack warns in a sharp tone.

I ignore him, knowing full well that I will do anything to save Taylor. "Anything," I repeat.

Seth grins at me. "I was hoping you would say that." He presses the edge of the blade to her throat, causing a fresh bead of blood to mix with mine on the metal. "Although, I think I'm jealous that you care for her so much."

I swallow and force myself to take another step forward. "If you want me to cut her out of my life, I will." It would protect her from any of my future fuck ups. "Just let her go, and I'll do whatever you want."

Jack moves towards me, but Seth snarls at him and presses the knife harder against Taylor's neck, making more blood spill onto the knife. "Stay back, Anubis! I don't trust you!"

"Please listen to him," I beg, flicking my eyes to his then back to the knife at Tay's neck. "Don't make this worse. I'll do what I must for my friend."

"That's what I'm afraid of," Jack growls, the base of his voice so low and deep it makes a shiver skitter down my spine. "Do not promise a god anything, Valkyrie. Especially not a demonic one. I can't save you from that."

"I'm not asking you to!" I screech, very aware of the despair in my trembling voice.

"That's my girl," Seth coos, oblivious to the churning of my stomach. "Now, for my first demand, I want you to give me what you denied me for months."

I blink at him. "A…kiss?"

"Yes," he purrs. "A kiss."

"Absolutely not!" Jack shouts, aura flaring again with his anger. "Don't get that close to him again!"

Taylor's lips tremble before she speaks. "No."

Seth turns a bewildered glare on her. "Shut up, you! You're in no position to say anything!"

But Taylor knows I don't kiss people. How could she possibly even think of trying to protect me when I'm the reason she's in this fucking mess?

"I'll do it," I say as I take a few more steps towards them. When I'm close enough to him, he shifts Taylor to the side. "Let her go, and I'll do it."

"No," he scoffs. "Do you think I am stupid? You're far too clever, Val. I don't want you trying anything until I get what I want."

I glance at Taylor, who's minutely shaking her head at me, then back to Seth. "Fine." I rub at the pawprint at the base of my sternum, trying to pass it off as wiping sweat from my hands. "Okay." I lick my lips and lean towards him. After a brief hesitation, I lightly press my lips to him.

Anubis' snarl is almost deafening in response, but before I can pull away, Seth cups the back of my head. He presses our lips harder together, his teeth almost bruising until I'm forced to part my lips. His tongue sweeps into my mouth, and I force back a gag at the slimy feeling.

It's nothing like Jack's kiss.

After an eternity of discomfort, he pulls back from me with a wide, satisfied grin. His eyes almost look dreamy as he sighs with pleasure. "Exactly how I thought you'd taste. Now that that's done, let's move on."

Before I can blink or make a single move to stop him, he slashes the knife across Taylor's throat.

Twenty-three

I stare down at my friend as she falls to the floor, blood gushing out from the gaping slit across her throat. A high-pitched whine escapes my throat even as the rest of my mind shuts down with denial. Still, I reach for her, but I'm stopped by a hard grip on my arm.

Fury and pain consume me as I meet Seth's mocking expression. "I'm a very jealous god, Val. I had to eliminate my competition for your affection."

Without hesitation or regard for the possible repercussion of my actions, I swing my fist with full force into the god's throat. I feel a satisfying crunch against my knuckles before he stumbles back from me. As soon as there's distance between us, Jack tackles him. He slams Seth's head into the tiled floor with a savage snarl.

It all happens in the blink of an eye, but it still feels like it takes too long for me to finally drop down next to Taylor. I quickly cover her neck with my hands, trying to staunch the flow of blood pouring from her neck.

"I'm here," I whisper, as if the volume of my voice will do more damage to her battered body.

"V-Val," she chokes on my name, a splatter of blood spilling across her lips.

"Shh, don't talk." I'm only aware of the tears rolling down my cheeks when they splash onto hers. "Just stay with me, Taylor. It'll be okay. You're going to be fine." I repeat these promises to her over and over, praying to whatever god will listen that I don't break them.

I can hear snarls and grunts as Seth and Jack fight, their auras rising and filling the small kitchen as they try to overpower each other. I try to ignore it and drown out the familiar sound of flesh hitting flesh so I can focus on the sound of Tay's breathing.

"No, no, no!" I cry when her eyes begin to flutter shut. I want to shake her, but I'm scared to hurt her more. "Don't you fucking dare close your eyes, Taylor! You're not giving up on me, do you understand me?!" Her eyes snap back open at my panicked shouting but take a second to focus on me. "You can sleep all you want later, okay? But not now. I need you to stay with me."

I flinch when there's a loud bang followed by the cracking wood of a cabinet. When I hear the screech of metal scraping against tile followed by a hollow thud, I tear my eyes away from Taylor's and glance over my shoulder to make sure Jack is okay. Jack is straddling Seth's body with the knife sticking out of his side. Jack pulls it out without a second thought and jabs it down into Seth's shoulder. Seth snarls and bucks his hips, throwing Jack off him. I watch as he yanks the blade free before jumping to his feet. Jack is already standing again, hands raised and poised to fight.

"You're coming back with me, Shezmu," Jack states in a low growl.

The blonde god glares back at him defiantly. "You'll have to drag me there," he sneers.

Jack lifts a brow at him. "You say that as if it'll be a problem."

"I'm going to enjoy beating you, Guardian," Seth hisses.

He's oblivious to the swirl of black shadows materializing behind him, but my tingling pawprint tells me all I need to know. I hold my breath as three sets of gleaming red eyes appear from the mist. Before Seth can turn around, an arm wraps around his neck in a chokehold.

"Cerberus," I breathe in a mix of relief and awe as the other two triplets appear on either side of Seth, caging him in. When Taylor makes a gurgling sound, I snap my attention back to her and shake my head at her wide, questioning eyes. "I'll explain everything later. Her lips part as if she's going to speak, but I gently shush her. "Don't waste your strength talking. I'll tell you every secret I have after this, I promise."

"Give him to me," Jack's deep voice commands.

"We think not," Cerberus says, the three voices an echo

of each other. "This is our mark, after all."

"Mark?" Seth chokes out indignantly. "What are you talking about? You can't interfere with other factions, you fool!"

I can't help it; I look over my shoulder again as Cerberus responds. "Normally, yes. However, you have been marked by one of my hounds and thus you are mine."

Seth's protest sputters to a stop when he finally sees me glaring hatefully at him. "You?!" he spits in disbelief. "You're a hellhound?!"

"Indeed, she is. One of my favorites," the triplet behind Seth comments, arm tightening around his prisoner's neck.

"You knew this would happen." Seth's face blooms red with anger as he continues to stare at me as if *I'm* the one who did *him* wrong. He begins thrashing against Cerberus, clawing at the arm at his neck in a futile attempt to get to me. "I will fucking kill you, Val. Do you hear me? I will utterly destroy you. I will—"

Jack's fist slams into Seth's face before he can finish his threat. The nose shatters, causing blood to drip down Seth's chin. "You won't ever touch her again," he snarls low, grey eyes glowing with his rage. He shoves aside a triplet when he tries to stop him and grabs Seth's face, thumb and fingers digging into the cheeks. "Because if by some small chance you do, you'll be begging to be fed to Ammit in order to end your suffering. And you will suffer tenfold for everything you did to Valkyrie."

My heart flutters at that. The backstabbing bitch.

The two triplets not holding Seth swing at Jack simultaneously, forcing him to release Seth and jump back to dodge the attack.

"He'll already be busy begging us for mercy," one of the triplets says, clasping his hands behind his back as they flank Seth once again.

"You can't have him," Jack growls.

A triplet smacks Jack's hand away when he steps forward to grab Seth's arm. "He has been marked by my hound in the living world fair and square. He's ours."

"It doesn't work that way and you know it," Jack counters, balling his hands into fists. "This is our realm's problem."

The triples all bare their teeth. "No, Anubis. As soon as this demon released Ammit into the living world, it became everyone's problem. Souls meant and destined for other realms have been taken from us. The balance has been shifted, thrown off. You, the one who weighs hearts, should know all about the scales of balance."

Another low rumble from Jack has me turning my gaze to him. "I know." His nostrils flare as his aura does, the spike in energy swelling in the room once again. "But Osiris will not allow you to just take him."

The triplets laugh. "Allow? I'd like to see him stop us." With identical wicked grins, smoke begins to swirl around them again. "Tell your daddy that Hades sends his regards."

Jack lurches for them as they disappear, but his hand passes through the fading smoke, the four already gone. "Fuck!" he curses and shoves his hands through his hair. "I have to get him."

Get him?

"Jack?" I ask, voice hardly louder than a whisper.

He whirls towards me and the rage in his eyes dims when he meets my panicked gaze. He quickly closes the distance between us, looking at Taylor then back to me. My stomach clenches when he looks at me with pure remorse. "I'm sorry."

I snap my head back to Taylor and see that her eyes have closed. My panic surges. When did that happen? When did she slip away from me? I whine and lean over her, refusing to move my blood covered hands from the wound on her neck. I tilt my cheek over her lips and almost cry in relief when I feel her soft breath against my skin.

"She's alive," I exhale and look at him again. My relief withers when I see him handing his phone out to me, that same regret in his eyes. I blink at it and furrow my brow in confusion. "Why are you handing this to me?"

"I have to go," he states in a solemn tone.

"…go?" I repeat. "Go where?"

Jack's eyes briefly close as he seems to fight some inner battle. I hate the determined look in his eyes when he re-opens them. "I must go get Shezmu from Cerberus. He can't have him. I have to take him to Osiris."

I stare at him in disbelief, my mouth floundering as I try to wrap my mind around what he's saying. I mean, I *know* what he's saying. But he wouldn't really leave me right now, would he? With my best friend bleeding out on the floor because some deranged, sick god kidnapped her?

"You can't," I whisper. My eyes widen when he looks away with a flicker of shame. "Jack. You can't leave me like this."

Anguish contorts his handsome face when he turns back to me. "I have to, Valkyrie. He must be punished for what he has done. It will be worse if I don't take him back to my underworld."

My chest heaves with anxiety, fear lurking behind it with savage intent. "You *can't.*"

When I refuse to take the phone from him, he bends so he can place it on my lap. Before he straightens, he lightly runs his fingers along my cheek. "I wish I didn't have to, but I do. I hate to leave you, truly I do."

I watch in complete horror and incredulity as he stands back up to his full height. "Then don't! Don't leave me like this," I beg, eyes brimming with tears as he turns away from me.

He hovers his hand over the back of his neck and drags it up, following the curve of his head. As he does, a gleaming gold and black headdress with two tall, pointed ears appears in its wake. It finishes with a black canine snout when his palm reaches the front of his face.

I'm facing Anubis in his official headdress, but all I care about is being left alone like this. "Please don't leave me, Jack." More tears spill down my cheeks. "*Please.*"

His hands twitch before they ball into tight fists. "I'm

so sorry, Valkyrie," he says in a soft, sad voice but without looking at me. That manages to hurt even more. "I already dialed 911. You only need to hit the call button."

Before I can plead with him more, a wall of black shoots up in front of him. I watch with helplessness as he hesitates for a moment before walking into the void of black without so much as a glance over his shoulder. As soon as he does, the wall collapses and disappears back into the floor as if it had never been there. As if Jack had never been there.

He *actually* left me.

Before I can completely fall apart, Taylor coughs causing her body to spasm. I focus back on her and realize I'm completely fucked trying to do this alone. With great care, I remove one of my hands from her throat and grab Jack's phone. It takes a few tries to awaken his phone, but after wiping the bloodied fingers off on my leggings, the touch screen responds.

"*What's your emergency?*" comes the dispatcher's calm tone.

Somehow, I manage to slide into Val the Detective, hiding behind her as my world continues to crumble. "This is Detective Valkyrie Dalton of the LVPCU, and I need an ambulance sent to my location immediately. LVPCU tech Taylor Meyers has had her throat slit and is losing blood."

I can tell the dispatcher immediately snaps into action by the sound of rapid keyboard clicks through the phone. "*Alright Detective, I'm sending out the order now. You said her throat has been slit?"*

She's dying! I want to scream into the phone, but I refrain. "Yes, I have pressure on it, but it's still bleeding. She lost consciousness but is still breathing."

"Keep the pressure firm." When my breath stutters, her voice softens. *"They're on their way, Detective."*

"I need to focus on her wound so I'm going to hang up. Make sure Lieutenant Scott Carter responds to this call. I need him here for the case."

"Yes, ma'am. I'll make sure he's notified."

I don't bother to thank her because I'm not sure the words will make it out coherently. I drop the phone next to me after hanging up and spot what remains of Jack's shirt not far away. Keeping a firm hand on Taylor's neck, I reach for the shirt. I bundle it up and quickly press it to Taylor's neck. I didn't want to, but in that brief glimpse, I saw the wide wound along her delicate throat, and my dam breaks a little more.

I bend over Taylor again and press my forehead to hers. Her skin feels frigid compared to mine, and it scares me. Completely, utterly terrifies me. Closing my eyes, I gently stroke her hair with a shaking, bloodied hand. "It's going to be okay; it's going to be okay," I whisper over and over again.

Maybe if I say it enough times, I'll believe it myself.

I'm pulled from my numbness when I hear the front door slam open, a cacophony of loud voices soon following it. I can't make out anything they're saying, but I yell out for them. Again, words are outside my current capabilities. The sound of pounding feet and the rattling of wheels come closer until I hear them in the kitchen.

"Detective? We're going to need you to step back," someone says, and I pull my forehead away from Taylor's to stare at him blankly. The EMT swallows but isn't to be deterred. He puts his gloved hand near mine, putting pressure on Jack's shirt. "We'll take over from here, Detective."

Slowly, I pull my hand away from Taylor's neck, leaving her in far more capable hands. Aware that I need to get out of their way, I try to rise to my feet but stumble. Someone's arms loop under my armpits, hoisting me the rest of the way up and making sure I stay upright.

"Come on, Dalton," Scott says as he practically carries me from the kitchen.

My eyes stay on the EMTs huddled over Taylor until I'm completely removed from the room and deposited onto the living room couch. I close my eyes and shake my head, trying to dispel the ringing in my ears, but that only makes it worse.

"What in the hell happened, Dalton?" Scott asks.

I look up to see him standing in front of me with his arms crossed. "Taylor—" I start, but I choke on the words. "Seth—he had her. The killer." Gods, I can't form a single cohesive sentence. I rub at my face and freeze when I realize they're still caked with Taylor's blood. I jump to my feet in a panic and try to wipe the blood off me.

"Hey, hey, calm down," Scotts says, stepping closer to

me.

Calm down? I don't know what those words mean. He has no idea what I went through the past couple hours.

Scott grabs my trembling hands and steadies me as I sway. He looks down at my thigh and curses. "Gods, your leg! No wonder you can't fucking walk." He turns his head and shouts, "We need an EMT in here!"

I rip my hands from his and shake them at the EMT who pops his head into the living room. "No! *Taylor*," I say, voice wobbling. "Please, Tay—" I turn towards the kitchen, but my abused leg buckles, making me sit down on the couch once again.

Seth's couch.

With a cry, I'm on my feet again, ignoring my leg's protest. My calf and thigh are not happy with me, but I have to get out of this apartment. I have to get away from anything Seth. "I can't," I pant, feeling the tightness in my chest appear again.

"You refuse medical attention? Fine. But Dalton, your stubborn ass needs to answer my questions. What happened? Why didn't you call for backup? Where's Khoury?"

Jack.

Jack.

Jack.

My heart is cracking in my chest, and it feels like it finally splits in two as the EMTs wheel the stretcher out of the kitchen. They bandaged Taylor's neck, but blood is already seeping through it. Her skin is ashen compared to the white sheet under her.

I can't do this. I can't handle any of this. I need to go, to leave. To put distance between me and this fucked morning. I turn to the door and Scott tries to stop me, but I shove hard at his chest.

He staggers back but rights himself before he can fall. "What the hell, Dalton?!" He blinks at me when tears start pouring freely down my cheeks. "Val," his voice softens with worry. "Talk to me."

I shake my head at him. "Can't," I reply desperately, clutching my hands to my chest as I back away from him towards the front door. "Please."

Scott's face contorts into a mask of concern as I hobble away from him. "Do you want to come to the hospital with me? For Taylor?" he offers in a gentle voice.

So I can ruin her life even more? Put her in more jeopardy than I already have? I don't think so. She's safer away from me. "No," I cry.

He lets out a heavy sigh and rubs the back of his neck. "Alright. Well, go get some sleep. We can meet up and debrief later." I'm already at the door when he adds a pointless, "Be careful!"

It's far too late for that.

Twenty-four

I don't know how or when I arrived back home, but I'm here. I briefly wonder how many traffic laws I broke, how many things I hit. I blink and I'm in my bathroom, pulling my hoodie over my head. Dropping it carelessly onto the floor along with my bra. I untie the makeshift bandage around my thigh and remove my pants, wincing as I pull the blood matted cloth off the stab wound. I stare at the gaping hole and the fresh blood welling with indifference.

Taylor's is much bigger.

I bite down on my trembling lip and slide the leggings down my bandaged calf. I look at Jack's handy work for a second before my heart clenches with pain. Unable to stand the reminder, I rip off the bandages and ignore the pain as developing scabs tear away from the puncture wounds. I drop everything in a pile at my feet and turn to the mirror.

I'm covered in blood.

Most of it Taylor's.

With a high pitched, desperate whine, I hurry to the shower. But as I fling open the curtain, I'm assaulted by vivid flashbacks of Jack. I can almost feel the cold tile against my nipples as he pressed me against the wall, the pleasure his thrusts brought as he powered into me. Worst, though, is when I remember how he held me as I sobbed, his cheek on my wet hair as I tried to pull myself back together.

"I'm here."

That's what he said to me, but where the fuck are you now, Jack?

Where are you when I'm truly broken?

With a frustrated scream, I turn back to my sink. Flipping the water on, I grab a towel and soak it in the cold water before scrubbing at my skin. I don't wait for the water to get warm because I can't. I have to get all this blood off me, have to wash away the evidence that tonight ever happened.

I leave the towel in the sink when I'm done, not able to stand the sight of the pink-tinged water. Robotically, I head to my closet and pull on a pair of panties, a tank top, and sweats that immediately get stained with fresh blood. Once I'm dressed, I turn to my bed and once again freeze when I see phantom images of Jack taking me there for the first time. In its wake are brief images of when Seth and I had sex there too.

Stupid, backstabbing *fucking* gods.

Nope.

With plans to burn my mattress and bedding tucked

away for later, I head straight to my kitchen for a glass of water. My throat still burns from my purge, and I need something to wash down my regret that won't sting more. As I lift a glass cup from the drying rack, I glance up at my cupboard of indulgences. The glass drops from my hand and shatters on the floor as I recall what's still in there. I literally tear the cupboard door from its hinges as I fling open the cabinet.

Seth's wine bottle stares back at me.

An inhuman scream tears itself from my throat as I grab the bottle by the neck and fling it into the sink with as much force as I can muster. Despite the shards of glass flying in every direction, all I care about is the pungent scent of blood and wine filling my nose. I turn away from the sink, but it's too late. The headless victims on my whiteboard surface to the front of my mind, and my body spasms violently in response. My stomach roils and lurches, and my esophagus constricts until I'm bending over and throwing up straight bile onto my kitchen floor.

I'm gasping noisily between each wave, panic and disgust gripping each side of my chest and tugging it in opposite directions to make my pulse skyrocket. Tears are stinging my eyes and rolling down my cheeks. I wipe futilely at the bile-laced snot dripping from my nose with shaking hands.

When my purging quiets into useless dry heaving, I brace my hands on my knees and try to pull in deep breaths to calm my racing heart. Hesitantly, I turn towards the sink and gag at the sight of the wine. I quickly flip the tap up and let it run to try and wash down the liquid. I give it a full minute before I dare to look at the sink again. There's a ton of pieces from the broken bottle in it, but at least most of the wine has gone down.

Pretending not to see the splatters of purple along the counter, I splash cold water onto my face, trying to cool down my burning skin. I then swish around some water in my mouth and spit it back into the sink, watching as it slides down the drain. With a groan, I turn off the water and glance down at the mess of my kitchen floor. I can't ignore the clear glass shards from my cup or the drops and small puddles of wine. Black spots dance along my vision as my head swims.

I'm back in Seth's kitchen.

My thigh is throbbing with pain and slick with blood. My heart, however, is squeezing as I watch Seth slit Taylor's throat. The blood on the floor is mine to start with, but hers steadily joins mine. It's spilling down, down her body, spilling and splashing into a puddle. Even then it doesn't stop; it spreads all the way to me and sinks into my shoes. It's deep now, almost to my ankles. When I turn to Jack for help, he leaves me despite me begging him to stay. Hurt but undeterred, I focus on Taylor again. I trudge through the blood, which now has the consistency of mud, determined to save my best friend.

Now, I'm bending over her. I'm holding her wound shut, but her eyes are closed and she's barely breathing. I can save her. I can! Then there's a muffled sound coming from under my hand, and I pull my hands back in surprise. The slash across her throat has become a wide mouth, the flaps of her skin moving like lips.

"You did this to me," it says in Taylor's voice.

"No, I—" I try to protest.

"*No?!*" she screeches at me. "If you hadn't spread your legs for this demented god then I wouldn't be dead!"

A pang of immense pain knocks the air of my lungs. "Dead?"

"Yes, Val, *dead*! What did you think would happen? He's a god! You think he would miss severing my jugular?! You stupid bitch!"

Tears fall pitifully from my eyes. "I didn't know, Tay. I didn't know!"

"And that's an excuse? You fucked him for two months. Two. Months. And you didn't have any idea that he was a blood thirsty murderer? What kind of detective are you? A pathetic one, that's what."

I wrap my arms around myself as I feel my body rock back and forth. "I'm sorry. I'm so sorry."

"Then, to make matters worse, I warned you to break it off with him, didn't I? Maybe you should have fucking listened to me! Gods, you're so stupid!"

"I am," I agree, still crying. "*I am.*"

The neck-mouth scoffs at me. "And then you start to fall for *another* god. Gods, you dunce, didn't you learn with the first one?"

"I didn't know," I whisper.

"Because you're *stupid*, remember? Keep up, idiot." Her

tone turns exasperated. "At least Anubis knew that you were more trouble than what you're worth. He wasted no time in leaving your broken ass behind, did he?"

"No," I mumble.

"Exactly. What was it that you once asked me? Oh, I remember: *what can I really offer him?* I was trying to be nice at the time because you're so pitiful, but the answer is *nothing*, Val. Nothing good at least. You come with baggage and damage. Of course, he would split at the first opportunity! I would have too." A heavy sigh comes from the skin-lips. "But I didn't get a chance to leave you on my own, did I?"

I swallow thickly. "No."

"*No*," comes the mocking echo. "Instead, I got killed by your murdering fuck buddy. Oh, if I didn't say so already, thanks again for that by the way. Either way, at least I'm free from your sorry ass."

"I'm sorry." I squeeze my eyes tightly. "*I'm sorry.*"

"I'm sorry!" I shout and startle awake. Blinking, it takes me a second to realize I'm staring up at a kitchen light fixture. Fear seizes my chest when I think I'm still in Seth's apartment, but a quick scan of my surroundings tells me I'm in my own kitchen.

Rolling over onto my side, my head spins and pulses with pain. I touch the back of my head, and it comes away bloody. It was the same place I hit my head when Ammit attacked me, but why would it be bleeding again? And why does it hurt?

Whether it was exhaustion, or stress, or a combination

of the two, I must have fainted.

One thing is for sure, my unconscious is not a place I want to be. It's too hurtful. Too real. But, just how real is it? *Is* Taylor dead? I look around for my phone, but I don't think I brought it into the kitchen with me. But, even if I had it, I don't think I can actually make the call. What if my nightmares are right?

I can't handle it. I'm not strong enough. I need a blank, black void to rest in.

Using the lip of the sink, I grab it and hoist myself to my feet. With shaking hands, I carefully reach and pull down each one of my seven alcohol bottles. Not having the energy to go anywhere, I gather them up in my arms as if I'm hugging an old friend and sit down. Resting my back against the cabinets, I unscrew the cap of a fresh bottle of whisky and take a hearty gulp.

I wipe my mouth with the back of my hand and toss the cap somewhere into the kitchen. I won't need it since I plan on finishing the bottle. My eyes fall on a puddle of wine near my feet, and I sputter out a curse. Before the images can plague me, I bring the bottle to my lips again and chug down a good amount. Maybe I can swallow down the nightmares of tonight.

Before I know it, I'm more than halfway through the bottle and my eyes are drooping. But behind my eyelids are the images from tonight. With a wail, I force my eyes back open and down the rest of the bottle, not caring that some dribbles out from the corners of my lips. I roll the empty bottle away from me and press my palms hard against my eyes.

Once again, I'm in Seth's kitchen, watching as he slits Taylor's throat over and over again. Each time he does, her neck spits its spiteful truths at me as the kitchen fills up with blood. This time, however, Taylor's eyes are open and glaring at me with pure hate. Seth is laughing at my distress as the blood rises to my knees, Jack looking on apathetically. Every time I turn to him for help, he adorns his jackal headdress and disappears.

"*Jack.*" His name is a cry on my lips as I come to on my kitchen floor once again.

Sitting up, I wipe away the tears and reach for another bottle.

Twenty-five

I think it's a loud but muffled bang that causes me to momentarily surface from the haze of unconsciousness. Even though it feels like there's cotton stuffed in my ears, I think I can make out someone calling my name. It's a man's voice, but I squash the hope that it's Jack. Instead, I try to curl up in a ball, but my body refuses to listen. My limbs feel as if they weigh hundreds of pounds.

So, I give up and drop back under the surface.

"Dalton!" The man's voice forces me back to the realm of the living. It's louder now, making me think he's closer to me. I try to pry my eyelids apart to look at him, but I can't muster the energy to do so.

Even though my body feels heavy and numb, I can feel the vibrations in the floor as he quickly closes the distance between us. He lifts my shoulders from the ground, and as my limp head lolls against his chest, my nose finally wakes up and registers his scent.

Why is Scott here? He should be with Taylor. Unless my haunting visions and their accusations are right, and Taylor *is* dead. Dead because of me.

My body spasms and Scott quickly angles my head to the side, making sure I don't choke on my liquid vomit. Bile mixed with whiskey, tequila, and vodka should burn coming back up, but I'm blissfully still numb. A part of me mourns the fact that all the alcohol I forced down my throat is now wasted on the ground.

"Gods Val, what did you do? You're freezing!" Scott says once fluid stops spewing from my mouth.

Am I? I don't feel anything.

"Val?" He shakes me suddenly, and my lungs respond with a sharp inhale as if they hadn't had air in a while. "Damn it, mutt! You better keep breathing!"

I just want to sleep.

I must have dozed off again because now I hear Scott talking sternly to someone. "—vomiting and has a slow pulse. She's cold to the touch and her lips are blue, but she's managing uneven breaths." A brief stretch of silence before he speaks again, this time more urgently. "She just started seizing! Get someone here now!"

Oh, he's right. If I concentrate on it, I can tell my body is trembling. No, not trembling, it's jerking spasmodically. Even if I had some semblance of control over my limbs, I doubt I could stop it.

Scott's arms lock around me, holding me tight to him.

"I'm going to kick your ass for this, Dalton!" he swears in a low hiss. "I swear to all the gods that once you're okay, I'm going to kick your fucking ass."

I think he means *if* I'm okay.

Still, I want to apologize to him. I let Scott down in more ways than one. The words are on my tongue, but my lips won't move. My body isn't my own right now, and I think that terrifies me a little.

A surge of regret swells in me with the growing fear that I might actually die. I think of all the people I won't see when I die. Unless they are marked for the Greek underworld, I won't see my loved ones ever again. Taylor is just at the top of my list, but Scott is there too. So is Jack. Then there is the family I have pushed away for a decade. My supportive, loving parents who never gave up on me, despite my silent treatment and brush offs.

And Athena, my younger sister by two years. She used to look up to me until I pushed her away and ignored her existence. I never told her, but I make it a point to know what show she's currently working with on the strip. Whether it's Broadway or the circus shows, I try to attend at least one.

I miss my family.

I never stopped missing or loving them. I only kept a distance between us to keep them safe from me, but I know I hurt us all in the process.

As the tide of black begins to swallow me down again, my fear turns into despair. I lost my chance to tell everyone how much I love them, and that's my biggest regret.

"Are you boarding?"

I blink my heavy lids open and am greeted with the sight of pale green. My toes twitch and curl into the silky sand. I marvel at its softness as I do each time I'm here. But wait, why am I here? When did I get to the underworld? Did Cerberus summon me?

"Valkyrie Dalton," the scratchy but kind voice calls. "Are you boarding?"

I lift my head and see a frail old man in a boat. His eyes and cheeks are sunken in, hair and beard grey with age. He's leaning on his pole for support, back bowed with what I presume is the weight of his job.

Charon, the ferryman.

My eyes run over his rust-colored robe before dropping to the ferry. The Styx's water laps at the side of the boat, ghostly hands rising from the surface to try and find purchase on the wood. The ferryman doesn't bother to bat them off; everyone knows the souls will never be pulled from the depths.

There's a splash on my toes as the ferry rocks, and I drop my gaze to my feet again. I startle at just how close I am to the shoreline. Too close. One more step and I'll be in the water. I go to take a step back, but my feet feel as if they're rooted in place. Panicked, I look up at Charon, but he offers me a small smile and holds out his hand.

"Coming?"

I open my mouth to ask him why I'm here, but I nearly choke as I realize there's something metallic on my tongue. I spit it into my hand and feel the blood drain from my face at the sight of the gold coin. My payment to the ferryman. Why am I so perfectly set up to cross the Styx? To journey to the afterlife?

"I will take your payment," Charon says, gnarled fingers gesturing at my gold coin.

Hesitantly, I start to hold it out to him. I pause, my fingers tighten on the coin as a sense of wrong washes over me. I can't figure out why I'm here or how I came to be here. What happened before I got here? What was I doing?

"Are you giving up then?" a familiar voice asks from behind me.

The same voice but with a slightly different inflection continues, "Pity. I thought you were stronger than that."

"What a waste," another comments.

I turn my head and see the triplets standing near me, hands shoved in their pockets. My brow furrows as I take in their words. "Give up?"

"Life became too hard, did it?" The one on the left says with a sigh.

The one in the middle rolls his blood red eyes. "Pathetic."

"We just assumed you were stronger, Val," the right one says with a disappointed frown.

I lick my lips nervously. "I don't—what do you mean?"

I ask.

The three of them scoff at the same time, but one asks, "have you already burned it from your memory? All the things that happened in Seth's apartment?"

"Or rather, Shezmu's apartment," another corrects.

My fingers squeeze the coin tightly as memories rush back to me. I tried so hard to drown them and push them away, but Cerberus resurfaced them with that name. All my hard work gone, like it was nothing. Was it too much to ask for a moment's peace after what I went through? I just wanted it all to stop. At least for a little bit.

I glance around nervously, looking for the Egyptian god that ruined my life. "I-is he here?"

They all tilt their heads at me. "No," they begin. "Your lover took him back."

It feels like they sucker punched me in the heart. "Jack?"

"*Anubis*," they correct.

"Right," I mumble and drop my gaze to the sand again. "You knew who he was the whole time, didn't you? He's your counterpart."

"We did, and he is."

I rub at my chest, trying to relieve the ache. "Did you also know it was Shezmu who was committing the murders?"

"Not exactly. We didn't know he was the one who released Ammit into your world, but we knew it had to be one of the underworld gods. That is why we wanted you to mark them so we could delve out our own punishment for them disrupting the balance."

My brows furrow. "Cerberus, I don't understand that

part. Why was I able to mark Shezmu, but not Jack? They were both in the living realm, like you said, so shouldn't it have worked on both of them?"

"No, not with Anubis," one explains. "He is our counterpart, as you said. He is the guardian of Duat, Egypt's underworld. He is there to judge the souls that enter the Hall of Maat. No soul gets past him, living or dead. We are both built into the structure of our underworlds, not simply a soul residing in it."

I bite at my bottom lip, picking at the skin there. "Kissing him was a relief." It was soft and sensual but could also be hard and unyielding in the best way. It was perfect. "It didn't come with any visions." Cerberus doesn't reply so I change the subject. "So, anyways, I take it Jack went back to Egypt's realm."

Again, they respond as one. "He did."

"But he had quite the tongue lashing for us," a triplet provides. When I snap my head up, I see it's the one on the left who has spoken. "He believes we took advantage of you at such a young, impressionable age."

My brows knit together even as a warmth spreads along my chest. "He yelled at you for making me a hellhound?" Why would Jack do that after abandoning me? What would be the point?

"Yes," the middle one grumbles. "As if we forced you to make the choice."

I loosen my fingers, letting the coin lay flat against my palm as I stare down at it. "You didn't force me," I whisper. "But the alternative wasn't really a choice, was it? What fourteen-year-old would choose to die, Cerberus?"

There's a beat of silence before he answers. "One that was weak," one starts.

"Your hardships at that young age made your spirit stronger, believe it or not," another continues.

"Your turmoil over being bullied for years groomed you to be a hellhound," the last finishes.

Anger surges into my veins as I lift my head to glare at them. "Excuse me? Do you know how fucking hard it was for me to go through all that? I still have hang ups from what those girls did to me!"

They nod, not even trying to contradict me. "We know. We understand that it was grueling and crushing but look at how strong it made you."

I sputter in disbelief. "Strong? How can you say that? Look at me now! I'm a fucking wreck!"

"We are talking about back then when you didn't cross the Styx," they say. "A weaker soul would have taken their chance to escape the hardships of life."

The defiance fizzles out of me. "Maybe I chose wrong then. Life only got so much harder after becoming one of your hounds. Look me now, Cerberus. I have no family, no friends, no lover. I'm an alcoholic who has seen better days."

Their eyes soften but not with pity. "We see you, Val. We only wish you could see yourself. You are stronger than ever despite your unnecessary sacrifices. Especially recently. Do not let these series of unfortunate events undo everything that you are. Do not let it stop you from *living* on. We were not lying when we said you're one of our favorites." They jerk their head towards Charon, who's still standing there with his hand out, patiently waiting for his payment. "That alone is why you are getting this rare third chance."

Third chance?

I look at the coin in my hand once again then at the souls wailing in the murky waters, their wails more audible now that Cerberus is here. Their begging falls on three sets of deaf ears as Cerberus keeps his attention on me.

Taking the offer, I tip my hand over and drop the coin onto the sand. It instantly disappears under the green grains, hiding away so that no one else can use it. Once it's removed from my person, I'm able to take a step back from the river. When I look at the ferryman, he gives me a peaceful smile and a bow of his head before pushing his boat off the bank. I watch as the water carries him away before turning back to the triplets.

"I don't want to die yet," I admit in a soft whisper.

"Then don't," they don't smile, but I think I can hear something akin to fondness in their tone.

"I *won't*," I reply haughtily, but with a small smile.

They lift a mocking brow, but it lacks any bite. "Then it's probably time for you to go back and wake up."

Twenty-six

*T*here's a beeping sound near me. I reach for my alarm clock, but there's some resistance before I smack against something cold.

What the hell?

I open my eyes but immediately close them with a flinch. Why is it so bright? I count a few seconds then pry them back open, ignoring how they burn in response. I blink them into focus and furrow my brow at the tiled ceiling above me.

Hearing the sound again, I roll my head to the side and see that it's not my alarm clock. Instead, it's a computer screen displaying vital signs. I drop my gaze down to my hand and see that the cold thing I hit is a metal rail guard for the bed. The resistance I felt is the IV nestled into the crook of my elbow.

I'm in the hospital.

I squeeze my eyes shut and take a deep breath, trying to

push back the memories of when I was fourteen and waking up in a similar way. Back then I had died. I was terrified at the idea of dying, of crossing the murky water of the river Styx, but then Cerberus gave me an option and I was sent back to the living after agreeing to become a hellhound.

Fragmented memories come back to me, and I realize that once again Cerberus gave me a choice. I chose to continue living, chose to remain a hellhound. I had too many loose ends, too many regrets to just die. Cerberus had called me one of his favorites, told me that was the only reason I was getting this rare third chance, but I think maybe he knew just how much regret I had.

"How long are you going to pretend to be asleep?"

I jolt at the sound of the voice and open my eyes. Turning my head to the right, I see Scott reclined in a chair, arms crossed tightly over his chest. It takes me three attempts to finally get out his name. "Scott?"

He hums in the back of his throat, eyes narrowing on me. "What the fuck were you thinking, Dalton?"

"What?" I croak.

"*What?*" he echoes in disbelief. He leans forward, hands on his knees. "I asked what the *fuck* you were thinking when you tried to kill yourself!"

I jerk back from the vehemence of his shout, but the pillow cushions my throbbing head. "I wasn't."

Scott stands from the chair so abruptly that it tips back and crashes with a loud smack on the linoleum. "*Don't,*" he warns with a baring of teeth. "Don't you lie to me when I'm the one who found you!"

I close my eyes and scrunch my brow as I try to remember what he's talking about. Brief clips of him calling my name and yelling at me. When I open my eyes again, I see his lips are now pressed hard together in a thin line. "Scott—" I start, but he cuts me off.

"Severe alcohol poisoning along with an infection in your leg. That's what the doctors said." His nostrils flare as he points to my legs hidden under the blankets. "You consumed so much alcohol, your body couldn't fight off the infection in your thigh! Luckily the wounds in your calf weren't infected, but they still had to pump your stomach and flush you with fluids to get your system somewhat regulated again!"

I keep my mouth shut as he angrily paces along my bedside. I honestly didn't realize I had done so much damage to my body. It wasn't my intention.

Scott stops at the foot of my bed and rubs his mouth before looking at me. "The damage had already been done to your leg by the time your healing could kick in. You have scars now, Val."

I swallow and give a small shrug. "They're just scars, Scott. It doesn't matter."

He hisses and slams his hands down on either side of my feet. "If you had just gotten the EMT to look at it, you wouldn't have any!" His hands ball into fists as he drops his gaze from me once again. "If I had insisted you be looked at, you wouldn't have them." His voice quiets. "If I had dragged you to the hospital with me, you wouldn't have done this to yourself."

Shame hits me like a freight train. "Scott, *no*. This isn't on you. Don't try to take the blame for my stupid actions." When he looks up at me, my eyes sting at what I see there. He really thinks this is his fault. "I wasn't trying to kill myself."

With a deep breath, he uncoils his hands and straightens. "What other explanation could there be?"

I fold my hands in my lap and look down at them. "I wanted everything to go away, but not in the way you're thinking. I didn't want to die. The images from that night—" I take in a shaky breath as the memories try to resurface. "They were too much. Every time I closed my eyes, I saw everything happening again and again. But it kept getting *worse*. My mind started to twist what happened, and it wouldn't leave me alone. I wanted to sleep without the nightmares, to fall into a black abyss and deal with everything later. I couldn't handle it, Scott."

"You found your abyss, Val," he states in a firm but not unkind tone. "At the bottom of four bottles. *Four*. Even for a wereanimal, that's an insane amount to consume in the nine hours I left you. And I don't even know how fast you drank them."

Four? Gods, I thought it was only two. "Every time I woke up from a nightmare, I drank more. It wasn't to kill myself," I reiterate. "It was to sleep without any dreams."

Scott walks over to the chair and steps on one of the legs so that it lurches itself back up into the correct position.

"At the scene, you looked more shaken than I have ever seen you. Despite needing answers, I tried to give you time to recuperate. But after listening to the recording, I realized just how traumatic it must have been for you.

"Still, I waited eight hours to give you ample sleeping time, but when you didn't answer any of my calls, I panicked. My instincts told me something was wrong, so I rushed to your apartment, blowing up your phone the entire way. Standing at your front door, I heard your phone ring, but you weren't answering. I pounded on the door, but still nothing. Your door was unlocked so I opened it and called your name. That was when I smelled everything."

There's a beat of silence before he continues. "You have no idea what it was like to find you like that," he says in a low voice, not looking at me. "Cold and barely breathing, then throwing up and seizing. I know we have our spats, Val, but I never wanted to see you like that." His voice gets a little wobbly as he continues. "I never had siblings, but I imagine if I had a little sister, she would be like you. A bratty one."

I let out a weak chuckle. "Does this mean I call you big bro?"

"Absolutely not," He sniffs and flops back down into the chair. There's a moment of silence between us, but then he asks the question I knew was coming. "Was it that horrible?"

"Yes," I whisper as I look at him. "It was all centered around my choices and I think that's what made it so much worse. If it had been some random person, I don't think it would have hit me so hard."

Scott crosses his arms over his chest again. "Like I said, I listened to the recording on the phone." He pulls Jack's phone out of his pocket. "I found this where you and Taylor had been in the kitchen. I went through it looking for answers."

I try to swallow the dry lump in my throat. "That's Jack's phone."

"Oh, I know. It became apparent when I was going through the pictures."

Scott gives me a pointed look, but I have no idea what it could mean. "So, the recording worked?" I ask.

"In telling me what happened? Yes. I'm still trying to wrap my mind around the fact that gods can freely walk among us. I mean, it shouldn't come as a surprise to us monsters, but the humans on the other hand…" He scratches at the stubble on his chin. "That's ultimately the problem, I suppose."

I frown. "I don't think they can freely walk among us. Shezmu escaped."

Scott lifts a brow at me. "What about Anubis and Cerberus?"

I shake my head. He had me there. "I'm not sure, but I think that there are rules they have to abide by."

"Either way," he starts. "How do you think the humans are going to handle that? Half of them still can't stomach the fact that monsters are real and live among them. What are they going to do about gods?" He doesn't wait for me to answer. "They'll panic. It'll be worse than the riots that broke out with the Monster Movement, Dalton. Everyone's religion will rebel. Think about Christianity and Catholicism. They reject any other god, so what do you think will happen when they find out there are many gods for all different realms?"

I bite at my chapped bottom lip. "It'll be bad," I agree. "I knew it was going to be an issue when we found out who was behind everything, but Jack insisted on giving the recording to you so that you knew what happened."

Scott gives me a look too close to pity for my liking before continuing. "I appreciate knowing the truth no matter how messed up it is. We'll have to spin the story and push the blame onto someone else. The Lord of Las Vegas owes us a favor for her vampire losing control." At my affronted look, he scoffs at me. "Gods Val, we aren't going to kill one of her vamps, but we'll have her come forward and confirm it was one of her people who did it. At least it will put the public at ease knowing the murderer is dead."

"Or whatever Jack is going to do to him," I mumble.

"You mean Anubis?" Scott corrects softly.

Why does everyone have to keep correcting me? Why can't he stay my Jack for a little while longer? I don't want the good memories I have of him tarnished. They're already wilting under his abandonment and lies.

He pushes on when I stay quiet. "To think I had Anubis and one of Cerberus' hellhounds working for me."

I startle and look at him, but he places the phone on the

mattress next to my leg. "Oh, the recording," I mutter lamely. I stare at Jack's phone but don't make a move to grab it. "Do you still want that hellhound working for you? Now that you know what she is? What she caused?" I ask quietly, almost scared of his answer.

"That depends." When I tear my eyes from the phone to look at him, he nods at the machines I'm hooked up to. "Is this going to be a problem? Your drinking?"

I shake my head. "No, this won't happen again, Scott. I promise."

His face grows serious once again. "What about here?" He taps his temple. "You went through a lot. If drinking was your way to escape what happened, then your trauma may try to manifest in different ways." He sighs at my guarded expression. "Look, I know it's not easy to admit you need help, but I really think you should try to talk to someone. You need to get out what happened."

Who in the world could I possibly tell what happened without censoring the fact that gods were involved? Still, I can't bear to let him down. "I'll think about it."

"Good." He nods in approval then stands. "Because not knowing for three days what was going to happen to you aged the human in me."

Three days? "That's how long I was out?" I ask in disbelief. "Three days?"

"Yep. Between you and Taylor, my tiger is going to grow grey stripes." He must have seen the color blanch from my face, or maybe it was the tightness in my shoulders, because his face turns into a mask of pity again. "If you weren't going to ask about her, I was going to bring her up."

"S-she-" I fist the thin blanket in my hands so hard a knuckle cracks. I'm saved from having to find my words when his head cocks to the side, ear tilted towards the entrance. A smile curls up his lips as he heads to the door and pulls it open.

Standing there in worn jeans and a cream sweater is my best friend. Her neck is covered in bandages, but there's no blood to be found. With her werewolf healing, most of the bruises have faded and her cheeks have filled back out. She looks freshly showered, blonde hair slightly damp and curling. She looks vibrant and clean and so alive that tears are filling my eyes.

Taylor is alive.

Alive.

I make a pitiful whine and let the tears fall again. Gods, I'm so tired of crying, but these are new and welcomed. These are relieved, happy tears. I bury my face in my hands as a wail escapes me, embarrassed at the outburst but not able to stop it. Nor do I really care to.

I hear heavy stomps across the floor coming to my bed followed by a soft "Val?"

Taking a second, I suck in a shaky breath and lower my hands from my face. I'm met with a furious blonde wolf. And I mean *furious*. "Tay?"

No sooner does her name leave my lips that a stinging slap meets my cheek. I go to lift my hand to touch the tender skin, but my arms are pinned down as hers wrap tightly around me.

"You stupid bitch," she wails, but it's not at all spiteful like in my nightmares. "How dare you?! I wake up in the hospital with stitches in my neck, but you're nowhere to be found. I thought he got you, that he killed you! I tried to leave so I could find you!"

She's making my ear ring with her yelling, but I won't push her away. Having her hug me is something I never thought would happen again. I wiggle my arms out, mindful of the IV, and wrap them around my small friend.

She cries harder at the contact. "But they wouldn't let me leave! My throat wasn't healed enough." She squeezes me harder. "And then Scott tells me you're here. That you almost died! He said it looked like a suicide attempt, but I told him he was fucking wrong because you're you! You'd never be so fucking stupid!"

"I didn't," I tell her firmly. "It was an accident. I didn't mean to."

She roughly pulls back from me but keeps her hands firmly on my shoulders. "I know that!" she shouts and gives me a hard shake. "But I was so worried!"

"Taylor, baby, come on. Let your friend go," a soft voice says.

We both turn our heads to look at the human woman at the door, Bryan standing beside her with a bemused expression.

"Hold on, mom!" Taylor says and whips her head back

to me with a fierce look. "You're not allowed to scare me like that ever again, you got me?"

I give her a watery smile. "Or what, you going to slap me again?" It's a shitty attempt at lightening the mood, but it manages to get a weak smile from her.

"Most definitely," she snips, but gives me another hug, this one gentler. "But seriously, never again, Val."

"Never again," I promise as I hug her back.

"Good." She pulls away from me again and wipes at her wet face before pointing an accusing finger at me. "And don't forget about the other promise you made me."

To tell her all my secrets? I didn't forget. She's going to get all the dirty, gritty details of my life. It's a payment I'm willing to make for her being alive.

"I won't," I tell her.

"Come on, Tay. We need to get your neck checked out," Bryan calls from the door.

I give her a smile when she gives me a worried look and watch as she walks to her intended mate. They hold hands while her mother lovingly strokes Taylor's hair. I'm hit with a pang of longing as they disappear from view.

Scott clears his throat to gain my attention. "I would have slapped you myself, but it's much more appropriate that she did."

I give him a faint smile and rub at my cheek. "I deserve it."

"You do," he agrees before gesturing at the tray to my left. "I also brought your phone. I wasn't sure when you would wake up, or if I would be here, so I wanted to make sure you had some communication with the world when you did."

"Thank you, Scott." My chest tightens as I realize just how inadequate those words are. He deserves so much more than those three words. "Really, I mean it. Thank you for saving my life. I wouldn't be here if you hadn't come to check on me."

He ducks his head in embarrassment before nodding once. "I'll leave you to get oriented. Let me know when they discharge you, okay?"

"I will." I'm making a lot of promises lately, but I intend to keep all of them.

After he leaves, I reach for my phone on the tray. I pull up my texts and read each and every one from Taylor. They range from worried to angry, but I cherish each one. Going back to my messages, my stomach clenches when I see I have a new one from my mom sent two days ago. I quickly click on it and read the message.

Hi honey. Your father and I saw your boss' press conference regarding the murders! Please be safe! We love you!

I read it three more times, my heart tightening more each time. Before I can talk myself out of it, I click on my mom's name. The machine next to me beeps as my pulse quickens, and I shoot it a venomous look for calling me and my nerves out.

It only takes two rings before the line picks up.

"*Val?*" My mom's voice is hesitant and concerned. Maybe a little breathy too.

Is she as nervous as I am to talk?

"Honey? Is everything okay?"

She probably suspects the worst since I never call her first. I cringe at myself, knowing damn well that I'm always the first to hang up.

Gods, I really have been horrible to her. To all of them.

"Mom," I wail, unable to help it. I feel like I'm that small, bullied child again.

"Valkyrie?" she calls back and I can hear her voice tremble. I can hear the love and worry she has for me in the way she says my name. *"What's wrong? Are you okay?"*

I'm struggling to find words again, but this time it's because I'm caught up in the sound of my mother's voice. How can she still love me so much when I've done nothing but hurt her?

"Honey, you're scaring me," she cries, a faint sniffle coming through the phone. *"Where are you? I'll come to you right now."* She hesitates briefly before adding, *"I mean, if you want me to?"*

I'm a total wreck, and all I want is my mom.

I choke on a cry as I try to hold it back long enough to get out one little word. "Yes."

Twenty-seven

*M*y mom and dad had showed up half an hour after
the call and spent the whole day with me in the
hospital. It was a tearful reunion, full of tight hugs and whispered apologies.

I gave them a very abbreviated explanation as to why I
was here. Obviously, I left out the gods and my own status,
but I told them my ex was the murderer and that he had tak-
en my best friend hostage. I explained how he hurt her and
that I couldn't do anything to stop it.

I was embarrassed to explain that I gave myself alcohol
poisoning. That my leg had been infected because I neglected to clean it or get it checked by a doctor. They didn't need
to know that it had been stabbed with a knife that had been
used to cut rotten fruit.

When I was done explaining myself, my mom and dad

were visibly upset. It was the second time I ever saw my dad cry, and that added to my shame.

They offered help. Offered to find me counseling, but I told them I would look into it myself. I wasn't sure how I was going to go about finding the right person, but it might be helpful to talk about my trauma to someone. Especially since I didn't sleep for shit last night.

"You all set, Val?"

I look up at my mom as she walks into my hospital room and give her a warm smile. The doctors said I can go home today so she insisted on being the one to pick me up. She looked so determined yesterday that I couldn't say no to her.

So, when Taylor called me yesterday and also volunteered to take me home, I told her my mom was picking me up, and she burst into tears on the phone. It's why I love my best friend so much; she knows exactly how big and important something is without me telling her.

"Val?" my mom says, gently touching my cheek. When I startle, she jerks her hand away and my heart hurts at the wounded look in her eyes.

From my sitting position on the edge of the bed, I wrap my arms around her, resting my cheek on her shoulder. One of her arms comes around my shoulders as her other hand pets my hair. "I'm sorry," I mumble into her shoulder. "You surprised me. I was staring off in space."

She hums in understanding. "Everything okay?" She clicks her tongue at herself. "Silly me, I know it's not. I'm just worried about you, Val. You went through so much."

I nod once, still holding her tightly to me, basking in the comfort only a mother can give. "I did," I agree in a quiet tone. "But I'll get through it."

"I know you will," she says confidently. She pulls back and cups my face in her hands. "You've always been the tough one. I mean, just look at you! You survived turning into a werewolf all those years ago."

Before I joined the LVPCU, I told my parents I had been turned by a werewolf my last year of high school. It was my cover story, and they needed to be aware of it since I was joining the preternatural branch of the police force. It's also the excuse I gave them as to why I needed physical distance between us. I claimed I was scared of losing control and hurting them. They believed me because why wouldn't they? When I was an asshole teen, they thought I was going through one hell of a rebellious phase. What excuse did I have as an adult?

I wanted to tell them the truth here in the hospital room, but I think a part of me was still scared of how my father would react to the hellhound name. Bringing up Cerberus after I died didn't go well the first time, and I didn't want anything to ruin our reunion.

"Yeah." I let go of her and stand up when she steps back. A sigh of relief escapes me when my leg doesn't protest in any way. "How's dad taking it?"

Mom purses her lips together and tucks her black hair

behind her ear. It's grown to the middle of her back, wisps of grey starting to show at her temples. There are laugh lines at the edge of her eyes and mouth, and I'm now a bit taller than her. But otherwise, she looks the same as when I was a kid.

"He's adjusting," she finally says with a sigh. "I think he feels responsible for you. A dad is supposed to protect his little girl, but he feels like he's let you down a lot." Her voice softens. "Especially when you were attacked, then when you were turned, and now with this near-death accident. It's hard on him."

"It's not his fault. None of it," I say as I grab my possessions from the bedside. "I know I didn't make things easier for us, Mom." I tuck my phone in one pocket of my jeans and stuff Jack's in the other. It feels much heavier than mine, but I know it's all in my head.

"Val," my mom begins, but pauses when we pass a nurse on our way to the elevator. Once it's only us in the elevator, she continues. "I understand you keeping us away after you were bit, but I'm not stupid."

I furrow my brow at her. "What do you mean?"

She turns towards me with a serious expression. "I know you saw something when you died. You said you met Cerberus, and I believe you." When I tense, she grabs my hand in hers. "I never agreed with what your dad said to you. We fought about it for days. When I was younger, I was really into Greek mythology. I even considered it for my undergrad."

My mouth drops open. "What? I had no idea."

She gives me a little shrug. "My grandmother was from Greece. She didn't follow any of the old gods, but she used to tell me some tales in passing. It sparked my interest." She squeezes my hands as the elevator comes to a stop. "But I believe you, Val. You changed so much after you died, and that was the only thing that would make sense."

I don't know what to say to her. "Thank you for believing me." What else can I add?

She leads me from the elevator to the exit and waits until we're alone in the parking lot to continue. "Did he do something to you?"

Her tone is so concerned that I'm answering before I can really think better of it. "Yes, but not like that."

She stops us at her car, one I'm not familiar with. "Val, you can tell me anything. I want you to know that, okay? I'll always support you."

I hug my mom again, closing my eyes so that I don't cry. "Thank you, Mom."

We stay like that for a few moments longer before pulling apart.

"Okay, let's get you home!" she says, wiping at a tear.

"Oh, Val..."

I wince with embarrassment as my mom trails off. We're

standing in my kitchen, taking in the pure chaos of it. Wine is splattered all over the cupboards, counter, and floor from when I threw it in the sink. Glass shards from both the bottle and my cup are scattered on the floor, mixed in with piles of vomit and smeared blood. Then there are the empty alcohol bottles lying carelessly on their sides.

The remaining full ones stare at me expectantly.

I turn towards her, forcing my gaze from the bottles. "Um, thanks for dropping me off, Mom. Tell dad and Athena I say hi."

She drops her purse on a clean section of the counter and begins to roll up her sleeves. "I'm not leaving you with this mess, Val. We'll do it together."

As embarrassed as I am, I'm also so relieved. I'm not sure I could have done this alone. "Thank you," I murmur. "Can you, uh, clean the wine then? I can't."

"Of course, honey." She doesn't ask why, and that makes me even more thankful.

It takes us nearly two hours to clean my kitchen. A couple of times I would spot some wine and start dry heaving. My mom would insist we take a break and made me drink apple juice. It was refreshing on my parched throat, and the sugar made me feel better.

"What do you want to do with these?" mom asks, gesturing at the bottles on the counter.

I walk over to them and grab the whiskey. With a sigh, I unscrew the top and pour the contents down the drain. I repeat this with the others until they're all empty. My mom holds open the trash bag as I throw each one away.

She ties the bag shut and gives me a proud but tired smile. "I'll take this down with me. Do you need anything before I leave? I can bring you dinner? Or I can order something in for you?"

I shake my head. "I'll be okay, Mom. I'll order something when I get hungry, but right now my stomach is still upset."

She nods and closes the distance between us to wrap me in a tight hug. "Thank you for calling me. You'll come for dinner one night, right? Maybe brunch?"

She tries to hide it, but I can hear the desperation. Does she think this was a one-time thing? Well, it's not like I've given her any reason in the past to think differently. "Of course," I promise. "Just let me know when. I'm off duty for a few more days to recover, but I'll try to work my schedule around it."

She pulls away and gives me a bright smile. "Good! Your dad and sister will be happy to hear that." She pats my cheek affectionately. "I love you, Val."

My whole body warms. "I love you too, Mom. Thanks again."

I follow her as she picks up her purse and hauls the trash bag with her to the door. She blows me a kiss and walks out. I lock the door behind her and let out a heavy sigh when silence encompasses me.

I'm so tired.

Nightmares kept me up, but the uncomfortable hospital

bed didn't help the situation. Reluctantly, I make my way to the bedroom and cross to my bed. I frown when I realize I didn't get a chance to change the bedding, let alone burn it. Tomorrow, I'll toss it and get something else, but for now it'll have to work.

I crawl onto the bed and flop down with a groan of delight. Rolling over, I bury my face in the pillow and try to sleep.

Except I grabbed the pillow Jack used. I can tell by the traces of sandalwood. My eyes sting, but instead of throwing the pillow across the room like I want, I rotate the pillow and curl my body around it. Keeping my face pressed to the side of it, I let myself drift off to sleep.

Epilogue

Drake

Oh, how the land of the living has changed. Rarely do I grace this realm with my presence, but it seems Shezmu has had quite the fun up here, so it piqued my interest. Not that he is now. Instead, he's chained and being tormented by my counterpart. Still, I'm intrigued.

My battle with my sworn enemy has gone my way once again. Rarely do I get the freedom of killing him. Not that either one of us ever stays dead. That's the reality of being a god, I suppose. Rubbing my swollen belly where my enemy lays, I look up at the solar eclipse and smirk at the evidence of my triumph.

The other gods will be on guard about my victory, but I

suspect they'll truly panic when they realize I'm no longer in the underworld. What is the human phrase? Shit themselves? Yes. Quite appropriate.

The jackal is already on thin ice with Osiris for Shezmu and Ammit escaping. Not that it was entirely Anubis' fault. In exchange for some of Shezmu's empowering wine, I agreed to help him escape to the living realm.

And shall I say that here is much better than that desolate area he first escaped to. It was so boring and plain. However, this city is bustling with chaos and sin. The buildings are so tall and flashy. Bright.

Too bright.

I wonder what this pitiful, bustling city will do if it falls into complete darkness? I already taste all the greed and indulgence radiating from the souls mulling around the streets. How sweeter will it become when these people succumb even more to the dark living inside them?

First things first, of course. I need to find a certain heart eating, soul devouring chimera.

I finally track Ammit down in the back parking lot of an old pink colored casino. She has a large dog between her paws, her massive jaws working at its sternum with audible snaps. Blood shines along the scales of her snout each time she moves.

Shoving my hands into the front pockets of my black jeans, I make my way towards her. When she senses me, her head snaps up with a possessive snarl. However, when I give a flare of my aura, she immediately becomes submissive. Ignoring her meal, she curls her tail between her massive, stumpy legs and drops her head to her paws. She doesn't look at me, instead keeping her gaze fixated off to the side.

I squat down next to her and place my hand on her head, smirking when she flinches. "You know he will come back for you." Her eyes flick to mine before glancing away again. "But I don't think you're ready to go home, are you?" Another quick look at me. I pet her lion's mane before running my fingers down her scaled snout. "I believe you and I can work here together. You'll get your souls, and I'll get my fun. How does that sound?"

This time when she looks at me, she holds my gaze with something akin to eagerness. With another pat to her snout, I straighten up to my full height. I tap the side of my thigh twice as I turn from her. "Well, come on then."

My smirk widens into a grin as I hear her claws scrape against the asphalt. When she's at my side, I cloak my new companion in darkness before making my way towards the busiest street of the city.

Thank you so much for reading! Marked is near and dear to my heart because I relate to Val in more ways than one. If you're interested in seeing more of this world, see where it all began in Skin!

Also by Ally Wagner

Skin

Shift